MY VERY OWN® PIRATE TALE

This book was created especially for
Logan Millward
who arrived on October 1, 2008

With Love From,
Mommy, Daddy & Riley
2013

Written by Maia Haag
Illustrated by Lisa Falkenstern
Designed by Haag Design, Inc.

I see Me!® Inc.
PERSONALIZED CHILDREN'S BOOKS

There once was a ship
full of pirates with hats,
and parrots with earrings,
and dozens of cats.
The captain was strong,
with a tooth made of gold,
and the funny thing was,
he was not very old.

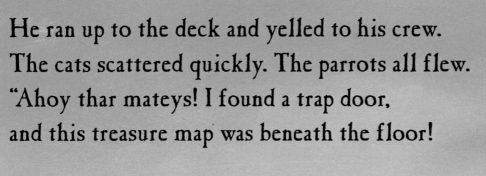

He ran up to the deck and yelled to his crew.
The cats scattered quickly. The parrots all flew.
"Ahoy thar mateys! I found a trap door,
and this treasure map was beneath the floor!

"It's a map of an island! Bless me boat!
I'll read these here words that somebody wrote:
      'If a captain wishes to be truly great,
      he must have a trustworthy, loyal first mate.
      Find a first mate who's the world's very best,
      if you want to open the 'ol treasure chest.
      The name of your fearless first matey lies
      in clues that are found in the sea and the skies.'

"Blimey! I'm wonderin' who this fine sailor might be?
I'm a-lookin' for clues in the sky and the sea."

"This Logical boy has sure learned how to think.
He'd avoid any rocks that could make your ship sink."

Leopard shark

Lo

"This Optimistic boy is a bright ray of sun.
He'd inspire your whole crew to get the job done."

Ocean sunfish

Log

"Choose this Generous boy
who is thoughtful like me,
when I share all my toys
with my friends in the sea."

Giant squid

Loga

"This Amusing young boy will make your crew smile
and leave them all giggling for quite a long while."

Anchovy

Logan

"Do you need a first mate
who'll inspire your crew?
This Natural leader
would be perfect for you!"

Napoleonfish

"The letters I'm seeing' in the sky and the sea
are beginnin' to make some more sense to me.
These creatures are playin' a jolly ol' game.
Is Logan the mysterious first matey's name?

"Me map has more words, and they might be a clue.
Listen up, me hearties. I'll read 'em to you:
  'Look for an island where monkeys are swinging,
  parrots are squawking and swallows are singing.
  There on this island a lone mango tree grows,
  on the shore where the warmest of sea breezes blows.
  If you find this quite secretive, white sandy beach,
  the ol' treasure chest will be close to your reach,
  but if you want the treasure that glimmers inside,
  you must have your trusty first mate at your side.'"

"Ahoy! On yonder lost island I think that I see
a sandy white beach with a lone mango tree!

"Sufferin' seagulls, I've just gotta know
me first mate's last name, and then we can go.
I'll ask some more creatures which mate is the best.
Once they spell his last name, we'll go to the chest!

"Callin' all creatures! Which young boy would be great?
Can you spell the last name of me loyal first mate?"

"This smart, Mindful boy
will not miss any clues
that your bold crew of pirates
might be able to use."

Manta ray

M

"This Intelligent boy is very well read!
He reads pirate books before going to bed!"

Ibis

Mi

"I know a Loyal sailor who'd be a great guide.
As you search for the treasure, he'd stay at your side."

Lionfish

Mil

"This Level-headed boy
would stay calm in a storm
and keep the ship steady
if big waves were to form."

Loggerhead sea turtle

Mill

Weedy seadragon

"This Well-spoken boy could give a great speech
describing the treasure that you're trying to reach."

Millw

Anglerfish

"With this light on my head, I swim deep in the sea.
My choice is a boy who's Adventurous like me."

Millwa

"Find a Reasonable boy
whose thinking is sound,
unlike all my friends here
who swim upside down."

Razorfish

Millwar

"This Decisive young boy
will help to define
the path to the treasure
by following the sign."

CORAL AVE

SHARKS REEF

DOLPHIN'S DEN

Discus fish

Millward

"Logan Millward, it's jolly good t' meet ye, mate.
The creatures been tellin' me how yer just great.
We followed the map to this lone mango tree,
but to open the chest, I need the right key.
Do ye have an idea of where it might be?"

"It seems," said Logan, "that my very own name
has been a big part of this fun treasure game.
Try saying my name now three times and we'll see
if that's what the magical code just might be."

"Aye, matey. We'll give it a good pirate's test.
Let's see if this opens the ol' treasure chest:

Logan Millward!
Logan Millward!
Logan Millward!"

"Bless my barnacles! Logan, by golly, yer bright!
These coins are a-shimmerin' in the evenin' light!

"What the creatures been sayin' about ye is right.
Arrr! Wear this hat to become a cap'n tonight.

"From this evening forward you will now be known
as Cap'n Logan Millward, with a ship of your own!"

Sea Animal Encyclopedia

Ahoy thar, Cap'n Logan! Let's play a fun game!
Find a coin on the pages that spell out your name!

Adélie penguin
My friends and I build nests out of
stones on the rocky beaches of
Antarctica. In the spring, we have to
walk over 300 miles (482 kilometers)
of frozen ocean to reach the open water.

Albatross
Squawk! In one day, I can fly as far over
the sea as you can travel for 9 hours in a
car on the highway. I can fly around the
entire globe during my life!

Anchovy
Phew! I spend my entire day trying not
to be eaten. I'm a little green fish with
a silver stripe down my back. Lots of
other fish are always trying to eat me!

Angler fish
Part of my spine sticks out of my
head like a fishing pole. I allow special
light-producing bacteria to live in my
"fishing pole" to attract other fish so
that I can eat them.

Barracuda
I am like a tiger in the sea because I have
sharp teeth and I like to hunt. Since I
don't have eyelids, I can't close my eyes
at night.

Blue whale
Did you know that I'm the largest
animal in the world? I am as long as
3 school buses, my heart is as big as a
car, and 50 people could stand on my
tongue!

Cowfish
I am a really slow swimmer because
my body is shaped like a box. If you
catch me with your hand, I will make a
grunting noise.

Crab
I am special because my teeth are in my
stomach. I have a very hard shell and my
eyes rest on my back like a snail's. I can
even grow a new claw if it breaks off!

Discus fish
When my babies are first born, they
feed off the mucous that comes through
the skin on the sides of my body.
Doesn't that sound delicious?

Dolphin
Did you know that I can see even while
I am sleeping? When I sleep, I rest one
half of my brain at a time so that one
eye is always open.

Eagle ray
My favorite thing to do is to swim fast
by flapping my fins, which look like
wings. I can leap high out of the water.
Watch out for my tail, which will sting
if you touch it!

Eel
My body is like a battery that sends
out electricity. The electricity from my
body is enough to light 12 light bulbs in
your house.

Elephant seal
My big nose helps me make really loud roaring noises. My nose also soaks in the moisture from my breath so that I don't have to drink water as often.

Hermit crab
Do you like this sea shell that I found on the shore? I wear it on my back all the time to protect me. When I become too big for this shell, I will find a new one to wear.

Emperor penguin
Brrr! To stay warm in Antarctica, 100 penguins and I lean on each other. We slowly shuffle around so that our friends on the outside of the group can come to the inside for warmth.

Ibis
My long, curved bill helps me to find and eat small fish when I wade in shallow water. I am known for my courage because I'm one of the last creatures to take shelter during a hurricane.

Fairy penguin
I live in Australia, where there is no snow or ice. I am only 16 inches (41 cm) tall and I weigh just 2 pounds (1 kilogram,) but I can sing more songs than any other penguin!

Iguana
I am a marine iguana. When I lie in the sun on the rocky beach, salt from the sea water that I've swallowed comes out of my nose and makes my face white.

Flying fish
I can take off and fly like an airplane. I swim fast underwater, and then I leap into the air and spread my fins to glide. Sometimes I soar onto the decks of ships!

Indigo hamlet
I am only 3 inches (8 centimeters) long and I am very shy. I like to stay in the same reef for my entire life without moving around much. It's my home!

Giant squid
I am over 30 feet (9 meters) long, and my eyes are as big as basketballs. My 8 arms and 2 tentacles have suction cups on them to help me grab and eat big fish deep in the sea.

Irish lord
I'm great at playing hide and seek! I can change the color of my body to red, pink, purple, brown or white to match what is around me so that you can't see me!

Green sea turtle
I hatched from an egg that was buried by my mom in the sand on the shore. My brothers and sisters and I crawled slowly to the sea, where we will live for over 70 years.

Jackknife drum fish
If you pull me from the water, I will make a knocking sound that sounds like a drum. My fins make me look as if I am two different fish. This confuses fish that are trying to eat me.

Hammerhead shark
My head is shaped this way because it helps me pin stingrays to the sea floor so that I can eat them. Since my eyes are far apart on each side of my head, I can see all around me.

Jellyfish
I am not really a fish. I don't have a brain, heart or bones, but I do have tentacles that can sting! Jellyfish have been around for more than 650 years. We were on Earth before dinosaurs!

Kelpfish

Guess how I got my name. I live amongst kelp and sea weed. My blade-shaped body helps me to blend in. My skin can even change color from red to brown to green to help me hide.

King penguin

My favorite sport is diving over 350 feet (100 meters) deep in the cold waters of Antarctica. Luckily, my 4 layers of feathers keep me really warm, and the outside layer is waterproof.

Leopard shark

While I am 7 feet (2 meters) long and my name is scary, I can't hurt humans because my teeth are small and I am shy. My spots help me to hide on the bottom of the ocean.

Lionfish

Some of my long striped spines are poisonous. I use my long fins to corner small fish into a space where I can eat them. It's a good thing that you're not a little fish!

Lobster

I'm all mixed up. My brain is in my throat. I listen with my legs and taste with my feet. My teeth are in my stomach! Lobsters have been around for nearly 100 million years.

Loggerhead sea turtle

I can weigh up to 800 pounds (364 kilograms.) Unlike other kinds of turtles, I can't tuck my head or arms into my shell. I spend most of my life in the ocean, where I love to swim.

Macaroni penguin

Do you know how I got my name? English explorers thought that the plumes on my head looked like a crazy "macaroni" hairstyle that was popular in England in the 1700's.

Manta ray

By flapping my big fins that look like wings, I can swim fast and leap high from the water! I use my flexible horns to direct small fish into my wide mouth.

Napoleon fish

Can you believe that I used to be a female fish, but I turned into a male fish as I got older? This hump over my head has also become more noticeable as I have aged.

Northern fur seal

When I swim, I use my whiskers to catch fish. My whiskers notice the vibrations made by passing fish! I spend most of my life hunting for fish, so my whiskers are very important.

Ocean sunfish

I'm a really big fish. I'm over 10 feet (3.1 meters) long and I weigh over 5,000 pounds (2,268 kilograms!) I am called an "ocean sunfish" because I like to sunbath at the surface of the water.

Octopus

I have a soft head with a big brain and 8 arms called tentacles with suction cups on them...but I have no body and no bones! When I'm scared, I spray ink into the water to distract my enemies.

Orca

I can make clicking and buzzing noises in the water. I listen to the echo that bounces back to tell me where other fish are located, how big they are and what their shape is! This helps me to hunt fish.

Parrot fish

I got my name from my parrot-like beak that is full of teeth. I use my teeth to grind up coral rock to eat the algae living on the coral. After I swallow the coral, it comes out of my body as sand!

Pelican

Do you know why I have a big pouch underneath my beak? I can catch fish by opening up my big throat pouch underwater. Before I can swallow the fish, I have to drain the water from my pouch.

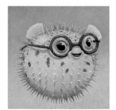

Porcupine fish

When I think that I might be eaten, I swallow water to become round like a ball so that the other fish need a really big mouth to eat me. I also stick out my sharp spines so that I don't look too tasty!

Queen angelfish

I got my name from the blue-ringed spot on my head that looks like a crown that a queen would wear. I have beautiful bright blue and yellow scales.

Razorfish

Some people call me a "Shrimpfish," and some people call me a "Razorfish" because of my sharp-edged belly. I like to swim with my head pointing downwards so that I blend in with the weeds.

Right whale

Did you know that my teeth are 7 feet tall and I am as long as 10 men lying in a row? People like to see me "breach," which means "jump out of the water."

Royal gramma

Do my bright colors make me look as if I'm wearing a royal gown? I'm only 3 inches (8 centimeters) long and I live in the colorful coral reefs of warm waters.

Saw shark

Guess how I got my name! My snout is edged with teeth and it looks like a saw. Other fish try to stay out of my way, but don't worry--I can't hurt humans. I am only about 3 feet (1 meter) long.

Sea otter

When I sleep, I float on my back on the surface of the water. My friends and I hold each other's paws while we sleep to keep from drifting apart!

Swordfish

The top part of my mouth looks like a flat sword with a point at the end. I'm a very fast swimmer and I take powerful leaps out of the water! I weigh more than a human adult.

Toadfish

I "sing" so that female toadfish will come to see me! My singing sounds like a hum or a whistle. Did you know that I can survive out of the water in low tides for as long as 24 hours?

Tripod fish

I stand all day long on the bottom of the ocean on my long, pointy fins. I wait for small shrimp to bump into my fins, and then I grab them with my fins and put them into my mouth!

Trumpet fish

I often swim with my tail up and my snout down so that I look like a stick floating in the water. It's a great trick! My body is about 2 feet (half a meter) long and it's thin like a stick.

Umbrella squid

My webbed tentacles look like a big umbrella. I love to swim deep in the Atlantic ocean. The main part of my body (called the "mantle") is about 1 foot (30 centimeters) long.

Unicorn fish

I got my name because I have a horn that looks like a unicorn's. I don't use my horn to fight, and I'm not sure why I was born with it. It just makes me special!

Vacquita porpoise

I'm the smallest porpoise in the world. My black lips make me look as if I'm wearing black lipstick! There are only about 200 of us left in the world, living in the ocean near California.

Yellow seahorse

I am called a yellow seahorse, but I can actually change colors from gray to yellow to purple within seconds. I can also look in two different directions with each of my eyes at the same time!

Velvetfish

Do you think that I'm handsome? I have thick skin that looks like velvet with little knobs on my body. When I hide between rocks, it is hard to see me because I look like a rock.

Yellowtail snapper

I'm not scared of the human divers that swim near me in the Atlantic Ocean near Florida. I swim up to see the divers! They like to look at the beautiful colors of my scales.

Walrus

My large tusks are actually teeth that can grow 3 feet (1 meter) long! I use my tusks to help pull my heavy body out of the cold Arctic water and onto the ice. I weigh as much as a small car!

Zanzibar butterflyfish

Do you think that this spot on my scales looks like an extra eye? My spot confuses other fish who might want to eat me. They can't tell which end of my body they're looking at!

Weedy sea dragon

My body looks just like sea weed! It is hard to see me when I float in the sea weed in the ocean by Australia. I move so slowly that I look like sea weed drifting in the water.

Zebra pipefish

I am a boy Zebra pipefish, and I like to swim with a girl Zebra pipefish. We greet each other by dancing in the water and making our long bodies form the shape of a circle or a cross.

Xeno crab

I am a tiny crab that is only as big as the tip of your finger. I live on whip coral in the ocean, and I'm hard to see. Some people call me a "whip coral spider" because I look like a spider.

It'll be helpful to know fun facts such as these when you sail your tall ship across the high seas!

PERSONALIZED CHILDREN'S BOOKS

www.iseeme.com / 1.877.744.3210 (toll free)

See all the personalized titles from I See Me! Inc:

My Very Own® Name
My Very Own® Fairy Tale
My Very Own® Pirate Tale
The Super, Incredible Big Brother
The Super, Incredible Big Sister
The World According To Me
Who Loves Me?
God Loves You!
A Christmas Bear for Me
A Hanukkah Bear for Me

14505 27th Avenue North, Plymouth, MN 55447

POPULAR JUSTICE

A History of Lynching in America

Manfred Berg

The American Ways Series

IVAN R. DEE   *Chicago*

www.ivanrdee.com

Berg, Manfred, 1959–
    Popular justice : a history of lynching in America / Manfred Berg.
        p. cm — (American ways series)
    ISBN 978-1-56663-802-9 (cloth : alk. paper) — ISBN 978-1-56663-920-0 (electronic)
    1. Lynching—United States—History. I. Title.
    HV6457.B47 2011
    364.1'34—dc22

                                                                2010041110

To my friend John David

Contents

Preface

IN 1905 the sociologist James E. Cutler introduced his book *Lynch-Law: An Investigation into the History of Lynching in the United States* with these words:

> It has been said that our country's national crime is lynching. . . . The practice whereby mobs capture individuals suspected of crime . . . , and execute them without any process of law . . . , is to be found in no other country of a high degree of civilization. Riots and mob executions take place in other countries, but there is no such frequent administration of what may be termed popular justice which can properly be compared with lynch-law procedures in the United States.

Although Cutler's study is outdated in many respects, its characterization of lynching as "popular justice" may yet be considered the best starting point to define the subject of this book. While anti-lynching activists and historians have endlessly argued over the proper definition of lynching, it is indisputable that since the term originated during the American Revolution it has referred to extralegal punishment meted out by a group of people claiming to represent the will of the larger community and acting with an expectation of impunity. Until the mid-nineteenth century, lynching or lynch law did not necessarily mean that mobs killed their victims. The terms also included nonlethal forms of communal punishment such as flogging or tarring and feathering. Whether deadly or not, lynching typically entailed a strong element of ritual aimed at reinforcing a sense of community among the executioners of popular justice. Hence some scholars have compared lynchings to rituals of human sacrifice designed to symbolically restore a disrupted world.

Lynching as an act of communal punishment must be distinguished from hate crimes on the one hand and riots on the other. Hate crimes are random acts of violence against racial, ethnic, religious, and sexual minorities without the pretext of punishing a particular crime and, at least in recent years, without community approval. Riots involve large-scale collective violence in which the participants make no claim to be agents of justice. To be sure, it is often difficult to draw clear lines between hate crimes, riots, and lynchings.

To speak of lynching as extralegal punishment takes for granted the principle that only government institutions have the authority to enforce the law, suppress crime, and punish criminals. In short, the word lynching assumes the existence of the modern state which, theoretically, holds a "monopoly of legitimate violence." In historical terms this is a fairly recent idea. Throughout most of human history the punishment of crime has been a matter of retribution by the wronged victims and their kinfolk. In Europe blood feuds persisted into the late Middle Ages, and it was generally accepted that a legitimate way to avenge a slain family member was to kill the slayer or members of his family. While blood vengeance may appear barbaric in modern eyes, it nevertheless provided a basic sense of protection in an age without a centralized power to ensure a general peace. Moreover the advance of formal law was slow and uneven. Among the rural populations of Europe, traditions of communal justice continued into the late nineteenth century. In American history the practice of lynching has often been attributed to conditions on the frontier, where the people were supposedly forced to take the law into their own hands because no effective system of law enforcement and criminal justice existed.

But it is misleading to see lynching primarily as communal self-help that ceased as soon as the state had successfully secured a monopoly of legitimate violence. On the contrary, American lynchers in the late nineteenth and early twentieth centuries, as the historian Michael Pfeifer has argued, were reacting to the establishment of a modern criminal justice system that attempted to replace the community's desire for "rough justice" with an "abstract, rational, detached, antiseptic legal process." Opponents condemned lynching as lawlessness, but its apologists justified it as an instrument of a "higher law" that heeded the values, traditions, and vital interests of the community. In order to dramatize their claim to meting out true popular justice, lynchers often staged ritualistic mock trials aimed at creating a semblance of "law and order" administered by a righteous community.

Mob violence can be found in most societies, but James Cutler, writing in the early twentieth century, surely had a point that the frequency and cruelty of lynchings singled out the United States among the so-called "civilized" nations of the time. What accounts for this "negative exceptionalism"? Why were Americans such a lynch-prone people, especially during the nineteenth and early twentieth centuries? In trying to answer these questions, historians have usually considered three core themes that will also be central to this book: the frontier experience, the race conflict, and the anti-authoritarian spirit of grassroots democracy.

The "lawlessness" of the frontier is the classic apology for vigilantism and lynching. The folkloristic image of hardened pioneers making short work of brazen outlaws has left a deep mark on American popular culture and greatly contributed to a highly ambivalent attitude toward mob violence. The significance of racism is equally evident, given that during the age of Jim Crow the vast majority of lynch victims were African Americans. White supremacists defended lynching as necessary to protect the purity of the white race against the allegedly insatiable drive of black men to rape white women. In contrast, readers may find it more difficult to accept that the spirit of grassroots democracy also was a wellspring of lynching in American history. Yet in claiming to execute the will of the people, the executioners of popular justice asserted their own ideas of democratic participation and local self-government. "In a democracy," James Cutler aptly noted, "the people consider themselves a law unto themselves. . . . To execute a criminal deserving of death is to act merely in their sovereign capacity."

The late Charles Tilly, a leading student of collective violence, once confessed that he preferred a "rough-and-tumble democracy" over a "nonviolent tyranny." But this is a false alternative. This book is predicated on the premise that liberal democracy has provided a solution to the problem of balancing order and liberty, namely the state monopoly of legitimate violence controlled by the rule of law, an independent judiciary, and the democratic process. Wherever this system works reasonably well, there is no need for law enforcement by private individuals and extralegal communal justice. American legal culture, in this regard, has been shaped by a striking contrast. While there has always been a strong tradition of popular justice and private violence, Americans have been rightly proud of their contributions to implementing a "government of laws, and not of men," as John Adams famously phrased it in the Massachusetts Constitution of 1780. Ordered liberty and the rule of law require the prudent self-restraint of the people, especially in the realm of criminal justice. It is no coincidence that the Constitution twice, in the Fifth and the Fourteenth amendments, mandates the fundamental principle that no person shall be "deprived of life, liberty, or property, without due process of law," binding both the federal and the state governments. Over the course of American history, lynchers ignored this pillar of liberty. They ignored the intent of due process, which exists not to shield criminals from justice but to protect all members of society from despotism, including the despotism of the people taking the law into their own hands.

The following chapters trace the history of lynching in America from colonial times to the present. They do not tell an uplifting story. Inevitably the record involves graphic violence and appalling injustice. Although there were numerous heroes in the struggle against lynching, many opponents were highly ambivalent in their views of its causes and its remedies. What is more troubling, lynching cannot be blamed on aberrants and the riffraff. Most lynchers were ordinary people and often respectable community leaders. And while the victims deserve recognition and sympathy, it would be disingenuous to pretend that they were all innocent of the crimes that had triggered their lynching.

There is also no redeeming end to this story. Unlike segregation or disfranchisement, lynching was not brought down by momentous court rulings or legislative acts. Rather, its demise was a slow process fraught with paradoxes and unacknowledged continuities, especially in the administration of the death penalty.

*   *   *

In writing this book I relied on the help and encouragement of many people. My editor and friend John David Smith invited me to write a history of lynching for the American Ways Series and suggested numerous improvements, constantly reminding me to keep an eye on the general reader. I also thank Ivan Dee for his constructive response to my proposal and his careful editing. Phil Racine read the entire manuscript and made numerous helpful comments. He also generously invited me to spend a semester at Wofford College in Spartanburg, South Carolina, where I could concentrate on writing and research. Kirsten Fischer read various drafts and helped me hone both my prose and my arguments. As always, my wife and colleague Anja Schüler not only served as a critical reader but patiently endured my preoccupation with a somber subject. I also thank my former doctoral student Claire Bortfeldt for sharing with me parts of her research on the Association of Southern Women for the Prevention of Lynching. Simon Wendt, my colleague and friend at Heidelberg University, provided valuable information on lynching scholarship. My students Christian Jauch, Stella Krepp, Jens Weimann, Onno Schröder, and Philipp Koeniger worked diligently in researching materials for this project. Because this book builds on the pioneering work of many historians, I acknowledge my special intellectual debts to W. Fitzhugh Brundage, Bill Carrigan, Stephen Leonard, Michael Pfeifer, Christopher Waldrep, Clive Webb, Amy Wood, and George C. Wright. I have found their work highly challenging and inspiring, whether or not I agreed with their views. Obviously, all errors and shortcomings of this book are exclusively my responsibility.

Popular Justice

1

The Roots of Lynching in Colonial and Revolutionary North America

SEVERAL COMPETING STORIES seek to explain the origins of the term lynching, including the tale of James Lynch Fitz-Stephen, the mayor of Galway, Ireland, who in the late fifteenth century allegedly tried, convicted, and executed his own son for killing a man in a fit of jealousy. But most historians consider Colonel Charles Lynch (1736–1796) of Bedford County, Virginia, as the most likely namesake for the practice of punishment outside the law. During the American Revolution, Charles Lynch presided over extralegal courts that claimed to fight lawlessness in general and loyalist activities in particular. Colonel Lynch himself spoke of "Lynchs [sic] law" in reference to irregular punishment. Although Lynch's associates executed several of their prisoners, they mostly limited themselves to severe corporal castigation. Subsequently, until the mid-nineteenth century, lynching did not necessarily mean lethal punishment. More typically it referred to violent forms of public humiliation, to whipping and to tarring and feathering. Moreover for several decades usage of the word remained confined to Virginia and scarcely appeared in writings before the 1830s.

Yet does the absence of the term before the late eighteenth century mean that lynching did not exist? At first glance this appears highly implausible. After all, British North America was a frontier society with no effective system of law enforcement in the modern sense. Thus, according to the theory that in a quasi state of nature the people have no choice but to take the law into their own hands, one might expect that lynch law was the rule rather than the exception, even if people had not yet coined a term for the practice. Indeed, as this chapter will demonstrate, the colonial frontier played a key role in shaping the American tradition of vigilantism. But while it is impossible to know how many people were executed without a legal warrant in the remote hinterlands, there is no evidence that extralegal punishment—in competition with the official administration of criminal justice—was a frequent occurrence or a major public concern during the colonial era. Still, a closer look at colonial institutions and practices affords a better understanding of the roots and patterns of lynching in the nineteenth and twentieth centuries.

The "classic" defense of popular justice held that, basically, lynching was a response to inefficient law enforcement and lenient courts in the face of rampant serious crime. Viewed from this perspective, British North America presents a paradoxical picture. On the one hand, historians describe the colonial system of criminal justice as ineffective, reflecting a generally weak administration of government. Distances were great and travel was slow. In many areas courts were few and far between, and court sessions were held rather irregularly. There were hardly any jails in which to lock up suspects, and most of them were in dismal condition. Not surprisingly, many prisoners easily escaped, including quite a few of those awaiting execution. On the other hand, the colonists apparently were not particularly worried about crime or about offenders not receiving their just punishment. Although there are few precise figures on crime rates for the seventeenth and eighteenth centuries, they appear to have been relatively stable, at least before about 1750, and not alarmingly high in the eyes of the colonial populace. This stands in sharp contrast to eighteenth-century England where the fear of rising crime perpetrated by the "dangerous classes" triggered intense public debate on the perceived weakness of the criminal justice system. Accordingly the English criminal code, the harshest in Europe, imposed extremely tough sentences on criminals.

This was especially true with regard to the death penalty, which was inflicted much more frequently than in the North American colonies and for a much broader range of crimes. In England the vast majority of criminals were hanged for property crimes such as theft, burglary, or robbery. This rarely happened in the colonies. And although crimes against morality and religion, including adultery, blasphemy, and sodomy, carried the death penalty during the early colonial period, these laws were rarely enforced. The only confirmed execution for adultery took place in

Massachusetts in 1643. By and large, the death penalty was reserved for murder and other serious felonies such as rape, arson, counterfeiting, or horse stealing on the frontier, and for supposedly incorrigible repeat offenders. Moreover a death sentence did not automatically mean that the execution would be carried out. The records of colonies such as Pennsylvania, New York, and North Carolina indicate that roughly half of all those condemned received a pardon or a commutation of their sentences and that most colonies, on average, had not even one official execution per year. One study of crime in North Carolina between 1663 and 1776, then mostly a frontier outpost, found a total of sixty-seven death sentences but only sparse evidence of executions. The same may also be true of severe corporal punishment like whipping, branding, or ear-cropping. Equally remarkable, there is little evidence that the colonists reacted to the supposed weakness of their criminal justice systems by taking the punishment of criminals into their own hands. For example, by the mid-eighteenth century the residents of New York complained about an alarming rise in crime which the courts were hard-pressed to deal with. Colonial authorities reacted by imposing more severe punishments, including a greater number of executions, but mob action against criminals did not seem to become a public concern.

One must be careful, however, not to read present-day ideas of "efficient" criminal justice into the premodern era. Colonial Americans and their European contemporaries viewed and experienced crime and punishment very differently from people living in the twenty-first century. By today's standards the colonial institutions of law enforcement may look weak. But in fact the small and predominantly rural communities of colonial North America were quite successful in enforcing their codes of behavior and morality.

Religion dominated the early modern view of criminal justice. No clear distinction existed between crime and sin. Offenders not only broke the law but violated God's commandments and therefore could bring His wrath onto the entire community. The key purpose of punishment was to restore the divine order by purifying both the community and the sinners, whose souls were saved by destroying their bodies. Since the root causes of crime were human depravity and sinfulness, to which all mortals were susceptible, punishment was staged as a moral drama in which the whole community participated and from which it would take a reassuring lesson. Of course there were important regional differences. The Anglican southern colonies were less rigid than Puritan New England in their equating of crime and sin, but it is nevertheless safe to say that moral and religious rules pervaded the early American concept of crime and justice.

In colonial America law enforcement and the administration of criminal justice were not yet exclusive prerogatives of governmental authorities and trained professionals but responsibilities of the entire community. All able-bodied men had the civic duty of assisting constables and sheriffs in apprehending criminals; members of the local community served as magistrates and jurors. In the relatively egalitarian colonial society, one's responsibility in the administration of justice could easily be construed as a right of the people. This communal character of law enforcement and criminal justice created a strong sense of legitimacy because the verdicts and sentences in criminal trials seemingly mirrored the will of the community, even if the fairness of individual cases was often contested.

The feeling of justice being done was further reinforced by the fact that most trials were relatively short and simple. Usually suspects were brought to trial swiftly after their capture, when memory of the crime was still fresh. Trials took no more than a few hours at most. By modern standards the odds were heavily stacked against the defendants. As a rule they had no lawyer and could not present witnesses in their behalf. The only question to be decided was whether the defendant had actually committed the deed of which he or she was accused. The notorious legal "technicalities" that many of today's advocates of speedy justice find so troubling, including the validity of evidence and the credibility of witnesses, rarely received attention. Finally, sentences were carried out soon after the verdict, though those condemned to hang were usually granted a few weeks to repent and prepare for death. The 1770 case of a burglar in Massachusetts who was executed less than a month after he had committed the crime exemplifies the importance that colonial Americans attached to swift punishment.

Hardly anyone questioned extreme physical pain and death as appropriate punishment for serious crimes. The death penalty, in particular, served three key purposes: deterrence, retribution, and penitence. To highlight these principles it was necessary that the sentence be carried out before the entire community. Typically, executions attracted very large crowds, often numbering into the thousands. Today the practice of publicly killing criminals is widely condemned as pandering to the voyeurism of the multitude. But it would be misleading to conceive of public executions in the seventeenth and eighteenth centuries as base popular entertainment. As a rule, hangings in colonial North America had the somber aura of a religious service, dramatizing the righteous indignation of the community and its claim to mete out retribution. In the late seventeenth century the Puritan minister Cotton Mather welcomed the hanging of several criminals as a "very profitable spectacle" because it provided him with an opportunity to expose the perils of sin before a large crowd. Until the late eighteenth century most people considered public executions as useful moral lessons. Many spectators brought their children to teach them respect for the law.

Deterrence was not the only reason why capital punishment was carried out in public. Executions were elaborate communal rituals lasting for hours. Extended parades, speeches, and prayers preceded the act of hanging. Indeed, the community deemed it an act of compassion to give the condemned an opportunity for public atonement and for bidding farewell to friends and family. As the main actors in a moral drama, the condemned were expected to maintain their composure, confess their crimes, ask for forgiveness, and exhort the audience to abstain from vice and sin. If their performance satisfied the audience, the crowd would respond with declarations of sympathy and perhaps even a call for mercy.

Some historians have argued that in the seventeenth and eighteenth centuries public executions should be viewed as expressing the consent of the people. In Europe time-honored customs allowed the people to grant clemency at the last moment. For example, a virgin might free a condemned man from the scaffold by promising to marry him. Supposedly the purity of the virgin served as a token of the man's innocence. Moreover if an execution failed—because the rope broke or the first strike by the sword was not deadly—this was seen as God's will. In fact botched executions could easily trigger violence to free the prisoner and to punish the executioner for doing a poor job. On the other hand, crowds might also lynch a criminal who, they believed, had not received a sufficiently harsh sentence or had been granted an undeserved pardon.

Although the authorities resented popular interference with the administration of justice and tried to prevent it by placing soldiers around the scaffold, the people stubbornly insisted on this tradition. One notorious case of a lynching in defiance of royal authority occurred in Edinburgh, Scotland, in 1736. When a local smuggler was hanged, the crowd, resenting the enforcement of British customs laws, began throwing rocks at the hangman. The commander of the city guards, one Captain John Porteous, ordered his men to fire at the mob, leaving several people dead. When a Scottish jury sentenced Porteous to death, the royal government pardoned him. Upon hearing the news of the reprieve, Edinburghers formed a mob, broke into the prison where Porteous was held, and hanged him at the city's usual place of execution.

We have no reports of such violent popular interventions in colonial North America. Yet the granting of clemency, often at the last minute when the rope had already been placed around the neck of the condemned, was not unusual. In 1731, for example, two burglars in Philadelphia were already standing on the scaffold when the sheriff suddenly read the pardon issued by the governor. The two men were overtaken by happiness, but the crowd, which had come to watch a hanging, also applauded the reprieve. In granting pardons to condemned men and women, authorities often responded to popular sentiment and appeals by respectable citizens. Because clemency was the only way to correct legal errors during the trial or to invoke mitigating circumstances on behalf of the defendant, petitions for granting pardons represented an important element of popular involvement in the administration of criminal justice. At least indirectly, clemency could be seen as an act backed by the community at large. But if clemency were denied, the people also participated in carrying out executions. Unlike in Europe, there were no professional executioners in colonial North America. Because no one coveted this unpleasant job, the task fell to the county sheriffs who, however, often tried to evade their duty by paying others. Sometimes condemned criminals acted as hangmen, but most of the volunteers were ordinary citizens of the community.

The communal and ritualistic character of capital punishment in colonial North America bears significant implications for the history of lynching in a later age. Although public executions were infrequent events, they nevertheless epitomized deep-seated ideas of popular justice as part of a larger moral and religious universe. In general, the way the death penalty was administered satisfied the people's sense of swift and harsh punishment for serious crime as well as their claim to an active role for the community. Until the late eighteenth century, Americans conceived of executions as participatory events which reflected the consent and values of the wronged communities. Under such circumstances there was no cause for the kind of extralegal punishment that would later become known as lynching.

As the process of modernization transformed the nineteenth-century Europe and North America into urban industrial societies, public executions ceased to be communal rituals of retribution and repentence. They degenerated into rowdy spectacles involving drunkenness and brawls. Respectable people no longer considered it suitable to consort with the rabble on such occasions. Some penal reformers even called for a wholesale abolition of the death penalty; many more favored banning public executions and drastically reducing the number of capital crimes. Gradually prison became the standard method of punishment for nearly all crimes short of murder. And although support for capital punishment remained high and public executions continued into the twentieth century, the state gradually monopolized the death penalty and deprived it of its former character as popular justice. Yet the idea of popular participation persisted, especially in the anti-authoritarian democratic political culture of North America. Hence the large crowds, mock trials, forced confessions, and collective infliction of cruelty that frequently accompanied lynchings in the nineteenth and twentieth centuries may well be interpreted as attempts to reenact the participatory traditions of a premodern era when justice was still close to the people.

Compared to Europe, criminal justice and methods of punishment were moderate in colonial North America. As a rule, torture was not used to extort confessions. Courts imposed the death penalty with less frequency than their European counterparts. Aggravated forms of execution, including burning, breaking on a wheel, and dismemberment or disembowelment while the condemned was still alive were reserved for extreme cases—as, for instance, in the execution of the New York insurgent Jacob Leisler in 1691. But the "regular" administration of criminal justice applied only to European colonists. The treatment of African slaves was an entirely different matter. The patterns of punishment and control of slaves that were established during the colonial era had a profound impact on both the history of criminal justice and lynching in

America. Racial slavery placed black people outside the "normal" law, including its protections, and legitimized a far-reaching system of extra-legal violence that whites could perpetrate against blacks with impunity.

As British North America, particularly the southern colonies, developed into a slave society from the late seventeenth century on, slaveholders found it necessary to impose a draconian regime of punishment on their human property in order to deter individual acts of defiance as well as wholesale rebellion. Because English common law did not recognize slavery as a legal institution, the colonies adopted special slave codes that fixed chattel slavery as lifelong and inheritable, established a separate penal code for slaves, and obliged all whites, whether they owned slaves or not, to participate in upholding slavery. In the realm of criminal justice, the slave codes meant that in punishing slaves colonial authorities were not limited by traditional English law or colonial penal codes. For example, torture was permissible in extracting confessions from slaves suspected of having committed a crime. For the slave population, their special legal status had dire consequences.

To begin with, African slaves were sentenced to death and executed at much higher rates than white criminals. In North Carolina a minimum of 100 blacks were executed in the period from 1748 to 1776, whereas only 43 free whites were legally put to death throughout the colony's entire history between 1663 and 1776. Virginia, with a much larger population, may have executed as many as 555 slaves between 1706 and 1784. Moreover African slaves were punished much more severely when charged with the same crime as whites. Rape, the offense most closely linked to the history of lynching, is a case in point. Colonial courts were highly reluctant to indict white men for rape, let alone to impose capital punishment on white rapists. Rape charges against white men were rarely taken seriously, especially if the alleged rapist belonged to the ruling elites. In colonial North Carolina no white man was ever convicted of rape. In contrast, blacks accused of having raped a white woman were invariably sentenced to death and executed. Blacks were also executed at higher rates than whites because the slave codes specified many more capital offenses than ordinary criminal laws. For instance, South Carolina threatened both slaves and free blacks with the death penalty if they deliberately burned grain or destroyed manufactured goods. Virginians, afraid of being poisoned by their slaves, prohibited them from administering medicine upon pain of death. In Georgia, any slave or free black who struck at a white person faced execution.

In addition the punishment of slaves, whether lethal or not, was extremely cruel, even by early modern standards. Condemned slaves were often singled out for aggravated forms of execution, especially for burning. Punishment was particularly brutal for rebellious slaves. After a slave insurrection in New York in 1712, the surviving rebels were burned to death, starved, or broken on the wheel. Twenty-nine years later, New York authorities ordered thirteen alleged slave conspirators to be burned at the stake and sixteen others to be hanged. To send a stern warning to other slaves, colonial judges sometimes had the head of an executed slave severed and stuck on a pole. After the suppression of the 1739 slave rebellion near the Stono River in South Carolina, the captured slaves were beheaded and their heads placed along the road to Charleston.

Colonial slave codes also allowed for horrible corporal punishment short of death, including savage whipping, branding, castration, nose slitting, and the amputation of toes, fingers, feet, or hands. Although many colonial masters abused their white indentured servants, the treatment of slaves had a different quality and often involved deliberately sadistic acts such as excessive whipping. Eventually the growing influence of Christian ministers inspired a more humane outlook among the colonists, which also affected the treatment of slaves. While branding or bodily mutilation remained permissible until the second half of the eighteenth century, the courts and individual slaveholders inflicted them less frequently, and public opinon began to regard them with reproach.

Colonial slavery set clear patterns for future racial violence in America. Most important, slave status and race determined the suitable degree of violent punishment. The slave codes singled out blacks for extremely cruel punishment, thus marking black bodies as innately inferior. By degrading blacks to hapless objects of nearly unlimited physical violence and sexual humiliation, whites demonstrated their belief that blacks must be less than fully human. Furthermore colonial slavery created a realm of private violence that whites could inflict on blacks. By definition, masters wielded almost unlimited power over their slaves. As objects of punishment, this placed the slaves in a highly ambivalent position. On the one hand, slaveholders, who were obviously interested in preserving both their property and their personal authority, could protect their bondsmen from criminal justice. Although the slave codes mandated financial compensation for the loss of executed slaves, most masters were reluctant to deliver their slaves to the authorities and preferred to settle matters of punishment outside the law. When slaves were sentenced to death, their owners could petition for a pardon. Interestingly, this kind of paternalistic protection survived slavery. In the age of Jim Crow, wealthy planters had considerable clout to shelter "their Negroes" from both lynch mobs and criminal prosecution, if they saw fit.

On a daily basis, however, slaves had much more to fear from their masters than from official law enforcement. While only a tiny number of them would ever be charged with a crime and brought to trial, all slaves were exposed to the arbitrary power of their owners to inflict punishment, including the power to kill. As early as 1669 the Virginia House of Burgesses declared that if a master or any of his agents killed a slave who resisted orders, he should not be prosecuted for murder since it was unreasonable to assume that any man would deliberately and with malice destroy his own property. To instill terror into their bondspeople, some masters went to extremes. In 1743 a North Carolina slaveholder forced his slaves to whip a "Negro girle" and then ordered the girl's mother to bring straw so he could set her on fire.

While masters had a first right and responsibility to discipline their own slaves, the duty of maintaining the institution of slavery fell on all white men of the community. In 1690 South Carolina established the first slave patrols in British North America. One year later Virginia passed an act designed to apprehend fugitive slaves and suppress slave rebellions by authorizing county sheriffs to raise necessary forces from among the local white populace. If fugitive slaves refused to surrender, they could be killed with impunity and the owners paid compensation. The slave patrols of the southern colonies later became a part of the militia system, with both slaveholders and nonslaveholders obliged to serve. Thus the entire white male population was enlisted in defending slavery while in effect every white slave patroller had authority to kill fugitive slaves. It does not seem far-fetched to draw a line of tradition from the slave patrols of colonial times to the lynch mobs and "Negro hunts" of a later era.

Colonial slavery contributed to the later emergence of lynching in that it established three crucial patterns of behavior. First, its racial character designated blacks as legitimate objects of excessive violence.

Second, it made the control of slaves a responsibility of the entire white community. Whites, as masters, overseers, or slave patrollers, could inflict violent punishment or even death on slaves, either with the explicit sanction of the law or with virtual impunity. Third, as a system of personalized violence, the institution of slavery must be seen as one factor that explains why governmental institutions in America could not establish a monopoly of legitimate force. When slavery was abolished and the law no longer permitted personal violence against blacks, many whites nevertheless considered it their right and duty to uphold the racial order by any means necessary.

In principle the slave patrols were not extraordinary in colonial society. Professional police forces had not yet been established, and law enforcement was considered the duty of the entire community. When a crime became known, local people raised a "hue and cry" and hunted down the suspects. In the eighteenth century, magistrates would typically form a *posse comitatus*, that is, "the power of the country" consisting of all able-bodied white men of the community, to assist the sheriff in apprehending criminals. In such a system of popular law enforcement it is obviously difficult to distinguish between posses executing legal force and mobs perpetrating extralegal violence. Moreover, effective law enforcement largely depended on popular consent. If the community sympathized with those who challenged the law—for example with smugglers or rioters—the authorities faced serious problems in raising a reliable posse. On the other hand, if the authorities failed to respond to popular grievances, the people felt entitled to defend the public welfare, as they saw it, by taking forcible action on their own. Not surprisingly, life along the frontier was especially conducive to this type of situation.

In December 1763 an infamous incident of frontier violence happened near Paxton, Pennsylvania, the present-day Harrisburg. Earlier that year Indians of the confederation forged by the Ottawa leader Pontiac had attacked English settlements in Cumberland and Lancaster counties and killed numerous colonists. When the colony's government, dominated by the Quaker establishment, paid little attention to calls for help, the Scotch-Irish settlers on the frontier resolved to form their own ranger companies. Rumors spread that some of Pontiac's raiders were hiding among the inhabitants of Conestoga, a small village of Native Americans who had lived peacefully alongside the

English for decades. On December 14, 1763, a ranger company of fifty-seven "Paxton Boys" descended on Conestoga, killed six Indians they found, and set the village on fire. The remaining fourteen residents of Conestoga fled to Lancaster where they were placed in the workhouse for safekeeping. All the same, on December 27, the Paxton Boys again attacked the Indians in their refuge and killed everyone, including the children. Following the massacre, the rangers moved on to Philadelphia to demand better protection from hostile Indians.

The Pennsylvania elite regarded the mass murder of peaceful Indians as an embarrassment. "The faith of this government has been frequently given to those Indians," Benjamin Franklin lamented, "but that did not avail them with people who despise government." Still, Franklin led the delegation that met with the Paxton Boys and assured them that the colonial assembly would now take their problems seriously. None of the participants in the massacres was brought to justice. Any attempt to do so would have been highly unpopular among the frontier settlers, many of whom viewed Indians as bloodthirsty savages undeserving of the same legal protections as whites. In most cases when the authorities indicted whites accused of crimes against Native Americans, either mobs freed the prisoners or local juries acquitted them. Because settlers on the frontier tended to view their relations with the Indians as inherently hostile and violent, many felt entitled to disregard legal procedure when dealing with Indians accused of crimes.

Large-scale violence between settlers and Native Americans also played an important role in the origins of the so-called Regulator movement that emerged in the backcountry of South Carolina in the 1760s. Many historians consider the Regulators to be the first major manifestation of organized vigilantism in American history. The Cherokee War of 1760–1761 had plunged the western part of the colony into devastation, misery, and chaos. The Indians killed countless settlers and burned down their homesteads. Destitute squatters and orphaned youths as well as war veterans who had gotten used to making a living by looting and robbing formed large gangs of outlaws who began terrorizing the backcountry. Planters and farmers lived in constant fear of raids, murder, torture, plundering, rape, and abduction. For all practical purposes, law enforcement collapsed. Still, the colonial government, dominated by the wealthy planters of the low country, made no attempt to redress the problem. By

1767 the situation had become so intolerable that the leading planters of the South Carolina backcountry formed an organization of Regulators to fight the bandits. In their methods the Regulators were relentless and harsh. While executions were not the rule, captured outlaws could expect to receive a brutal whipping and banishment from the area. Those regarded as redeemable were assigned a piece of land and ordered to work.

The Regulators quickly succeeded in reestablishing a degree of safety and order to the South Carolina hinterlands, but they also incurred much criticism for their arbitrary and excessive brutality. Moreover the colonial government began to fear that they might become a danger to the political order. Eventually a direct confrontation between the vigilantes and the colonial authorities was averted. In 1769 the Regulators agreed to disband when the South Carolina legislature appropriated new courts, jails, and sheriffs for the backcountry.

In contrast, the Regulator movement in North Carolina escalated into violent conflict in 1770 when the governor ordered the militia to quell a popular uprising, leaving roughly two dozen people dead. Unlike in South Carolina, the main grievance of the North Carolina Regulators was not so much the colony's failure to suppress lawlessness but the demand for fair trials and unprejudiced justice. The insurgents viewed the existing court system as highly corrupt and mostly serving the interests of the wealthy elites. Thus in 1770 mobs of Regulators directly assaulted a court session, beating up lawyers and government officers and threatening an associate justice of the North Carolina Superior Court with violence.

The confrontation between the Regulators and the government of North Carolina was not a singular event in the history of colonial America. The period from 1645 to 1760 saw no fewer than eighteen major insurrections and roughly a hundred riots. These incidents reflected a strong anti-authoritarian sense that developed in the political culture of colonial America. Traditionally, English common law defined riots as uprisings of three or more persons who committed unlawful acts for private purposes. But unlawful acts and private aims were, of course, matters of opinion. Many historians have argued that eighteenth-century mobs, both in England and in the American colonies, should not be dismissed as unruly rabble primarily interested in bawdy excitement, vandalism, and disorder. Rather, these historians argue, local people often acted to enforce the law and defend the interests of their community. When the authorities failed to address their grievances, the people felt that they themselves must take action to secure safety and justice.

Government officials often tacitly accepted mobs as extralegal instruments of law enforcement for several reasons. To begin with, they were mostly powerless to stop the mobs even if they wanted to. As long as the people exercised restraint and discipline in meting out communal punishment, there appeared to be no need to interfere. Killings, excessive violence, or the wanton destruction of property were exceptional and usually blamed on outsiders to the community, such as foreign sailors. Also, the purported goals of the mobs generally enjoyed broad popularity, especially the enforcement of moral norms like the whipping of unfaithful husbands and wife beaters or the shutting down of brothels. In 1774, for example, a mob in Massachusetts burned down a hospital with smallpox patients who refused to obey a quarantine. Finally, if the people felt compelled to take action this was widely taken as evidence that something was indeed wrong. Thus mobs and riots, to some extent, appeared as a necessary part of free government.

As the conflict between the British crown and the American colonists escalated in the late 1760s, mob action developed into a crucial driving force of colonial resistance. Customs officials, tax collectors, informants, or merchants disobeying the boycott of British imports became the targets of violent retribution by the patriots. The preferred methods of punishment were whipping and tarring and feathering. The latter procedure, in addition to inflicting severe pain, exposed the victims to spectacular public humiliation but normally did not claim their lives. In January 1774, for example, a Boston mob seized John Malcom, a hated customs commissioner. After they had stripped and beaten him, the vigilantes tarred and feathered him and then paraded their prisoner around town for hours. At every stop he received more lashes. Eventually his tormentors forced the official to drink tea until he vomited and then left him half dead. Although many Bostonians protested the incident as excessive, tarring and feathering became a popular sanction against officials and sympathizers of Britain during the American Revolution. Hallowed as a patriotic tradition, the practice remained a favorite punitive ritual of Americans for many decades thereafter.

In January 1774 British customs officer John Malcolm was tarred and feathered in Boston.

Before 1776, mob action against representatives of the British crown was mostly confined to whipping, tarring and feathering, and the throwing of rocks and rotten eggs. Revolutionary mobs also routinely destroyed the property of unpatriotic merchants, as in the famous Boston Tea Party of December 1773, when the patriots famously made a point of their orderly conduct. Likewise, crowds seized or crushed the printing presses of loyalist editors. In extreme cases riots resulted in the ransacking or burning of buildings. As hatred for the crown grew among the colonists, mob violence threatened practically all loyal officials, including sheriffs and judges charged with enforcing the law. In general, though, historians have praised the mobs of the American Revolution for their restraint, particularly for refraining from deadly violence. After the conflict turned into a full-blown war in 1775, incidents of mob violence declined because military action became the predominant mode of confrontation. Once the United States declared its independence, many former loyalists either accepted the new order or went into exile. Nevertheless personal violence continued to play a salient role in the American Revolution.

In many regions the War of Independence turned into a vicious civil war between patriots and Tories. Political conflict and private feuds became inextricably linked, and both sides committed numerous outrages. In May 1781 patriots in South Carolina, where the war was fought with special cruelty and bitterness, killed fourteen defenseless Tories near Orangeburg. Later that year loyalist militias massacred scores of patriots in their "Bloody Scout" through Edgefield County, South Carolina. Three years later the victorious patriots arrested one of the Tory participants in the "Bloody Scout" who had been careless enough to remain in the area. Surprisingly, a judge ordered the prisoner released. On his way home, relatives of the "Bloody Scout" victims captured the man and hanged him from a tree opposite the courthouse. In the same vein, twelve loyalists who refused to leave their homes were killed by their former enemies.

Compared to these atrocities, the actions taken by Colonel Charles Lynch of Bedford County in central Virginia appear relatively moderate and restrained. Born in 1736 as the eldest son of a wealthy planter, Lynch was a leading citizen of Bedford County. He had been brought up as a Quaker but was excluded from the Society of Friends when he took an oath as a justice of the peace in 1766. Three years later he was elected to the Virginia House of Burgesses. A supporter of the patriot cause, Lynch also served in the Virginia constitutional convention of 1776 and remained a member of the House of Delegates until early 1778 when he was appointed a colonel of the state militia. In this capacity Lynch, like other leaders of the patriot militia, was responsible for suppressing Tory insurrections. The militia men dealt harshly with their enemies. In July 1779, for example, a patriot detachment in western Virginia apprehended a band of Tories and shot one man, hanged another, and flogged several others.

By 1780 the court system of central Virginia had virtually broken down due to the chaos of the war. In addition to loyalist insurgents, roaming bandits constantly threatened public safety. In this situation Charles Lynch and his patriot neighbors resolved to hunt down outlaws and traitors and bring them to justice. Since hauling their prisoners before the court in Williamsburg was practically impossible, they held their own tribunals. Although undoubtedly extralegal, these trials showed some degree of fairness. Lynch and his associates routinely confronted the defendants with their accusers and charged them with specific offenses. Also, the prisoners could call witnesses in their own behalf. Conviction was not a foregone conclusion as several prisoners were acquitted and released. Those found guilty received thirty-nine lashes on their bare backs and were forced to shout "Liberty Forever." If they refused, they were hung by the thumbs until they changed their minds.

In the summer of 1780 the efforts of Colonel Lynch and his fellow patriots to suppress loyalism reached their peak and resulted in several extralegal executions. Hoping for the imminent arrival of Lord Cornwallis and his redcoats, the Tories of central Virginia had prepared for an uprising and attempted to seize the lead mines near New River. But the patriot militias received word of the loyalists' plans and moved to thwart them. In early August 1780, Colonel William Preston informed Governor Thomas Jefferson that his troops had arrested nearly sixty leading loyalists. After conducting inquiries, Preston ordered most of the prisoners whipped. If no evidence of treason could be found, he enlisted them in the Continental Army. Yet he was unsure what to do with those who fell under the state's treason law, partly because he had not received a copy of the act only recently passed by the Virginia Assembly. Unconcerned with legal considerations, his soldiers insisted that the property of the traitors be seized and divided as plunder. Finding himself in a similar situation, Charles Lynch reported that he had decided to release some of his prisoners for want of criminal evidence but believed that "perhaps Justice to this country may Require [that others] shou'd be made Examples of." Indeed, Colonel William Campbell ordered the hanging of a prisoner named Zachariah Goss because the man was known to be a member of a gang of "noted murderers, horsethieves, and robbers." It is unclear whether Lynch ever ordered an extralegal execution himself. Evidently some people believed he would do so. The wife of a suspected Tory conspirator feared that Lynch might order her husband hanged because the colonel disliked Welshmen. The fate of this prisoner is unknown. But evidence suggests that Lynch, without proper legal authority, sentenced several loyalist insurgents to imprisonment ranging from one to five years.

Governor Thomas Jefferson commended Lynch for his "vigorous, decisive measures" in a situation of great peril. He nevertheless emphasized the need to bring traitors before a regular court, if only so that procedural errors might not allow conspirators to escape their due punishment. Clearly many Virginian patriots felt uneasy about the high-handedness of Lynch, Preston, and others in arrogating to themselves the power to punish. As soon as the guns fell silent and wartime anxieties were calmed, some of their victims threatened the militia leaders with a lawsuit. In response, Lynch appealed to the Virginia Assembly for indemnity. In October 1782 the Assembly finally granted the request, but, far from celebrating Lynch and his companions as heroes of the patriot cause, the indemnity act matter-of-factly described their measures as "not strictly warranted by law, although justifiable from the imminance of the danger." After the Revolutionary War Charles Lynch served in the Virginia Senate from 1784 to 1789; he died in 1796 as a highly respected citizen.

In light of the historical record it seems ironic that in later years Colonel Charles Lynch's name became associated with the bloodthirsty fury of mobs in the nineteenth and twentieth centuries. The "lynchers" of Bedford County obviously were fully aware that they violated established principles of due process and that their actions could be justified only by a clear and present military threat. Even so, under the circumstances they demonstrated remarkable discretion in judging individuals and reluctance in imposing the death penalty. While "Lynch's law" undoubtedly lacked legal authority, it was not simply mob violence in the guise of the law.

Although the Virginia legislature later exonerated Lynch and his associates, the "revolutionary justice" they exercised never deteriorated into a regime of state terror that has become the hallmark of most revolutions in modern history. The early phases of the French and Russian revolutions saw huge waves of popular violence, including spontaneous killings of thieves and other "enemies of the people." Even before they stormed the Bastille, the crowds of Paris began practicing their own ideals of justice and order by instantly hanging alleged evildoers from the lanterns in the streets. The ensuing terror of the Jacobins, many historians believe, resulted from the widespread popular demand for harsh justice. Similarly, in late 1917 the Russian author Maxim Gorky, a sympathizer of the revolution but also a staunch supporter of civil liberties, claimed that he had counted more than ten thousand lynchings since the fall of the tsarist regime. The unchecked cruelty of the mobs, Gorky feared, greatly jeopardized the prospects for a civil and humane democracy in his country. To some extent the Bolshevik terror may well be seen as a response to the popular "violence from below."

The American Revolution also had its share of ideological fervor and popular violence. Nevertheless neither revolutionary mob action nor the political suppression of loyalism during the War of Independence escalated into a regime of revolutionary terror backed by the masses. Among the many reasons for this, the most important was the dominant political culture of rights in British North America. The American revolutionaries cherished English traditions of individual liberty, the rule of law, and due process. Even as they exposed Tories as "enemies to American liberties," they recognized that they themselves were curbing the rights and freedoms of their opponents in the name of liberty. Moreover many of the elite patriot leaders, while praising popular rebellion against tyranny, harbored deep-seated fears of mob rule and anarchy. As soon as ordered liberty was secure, "respect [was] due to Constitutional authority," Samuel Adams declared in 1784, "and those Men, who under any Pretence or by any Means whatever, would lessen the Weight of Government lawfully exercised must be Enemies to our happy Revolution and the Common Liberty." After the Revolution, most of the states passed so-called Riot Acts to enable governments to deal effectively with civil unrest. Attempts to rekindle the flame of popular rebellion, such as the 1786 Shays's Rebellion of desperate debtors in Massachusetts, or the 1794 anti-tax Whiskey Rebellion in Pennsylvania, were forcefully quelled. President George Washington himself led federal troops against the Whiskey insurgents, who disbanded in the face of the hero of the Revolution. The message was clear: the free institutions of the American Republic had rendered the need for popular insurgencies obsolete. Mob action and riots could no longer be tolerated.

Of course not everyone agreed. In 1787 Thomas Jefferson famously asked, "What country can preserve it's [sic] liberties if their rulers are not warned from time to time that their people preserve the spirit of resistance?" As a healthy precaution to despotism the future president recommended that "the tree of liberty must be refreshed from time to time with the blood of patriots & tyrants." This idea that the people have a right to resist tyranny, if necessary by violent means, has remained highly influential in American political culture. Most Americans cherish the libertarian spirit forged in the American Revolution as a great national tradition and would not even think of linking it to the unsavory history of lynching. Yet there is some ambivalence in this legacy. "Perfected during the revolutionary epoch," the historian Richard Maxwell Brown has argued, "were techniques of civil violence that Americans put to frequent use in later centuries. In the realm of ideas, the concept of popular sovereignty emerged as a powerful rationale for extralegal violence against those deemed to be enemies of the public good." A disposition to form mobs and kill such enemies of the community, a practice that was soon universally known as lynching, must be counted among the "demonic sides" of American history that Brown identified as a vital part of this legacy.

2

The Rise of Lynch Law
in Antebellum America

IN SEPTEMBER 1835 *Niles' Weekly Register*, one of the most influential popular magazines in the United States at the time, voiced its deep concern over a wave of mob violence that was sweeping the country. Claiming that it had collected more than five hundred reports of recent incidents, the weekly painted a bleak picture. "Society seems everywhere unhinged and the demon of 'blood and slaughter' has been let loose upon us," the article lamented. "We have executions, and murders, and riots to the utmost limits of the union. The character of our countrymen seems suddenly changed, and thousands interpret the law in their own way." Such lawlessness held up Americans "to the contempt and scorn of the old world," prompting the magazine to implore its readers: "Let the laws rule. And let no one do anything . . . to bring them into popular disrespect." Other newspapers, both in the North and in the South, agreed that America was teetering on the brink of "mobocracy."

Despite their alarmist tone, these warnings were clearly supported by facts. According to one historian's count, the United States experienced 147 riots in 1835, with 109 incidents occurring between July and October alone. Unrest spread across the entire country, from Maine to Arkansas, and included clashes between Irish immigrants and native-born New Englanders, the sacking of a brothel in New York, attacks on religious dissenters such as the Mormons, violent political confrontations, and the lynching of alleged criminals. In two-fifths of the 1835 riots, the increasingly volatile issues of race and slavery played a key role. In 46 cases, proslavery mobs acted against abolitionists or putative slave insurrections.

Observers also noted correctly that mob violence had taken on a new quality in the 1830s. The decade marked a watershed not only because riots and lynchings became more frequent but also because they took a deadly turn. Whereas in the era of the American Revolution mobs had rarely killed their victims, the 1835 riots claimed at least seventy-one lives. A few accidental fatalities notwithstanding, most victims died at the hands of mobs acting with intent to kill. In the most conspicuous lynching of the year, vigilantes hanged five gamblers in Vicksburg, Mississippi. These events stood in stark contrast to the the first three decades of the nineteenth century, when most victims of mob action suffered flogging and banishment rather than death.

Why did mob violence explode in the 1830s, and why did mobs become so bloodthirsty? Why did lynching develop into an integral part of American life in the decades before the Civil War? The answers to these questions involve three key factors: the rise of mass democracy, the conflict over slavery, and the expansion of the frontier beyond the Mississippi. This chapter looks at the changes in antebellum society and at the link between slavery and lynching.

Antebellum America was a highly dynamic society. Between 1790, the year of the first census, and 1840 the population of the United States grew from fewer than four million to more than seventeen million, even before the impact of mass immigration. Hundreds of thousands of farmers pushed into the trans-Appalachian West, eager for land to grow cash crops for expanding markets in the East, where early industrialization was driving urbanization and the emergence of a large working class. In 1820 only 6 percent of all Americans lived in towns with 2,500 or more residents; the United States had only two cities, New York and Philadelphia, with more than 100,000 inhabitants. Forty years later, 20 percent of the population were urban dwellers, and eight cities boasted more than 100,000 residents, with New York approaching one million. During the same period the so-called Transportation Revolution, including overland roads, canals, steam-driven riverboats, and railroads, was bringing Americans closer together and spawning the rise of new commercial and industrial centers in the Great Lakes area and along the Mississippi River. The invention of the electric telegraph by Samuel F. B. Morse in 1844 revolutionized long-distance communication.

Inevitably the forces of modernization disrupted traditional ways of life and social values, and created anxieties that provided a fertile breeding ground for collective and personal violence. Immigration is an excellent case in point. From 1815 until 1840 approximately 800,000 immigrants arrived in the United States. Over the following 20 years, their numbers soared to a total of 4.2 million, with three million coming in the decade between 1845 and 1854. In proportion to the total population, this movement of people amounted to the largest immigration wave in all of U.S. history. Among the newcomers, Irish led the way with Germans a close second. By 1860 three-fourths of the more than 4 million foreign-born residents of the United States belonged to either of these two ethnic groups whom the dominant Anglo-Protestants viewed as significantly different in their language, culture, and religion and as unwelcome economic competitors. Not surprisingly, mass immigration triggered a strong nativist reaction. Violent clashes between immigrants and nativists as well as among the different immigrant populations became a hallmark of antebellum urban life.

Nativist violence often dovetailed with religious resentment. In 1834 wild rumors among Bostonians that a Catholic convent in nearby Charlestown contained secret dungeons and chambers of torture prompted a mob to burn down the building. Protestant nativists viewed Irish Catholic immigration in particular as part of a vile conspiracy by the Vatican to destroy American Protestant liberty. When in 1844 the Catholics of Philadelphia protested the use of the Protestant King James Bible in public schools, xenophobic hysteria boiled over. Mobs descended on Catholic neighborhoods, and fierce fighting ensued until the militia intervened. The so-called Philadelphia Bible Riots left at least sixteen people dead, mostly nativist assailants, and dozens of houses in ruins. In the 1850s, when the nativist Know-Nothing movement briefly swept American politics, political riots with scores of people killed or injured raged through most major cities in the North, the Midwest, and the South. But urban unrest triggered by ethnic, religious, and political tensions must be distinguished from lynching. Typically, hostile mobs fought and sometimes killed each other in open street battles rather than staging extralegal executions of hapless victims.

The emergence of mass-circulation newspapers, another aspect of modernization, also fostered the rise of collective violence. Improvements

in printing technology sharply reduced costs and sale prices. In the 1830s
the *New York Sun* and the *New York Herald* became the first newspapers with a mass appeal, running a combined circulation of 40,000 copies
daily. Nationwide newspaper circulation multiplied from roughly 80,000
to more than 300,000 by the end the decade. A drastic change in reporting styles boosted the allure of the penny press. Sensational sex and crime
stories featuring murder and rape whipped up emotions and might easily
be read as encouraging mob action.

This upsurge of mass journalism advanced the rise of mass politics in
the 1830s. The presidencies of Andrew Jackson (1767–1845) and his successor Martin Van Buren (1782–1862), encompassing the years from 1829
to 1841, marked the transition from a rather elitist political culture toward mass participation. The expansion of the suffrage ensured that by
the early 1840s practically all white male Americans twenty-one years of
age and older had the right to vote. And vote they did. In the presidential
election of 1824 merely one-quarter of all eligible voters had exercised
their franchise; in 1840 the turnout approached 80 percent. Jacksonian
Democrats and Whigs emerged as modern parties keenly competing for
a mass following. Political rallies tended to be rather rowdy and drunken
affairs, and fists and bludgeons were often more instrumental in settling
political disputes than the power of the reasoned word.

The arrival of the "common man" in politics advanced a new understanding of popular sovereignty, including the power of the people to
take the law into their own hands. More than any other public figure
of his time, President Andrew Jackson, whose name came to signify the
era, embodied the spirit of popular empowerment. Born in the Carolina
backcountry as the son of humble immigrants from Northern Ireland,
Jackson spent his early adult years as a self-taught lawyer whose understanding of the law was shaped by its practical application on the frontier.
Although he prospered as a planter and slaveholder, "Old Hickory," as
his admirers fondly called him, owed his political career to his reputation
as a champion of the plain folk, a ferocious Indian fighter, and the hero
of the 1815 Battle of New Orleans in the war against Britain. To Andrew
Jackson, resorting to violence in defense of personal honor or the public
interest appeared perfectly legitimate, even if this meant stepping beyond
the boundaries of the law. Famously, his mother had admonished her
son that in matters of honor the law "affords no remedy that can satisfy

the feelings of a true man." Indeed, as an adult Jackson did not shy away from duels that ended with the death of his opponents.

As a military commander and public official, "Old Hickory" was no less audacious when it came to situations that seemed to require determined action rather than legal hairsplitting. During the 1818 campaign against the Seminole tribe of Florida, he ordered the execution of two Indian chiefs and, shortly thereafter, of two Englishmen whom he charged with inciting Indian attacks on American citizens. While the Indians were hanged without further ado, the British prisoners at least received a military trial, albeit one of questionable legality. When the court-martial revoked the death sentence against one of the defendants, Jackson ordered him executed all the same.

Critics accused Jackson of overstepping his authority and setting a dangerous precedent of executions outside the law, but his admirers celebrated him for vindicating American honor and power. After he was elected president in 1828, Jackson continued to conceive of the law as the servant of the people. If it failed to advance the popular will and interest, the law had to be changed or, if necessary, ignored. When in 1832 the U.S. Supreme Court found that the Cherokee Indians were entitled to federal protection against infringements by the state of Georgia, "Old Hickory" chose to disregard the ruling because the decision potentially hampered his policy of Indian removal. Allegedly Jackson scoffed at the Court's chief justice: "John Marshall has made his decision; now let him enforce it." Such an attitude did not help promote popular respect for the law.

Jackson's critics complained that the democratic and egalitarian spirit of the age encouraged anarchy and mob rule—an argument that detractors of democracy have put forth throughout history. But there can be no doubt that many antebellum Americans were deeply worried about the rise of violence. To counter rioting and soaring violent crime, larger cities established professional police forces. Still, American homicide rates continued to grow at an alarming pace and may have been twice as high as in Europe. Some historians believe that the harsher administration of criminal justice by authoritarian European states explains this difference. In the early nineteenth century the per capita execution rate in England was 20 percent higher than in the United States, though supposedly the English committed less crime and fewer

homicides. In contrast, law enforcement in America was notoriously
weak. A study of murder in New York City has found that in the nineteenth century only about half of all homicides resulted in an arrest;
half of those arrested were tried, and half of those brought to trial were
actually convicted. Thirty percent of those sentenced to prison terms
for homicide were pardoned before serving their full terms.

Then again, the efficiency of law enforcement in the urban North
compared favorably to that of the South, where nothing even remotely
resembling a state monopoly of force existed. Personal violence was rampant and widely condoned, especially if committed by a man in defense of
his honor or that of his kin. This peculiar code of honor, requiring a violent response to even the slightest perceived insult, was often celebrated
as a distinguishing feature of Southern culture. Yet all too often the claim
to defend one's honor was only a cheap excuse for unruly behavior and
lawlessness. Moreover much of the violence allegedly perpetrated in vin-
dication of personal repute did not at all resemble fair fights but rather
consisted of treacherous assaults committed for sordid motives. In 1831
Robert Potter, a member of the North Carolina legislature, castrated two
men whom he accused of having had adulterous relations with his wife.
In reality Potter had invented the charges to disgrace his wife so he could
marry another woman. All the same, he served only a brief jail term and
was reelected upon his release. The case was not exceptional. Southern
society was extremely tolerant of physical violence and homicide whenever honor, revenge, or similar passions were involved. Many homicides
resulted in no criminal prosecution at all; those cases that came to trial
were most likely to end with acquittals or token fines. For the victims of
violent assault, safety and justice were not to be found in the law but in
resorting to their own vengeance.

In a society that glorified extralegal violence and maintained only
weak legal institutions, many Southerners regarded lynching and mobs
as acceptable instruments in meting out punishment. To be sure, mob
violence also occurred in the North, claiming numerous fatalities. But
most casualties north of the Mason-Dixon line were rioters killed or injured by police who were trying to preserve law and order. In the North,
rioters also faced a much greater risk of arrest and criminal prosecution.
In striking contrast, in the South the forces of the law rarely interfered
with the work of mobs; hence the vast majority of those killed were the
lynchers' targeted victims.

The extralegal execution of five gamblers in Vicksburg, Mississippi, in early July 1835 became a defining moment in the history of lynching in America. Although mob violence had been on the rise for years, the hanging of five men by a crowd allegedly numbering in the hundreds was an extraordinary event. Newspapers throughout the country reported the incident, describing it as a "lynching" or "lynch law," thereby helping establish these terms in the parlance of ordinary Americans. For years to come both advocates and critics of popular justice cited the Vicksburg incident in support of their positions, making it into a paradigm for the communal punishment of crime and vice in antebellum America.

In the early 1830s Vicksburg, a booming town at the confluence of the Mississippi and Yazoo rivers, had developed into a hotbed of gambling and prostitution. Apparently the brazen conduct of the gamblers offended many Vicksburg citizens, who feared they were being overtaken by outlaws. When the local militia, known as the Vicksburg Volunteers, held a barbecue on Independence Day 1835, the simmering pot boiled over. An unwelcome gambler named Cabler became unruly, insulting and beating up one of the other guests. Shortly after he had been forcibly removed from the celebration, Cabler returned wielding a knife and a gun and threatened to kill one of the militia men who had thrown him out. Having once again subdued the troublemaker, the Volunteers decided to teach him a lesson. They took him to the woods and "lynched" him by giving him a severe whipping, followed for good measure by tarring and feathering. The next day they issued an ultimatum to all gamblers to leave town within twenty-four hours. Most of the unwanted residents got the message and absconded. But when the Volunteers and other townspeople raided the gambling houses on the morning of July 6, they discovered that one group of gamblers refused to leave. Upon entering the building through the back door, the Volunteers were greeted by shots that killed one of the militia leaders, Dr. Hugh S. Bodley. The enraged citizens quickly overpowered the gang and resolved to make short work of them. They let go one man who apparently had nothing to do with the shooting but instantly hanged the remaining five prisoners, including one fatally wounded by a gunshot. The bodies dangled for another day and then were buried in a ditch.

A few days later the local newspaper, the *Vicksburg Register*, published a narrative of the events that encompassed the standard rationale in defense of lynching. According to the paper, the community had exercised self-defense against wicked scoundrels who had terrorized the town to a point so intolerable that action was imperative. The laws were "wholly ineffectual" for suppressing and punishing their "shameless vices and daring outrages." In liberating itself from this pest, a unanimous community had shown a marvelous "public spirit." No matter what "sickly sensibility or mawkish philanthropy" might say, the *Register* praised the lynching as a "purifying storm" and a "revolution . . . conducted by the most respectable citizens." The gamblers deserved their fate because they were depraved wretches, "unconnected with society by any of its ordinary ties," who "poisoned the springs of morality."

Such righteous indignation raises the question of who actually frequented the "tippling houses" run by the gamblers if not many of the respectable townspeople. One might suspect that, by killing the outlaws, the good citizens of Vicksburg had staged a ritual of self-purification and made the gamblers the scapegoats for their own less than perfect virtue. Following the hangings, "the whole procession then returned to the city, collected the faro tables into a pile and burnt them," as the *Register* described this quasi-religious ceremony.

On closer look, the justification for the Vicksburg lynching falls apart. Whatever immediate threat against the community may have existed, the militia could have easily controlled it. They restrained Cabler, chased most gamblers out of town, and quickly overwhelmed those who refused to leave. Nothwithstanding the *Register*'s moral outrage against the "vile and lawless machinations" of the gamblers, their actual crimes remain suspiciously unclear. After all, as Abraham Lincoln, then a young Whig politician, who discussed the Vicksburg lynching in one of his earliest speeches, correctly pointed out, while gambling was not exactly a "very useful, or very honest occupation," it was nevertheless legal under Mississippi law. The *Register* itself admitted that lynch law was necessary because it would have been difficult to obtain a court conviction of Cabler or any of the occupants of the house where Dr. Bodley was killed. An impartial jury might well have concluded that these men had acted in justifiable self-defense against a mob.

Public reaction to the Vicksburg lynchings throughout the country was sharply divided and included numerous critical voices who decried that American citizens had been executed without due process of law and trial by jury. Vigilante committees claiming to exercise the higher

The hanging of the Vicksburg gamblers, 1835 ("Our Peculiar Domestic Institutions).

law of necessity and popular will, one critic wrote, were little more than mobs made up by "a large number of boys and drunkards" whipped into a frenzy by "inflammatory speeches." On the other hand, the Vicksburg hangings also met with considerable approval, especially in the South, where anti-gambling committees formed in several towns to drive out the unwelcome residents. In 1836 the governor of Mississippi, incidentally named Charles Lynch, referred to Vicksburg and other recent mob killings in the state when he advised the legislature "that necessity will sometimes prompt a summary mode of trial and punishment unknown to the law."

Southerners often saw occasion for acting upon such necessity. From 1830 to 1860 Southern mobs claiming to punish crime killed approximately 130 white people and whipped and banished many more. Many Southerners viewed mob violence as an acceptable alternative to the official court system. In defending the need for popular justice, its proponents often cited the corruption of the criminal justice system that allowed the wealthy to buy themselves impunity or simply profit from their social status. In one infamous case that occurred in Natchez, Mississippi, in January 1835, a mob seized James Foster, Jr., a member of a prominent planter family but a notorious drunkard and gambler. Although strong circumstantial evidence implicated Foster in the murder of his young wife Susan, who supposedly came from a humble social background, the judge dismissed the case and set the defendant free. As soon as Foster left the courthouse a crowd of several hundred snatched him, tied him to a tree, and flogged him until "the flesh rung in ribands from his body." Next the lynchers scalped him partially, drenched his body with hot tar, and covered him with feathers, reducing him to the appearance of a "shapeless fowl." Yet even though some called for hanging or drowning Foster, he was eventually allowed to escape after several gentlemen persuaded the mob that justice had been served. Even in disgrace the victim's social rank could not be entirely ignored. In contrast, social outcasts such as the Vicksburg gamblers faced much greater odds of being killed.

Whether deadly or not, few white Southerners publicly questioned the legitimacy of communal punishment. For one thing, open criticism of lynchings could have provoked retaliation by the mob. But intimidation only partly explains the absence of opposition. Although lynching and mob violence did not happen every day, week, or month, the notion that they were indispensible elements of true popular justice became deeply ingrained in Southern culture. In those few cases when legal action was brought against the perpetrators, "respectable citizens" flooded the authorities with petitions vouching for the good character and pure motives of the defendants. Sheriffs looked the other way when prisoners tried to break jail, and juries generally sympathized with the lynchers. In fact, public approval of and mass participation in a lynching could serve as evidence that the act itself was justified. After a large mob had burned a free black man to death in St. Louis, Missouri, in 1836, Judge Luke Lawless—another appropriate name—informed the grand jury that if the deed represented the "mysterious, metaphysical, and almost electric phrenzy" of an "infuriated multitude . . . the case then transcends your jurisdiction—it is beyond the reach of human law." In other words, the righteous ire of the people trumped the law.

True, lynchings also occurred in the North, and some Northern lynchers went unpunished, especially if their victims were blacks or unpopular outsiders. The leaders of the Illinois mob that killed the Mormon prophet Joseph Smith in 1844 claimed that they acted in self-defense against a dangerous threat to the public; they were merely executing the will of the people. A jury that included no members of the Mormon church later issued an acquittal. Nevertheless there can be no doubt that violence and lawlessness were not only more frequent in the South but also based on much stronger popular consent. The root cause of that consent was slavery, perhaps the single most important wellspring of mob violence in antebellum America.

From the colonial era, the institution of slavery in America had undergone profound changes. The libertarian and egalitarian spirit of the American Revolution triggered a process of gradual emancipation in the North, where slavery had always been of marginal economic importance. Even most Southern slaveholders conceded that human bondage was a moral and social evil, albeit one that could not be abolished all at once but would fade away over time. Their misgivings did not last very long, however. During the 1787 Constitutional Convention in Philadelphia, the slaveholders succeeded in obtaining a tacit recognition of and legal safeguards for their human property, including the so-called fugitive slave clause which obliged the free states to return escaped slaves to their owners. Moreover the introduction of the cotton gin and the ensuing cotton boom provided slavery with a new and rock-solid economic base. Between 1790 and 1860 annual cotton production exploded from four thousand bales to four million, making it by far the country's most important export commodity. During the same period the slave population, driven by vibrant natural reproduction, surged from roughly 700,000 to around four million. On the eve of the Civil War the American South was the largest slaveholding society in the world. Human property represented its second most valuable capital stock, surpassed only by the land itself.

Naturally the prosperity that cotton production and slave labor generated for the Southern planter class affected its ideological outlook on slavery. The defenders of the South's "peculiar institution" dropped all apologetic pretenses and began to praise slavery as a positive good. Masters depicted themselves as paternalists who fondly cared for their "children" and taught them the blessings of civilization and Christianity. At the same time they appealed to the racial solidarity of the nonslaveholding majority of white Southerners, warning them that the abolition of slavery posed a deadly menace to all white people. The end of slavery, the defenders of bondage argued, would set free hordes of savages intent on murder, plunder, and rape.

In the 1830s the pro-slavery discourse of the South grew increasingly shrill and aggressive. In part this was a reaction to the emergence of organized abolitionism in the North, which the advocates of slavery vociferously condemned as a sinister conspiracy against the Southern way of life. Equally important, the Nat Turner slave rebellion of 1831 seemed to confirm the worst nightmares of the South. Turner, a charismatic slave preacher living in Southhampton County, Virginia, led an insurgency of roughly seventy slaves who attacked several plantations and killed as many as sixty whites, including women and children. Although the rebellion was quickly crushed and remained the only major slave insurrection of the antebellum era, the Nat Turner revolt nevertheless had a deep impact on how white Southerners reacted to even moderate criticism of their peculiar institution. Anyone who questioned slavery in whole or in part appeared as the South's mortal enemy. Abolitionists, South Carolina planter and politician James Henry Hammond wrote to a New York editor in the summer of 1835, "can be silenced in but one way. Terror and Death." In 1848 U.S. Senator Henry Foote of Mississippi warned a Northern anti-slavery colleague that should he ever come to his state, "he could not go ten miles into the interior, before he would grace one of the tallest trees of the forest, with a rope around his neck; and that if necessary, I should myself assist in the operation." For all practical purposes, mob violence and lynching became officially condoned instruments in defending slavery. Slaves and free blacks, suspected and real abolitionists both in the North and the South, all fell victim to the furor of pro-slavery mobs.

While the Southern states rigidly suppressed all anti-slavery propaganda or publications, the North refused to curtail freedom of speech. This does not mean, however, that abolitionism was popular in the free states. On the contrary, many Northerners, especially Jacksonian Democrats, despised abolitionists as self-righteous and hypocritical fanatics who jeopardized sectional peace and undermined white supremacy. Many Northern newspapers echoed Southern demands for banning anti-slavery activities and openly encouraged mob violence, insinuating that the troublemakers were asking for it. Their calls did not go unheeded. Between 1830 and 1860 more than seventy anti-abolitionist riots occurred in the free states.

Yet Northern attacks on abolitionists very rarely resulted in fatalities. The only known lethal incident occurred in November 1837 in Alton, Illinois, when the Reverend Elijah P. Lovejoy lost his life in a gun battle with a mob trying to ransack his printing presses. During the confrontation one of the assailants also died. Typically, Northern anti-abolitionist violence targeted property, particularly newspaper offices, and rioters confined themselves to beating up their victims. In 1843, for example, Frederick Douglass, the escaped slave and prominent black abolitionist, was battered by an Indiana mob. Moreover the instigators of anti-abolitionist violence in the North could not count on impunity. In the fall of 1837 a crowd pelted anti-slavery activists in Connecticut with stones and rotten eggs and forcibly broke into a church. By the standards of the time, this was a minor case of disorderly conduct, but it nonetheless resulted in eight arrests and two rioters being sentenced each to two months in prison. The leader of the mob faced court costs amounting to $1,000.

In the free states, violent anti-abolitionists targeted known and self-professed opponents of slavery. Abolitionists did not advocate slave rebellion or racial mixing, as their detractors charged, but they vocally condemned human bondage as a moral and social evil that must be ended as soon as possible. Although a small and unpopular minority, Northern abolitionists constituted an active and visible social movement. In glaring contrast, open and organized abolitionism was practically absent in the slave states. Cassius M. Clay, the maverick anti-slavery editor and politician from Kentucky, who for years physically fought hostile mobs before he was finally driven from the state in 1845, was a rare exception. Nearly all Southerners who had doubts about slavery were cowed into silence and conformity. Still, mobs eagerly looked for and found "abolitionists" plotting racial mayhem and the destruction of the South. Almost all of their victims turned out to be "phantom abolitionists" who had somehow aroused suspicion. Strangers who came from the North were especially at risk of being accused as abolitionist intruders.

Wild rumors and hysteria inevitably produced situations of comical absurdity, except of course for the injured parties. Shortly after the Nat Turner uprising, for example, a Virginia mob savagely whipped an English traveler named Robinson for allegedly having advocated emancipation in a private conversation. Over the next several years rumors lingered on that an Englishman who had aided Nat Turner was roaming the South and instigating slave rebellion. As a consequence, two British subjects named Robertson and Roberts, respectively, became mob targets because their nationality and their names coincided with those of the imaginary English "abolitionist." In 1859 and 1860, when the militant abolitionist John Brown staged his notorious raid on the federal armory in Harpers Ferry, Virginia, aiming to ignite a slave insurrection throughout the South, and when the anti-slavery Republican party became the dominant political force in the North, the Southern abolition scare reached new heights. Possession of Northern state banknotes or, for that matter, a copy of the U.S. Constitution could be construed as evidence of abolitionist sympathies and provoke popular wrath. In Mississippi a mob hanged a man merely for wearing a red sash, which, the lynchers claimed, proved his affiliation with a clandestine abolitionist society.

It is uncertain how many white persons were killed by Southern anti-abolitionist mobs. In 1856 the abolitionist newspaper *The Liberator* declared that during the preceding two decades more than three hundred whites had been murdered for allegedly criticizing slavery. In contrast, a leading modern historian of antebellum mob violence maintains that, as a rule, Southern mobs were content with expelling suspected abolitionists. According to his count, while lashing and tarring and feathering were more common, only eighteen white victims died at the hands of abolition mobs, and another twenty-six perished by summary execution during the repression of putative slave insurrections. In addition to the abolitionists' desire to dramatize Southern cruelty and lawlessness, the vague use of the terms lynching or lynch law, which still included nondeadly forms of communal punishment, may have inflated the number of fatalities. But there is no question that the term lynch law was a proper description of how Southern mobs treated alleged abolitionists. Public floggings and execution-style hangings were meant to convey the message that the people would mete out just punishment for abhorrent crimes against the local community and the South at large.

In the South, whites might risk being beaten up or lynched merely for expressing dissenting ideas about slavery. Yet those suspected of inciting slave revolts faced certain and merciless retribution without benefit of due process. In early July 1835, at the same time the Vicksburg gamblers were lynched, the adjacent County of Madison, Mississippi, experienced an insurrection panic. In all likelihood it was a figment of excited fantasies, but it resulted in the deaths of seven whites and at least a dozen slaves. After torturing the slave "ringleaders" into confessing to a plot and implicating their white "accomplices," the vigilantes seized two white suspects, Joshua Cotton and William Saunders. An apologetic report of the events, published later in the year, articulated the logic of lynching in words that strike modern readers as inadvertently candid. Under ordinary circumstances, the report's author Thomas Shackelford reasoned, the suspects should have been handed over to the civil authorities. But "it was well known that much of the testimony which established their guilt beyond all doubt, would, under the *forms* of the law be excluded; and, if admissible, that the witnesses were then no more." In other words, Shackelford insisted that extralegal action was necessary because the "confessions" by the slaves were based on legally impermissible torture and because Southern law did not permit slaves to testify against whites in the first place. But even if these rules could have been disregarded, the mob had already killed the slave informants, who could no longer repeat their testimony. According to this logic, the first act of lawlessness justified the next one.

Moreover, Shackelford argued, if the men had been brought into the "custody of the law," a mob would have seized them anyway. Hence it was preferable that an orderly "Committee of Safety" deal out summary and exemplary punishment, predicated on the venerable "law of self-preservation, which is *paramount to all law*." To underscore the social standing and respectability of the vigilantes, Shackelford thought it fitting to quote their guiding principle in Latin: "salus populi est summa lex"—the "safety and welfare of the people is the supreme law."

In addition to the need of nipping an awful conspiracy in the bud, Shackelford offered another telling reason why Cotton and Saunders must hang. "It was not believed that the execution of a few negroes, unknown and obscure, would have the effect of frightening their *white* associates from an attempt to perpetrate their horrid designs." Because black slaves were supposedly incapable of independently plotting an uprising, there had to be white masterminds. White leaders were also necessary to prove the theory that abolitionists posed a mortal threat to the South. Consequently the vigilantes forced Cotton and Saunders, with the help of the lash, to incriminate other white conspirators. Following

their hanging on July 4, five more white men were executed in Madison
County over the next two weeks. Another man committed suicide after a
mob had viciously tormented him for hours. Because most of the victims
did not live in the county and three were native New Englanders, they
nicely fit the description of what Shackelford called "emissar[ies] of those
deluded fanatics at the north—the ABOLITIONISTS."

In the heated imagination of the Madison County vigilantes, abolitionist conspirators had allegedly joined forces with a fabled criminal
gang known as the Murrell clan from Tennessee. Presumably the white
criminals were eager to benefit from the chaos created by a slave uprising. Thus fears of an impending race war merged with concerns about a
criminal white underclass. In contrast, Shackelford portrayed the "Committee of Safety" as an organization of high-minded and respectable citizens. The Committee, he claimed, made every effort to pay tribute to the
requirements of a fair trial, "if not *formal*, at least *substantial*." To emphasize his point, he cited the "confessions" most of the condemned men had
made under the gallows. Of course Shackelford's report conveniently
ignored that all "confessions" had been rendered under torture and in
the vain hope of clemency. The admission of guilt in the face of death,
as noted earlier, had been a key ritual of public executions for centuries
and was required to attest to the justice of the verdict. By the same token, lynchers needed confessions in order to validate their claim to being
agents of a "higher law." Then again, torture prolonged the victim's suffering and gave more people a chance to inflict pain, turning lynch law
into a truly communal ritual of hate and violence. As one eyewitness of
the 1835 frenzy in Madison County put it bluntly, the people were "blind
with excitement" and simply "out for blood."

Throughout the antebellum era the omnipresent fear of slave revolts
fueled numerous insurrection scares that repeatedly swelled into waves
of hysteria, especially in the 1830s and the late 1850s. During the Texas
panic of 1860, mobs lynched up to ten white persons, including several
ministers believed to be affiliated with Northern anti-slavery churches.
But, of course, most victims of the insurrection scares were slaves who
bore the full brunt of white nightmares. By conservative estimates, more
than four hundred slaves perished in such violent crazes, not counting
those who were legally executed.

But as desperately as many slaves may have wished to rise against their oppressors, nearly all their alleged plots existed only in the fantasies of the vigilantes. They were based on nothing more than rumors and "confessions" obtained by torture or promises of freedom. Fires or the outbreak of mysterious diseases could easily trigger accusations of arson or the poisoning of wells. Such acts, many whites believed, would serve as signals to precipitate a slave rebellion. Once the scare gained momentum, mobs, vigilante committees, or slave patrols—often indistinguishable from one another—began hunting down the "ringleaders" and beating "information" out of frightened slaves. To quell the looming danger and to instill terror into potential rebels, summary executions followed, often administered with deliberate cruelty such as burning the victims and maiming them before they died. The custom of cutting off the heads of executed slaves and displaying them on poles, practiced since colonial times, was continued throughout the antebellum period.

Some sober-minded Southerners recognized that the panics were little more than the products of hysteria and bloodthirst. During an 1856 scare in Tennessee, which resulted in the killing of more than fifty slaves, a planter privately mused: "We are trying our best . . . to produce a negro insurrection, without the slightest aid from the negroes themselves." Clearly many slaveholders were not happy to see their human property destroyed by raging mobs. Still, they had to be careful not to question the right and duty of the community to control and punish slaves, because slavery depended on the collusion of nonslaveholding whites. Thus the recurring insurrection scares exposed the bleak truth that in the last resort the peculiar institution rested on violence. The rhetoric of paternalism notwithstanding, masters relied not only on asserting their own absolute power but also on the brute force of mobs euphemistically called slave patrols or "committees of safety."

Slaveholders were loath to acknowledge the role of mob violence in upholding slavery. Rather, they took great pride in the legal protection that the law supposedly afforded their slaves. In an 1860 verdict on the appeal of a slave who had been sentenced to death for raping a white woman, the Florida Supreme Court called it "the crowning glory of our 'peculiar institution,' that whenever life is involved, the slave stands upon as safe ground as the master." Historians have echoed these claims,

pointing to the amazing degree of due process that Southern courts extended to slaves, even when they stood accused of raping a white woman.
In the majority of rape cases slaves received a fair trial; neither a guilty
verdict nor execution were foregone conclusions. Instead, class and gender often worked in favor of black defendants. Masters provided their
slaves with legal counsel and initiated appeals, because the execution
of a slave usually meant a significant financial loss given that the compensation to which slaveholders were entitled did not match the slave's
market value. Moreover nineteenth-century standards of evidence in
rape cases were extremely high, requiring, for example, proof of physical resistance by the victim. Thus if a woman pressing rape charges was
poor and perhaps had a reputation for loose morals, especially of enter-
taining illicit sexual relations across the color line, her credibility might
not match that of a black slave backed up by his owner.

   In 1848, for example, three slaves stood trial in Gloucester County,
Virginia, for raping a white woman who claimed that she could identify
at least two of her assailants. Other eyewitnesses corroborated her testimony. The jury acquitted one of the defendants for want of evidence
and sentenced to death the two others, including an adolescent named
Edmund. Although there was little doubt that Edmund had actually
committed the crime, no fewer than 182 respectable citizens of Gloucester County petitioned the governor to commute Edmund's sentence to
transportation out of the state, citing his youth and the "notoriously bad
character" of the victim who had allegedly provoked the deed by her
lewd behavior. Eventually none of the three defendants was executed.
The outcome of this case was no rare exception. Of the roughly 150 slaves
sentenced to death for rape in antebellum Virginia, half of them escaped
the hangman, either because they were pardoned or because their convictions were thrown out on appeal.

   In striking contrast to the obsession with the putative menace of
the black rapist that took possession of the Southern white mind and
served as the key justification for lynching in the late nineteenth century, it appears that rape charges against slaves before the Civil War
were calmly handled by the courts. Then again, a caveat must be raised:
it is impossible to know how many slaves accused of raping, assaulting, or murdering whites were killed by their masters or by lynch mobs
before their cases could ever reach the courts. Moreover, because the

terms lynching or lynch law were rarely used in connection with the killing of slaves, many such murders may have escaped the attention of both contemporary chroniclers and later historians. Those cases for which there is some documentation add up to considerable numbers. For the period from 1828 to 1861 there is evidence of at least forty-nine Southern mob actions against alleged black criminals, all of them ending in the death of their victims. Half of these cases involved aggravated cruelty, especially burning.

A few instances may illustrate this point: In 1835 lynchers incinerated two slaves in Mobile, Alabama, for allegedly killing two white children. One year later a large crowd in St. Louis gleefully watched a free man of mixed ancestry who had stabbed a sheriff to death being slowly roasted on a fire. In 1842 a posse in Louisiana apprehended and burned two runaway slaves who had purportedly murdered and raped several whites. In 1853 the same fate befell a slave in Missouri accused of having raped and slain a white woman. The next year lynchers in Natchez, Mississippi, reportedly forced four thousand slaves to watch a burning in order to make an example of a bondsman who had presumably struck at a white man. In September 1855 a mob in Tennessee broke into a jail and hanged a fugitive slave charged with the murder of a white woman. A few months later a slave who had killed his master was lynched in Missouri. In 1857 a vigilante party in Arkansas cremated several runaways accused of rape and murder while a Kentucky mob massacred three slaves charged with the slaying of a white family. The evidence for the 1850s suggests that of those slaves accused of killing their masters or overseers, more were put to death outside the law than were legally executed. This group includes two slave women, one of whom was burned at the stake for allegedly poisoning her owner.

In the summer of 1859 four slaves were lynched in Saline County, Missouri. The white residents of the county had become alarmed by a streak of crimes committed by slaves—murder, assault, and rape—which they interpreted as a dangerous sign of insubordination requiring a stern show of force. Although the county court was in session and quickly sentenced one of the black defendants to death, a crowd stormed the jail and murdered four prisoners. In defense of the lynchings the local newspaper made the usual claim that the law did not provide sufficient punishment and deterrence. Unless the legislature revised the criminal code to satisfy public sentiment, the paper declared, lynching would continue. "The law that is not based on public opinion is but a rope of sand," wrote the author James Shackleford, a magistrate of Saline County. "An enlightened public opinion is the voice of God, and when brought into action it has a power and an energy that cannot be resisted." Countering the charge that lynching constituted mob law, Shackleford pointed to the venerable precedents of American history, including the extralegal executions ordered by Andrew Jackson and, for that matter, the Boston Tea Party. "I know no reason why we should not have a little mob law in the state of Missouri, and County of Saline, when the *occasion imperiously and of necessity* demands it."

While its Southern defenders hailed lynching as true to the spirit of American democracy and essential in upholding the peculiar institution, abolitionists denounced Southern mob violence as proof that slavery encouraged violence and represented the very opposite of American ideals of justice and the rule of law. To highlight the savagery of slavery, abolitionist narratives often depicted lynch victims as Christian martyrs. A writer for the *Liberator*, who claimed to be an eyewitness to the 1836 burning in St. Louis, celebrated the victim, a free black man named Francis McIntosh: "Never [a] martyr suffered more courageously. Not a single scream escaped him . . . , all he said was 'God take my soul—God take my life.'" In a similar vein, the anti-slavery *New York Tribune* quoted the last words of a slave burned to death in Natchez, Mississippi, in 1854: "Now, set fire, I am ready to go in peace." Literary conventions of martyrdom notwithstanding, black lynching victims were not passive and pious sufferers. As a matter of fact, McIntosh was lynched because he had killed a white officer of the law while resisting arrest; the Natchez slave died for beating a white man. As these incidents demonstrate, the lynching of slaves and free blacks and the sadistic torture administered by the mobs revealed deep-seated white fears of black resistance.

Free blacks in the North had considerably more latitude to challenge slavery, and in doing so they did not shy away from collective violence. When slavecatchers roamed the free states in order to claim fugitives, they often provoked opposition from black communities and their anti-slavery white allies. In dozens of cases such resistance developed into major riots, involving shoot-outs with slavecatchers and large-scale confrontations with the forces of the law, resulting in serious injuries and sometimes in the death of policemen, slavecatchers, rioters, and fugitive slaves. Surprisingly, most of these riots were successful in that they prevented the reenslavement of the fugitives. Even more surprising, black participants in anti-slavery mobs who faced court charges usually received very light sentences, either fines or short prison terms. Such lenient punishment reflected the resentment of many Northern white communities toward the intrusions of the Southern slave power as well as their remorse for colluding in the enforcement of slavery under the federal fugitive slave laws.

Still, Northern blacks fighting slavecatchers were not lynch mobs, though sometimes they manhandled their adversaries to persuade them not to come back. Also, blacks who informed to the slave catchers risked being beaten up or seeing their homes set on fire, as happened to one suspected traitor in Christiana, Pennsylvania. The town was a sanctuary for runaways from Maryland and the scene of a major standoff between an anti-slavery mob and a slaveholder's posse in 1851. The posse was met by a large crowd of African-American vigilantes aided by a few whites. When the confrontation ended, the slaveowner who had come to claim his property lay dead. In order to assuage Southern outrage, federal authorities indicted twenty-seven blacks and three whites for treason and made sure that six fugitives were reenslaved. Despite this outcome, where anti-slavery sentiment among the white community was strong, even African Americans could successfully appeal to a higher moral law in justifying extralegal violence, though their actions involved defying white authorities.

Abolitionists were incontrovertibly right that slavery, apart from being an intrinsically violent institution, encouraged mob violence and lawlessness throughout American society. When in the mid-1850s pro- and anti-slavery forces clashed in "Bleeding Kansas," both sides justified mob violence and extralegal punishment in terms of higher law and popular will. Those residents of Kansas who demanded that slavery be legalized on the basis of popular sovereignty also called for meting out popular justice against abolitionists and "slave stealers." Conversely, when John Brown and his sons infamously butchered five pro-slavery men who were not known to have committed any particular crime, they sent what many anti-slavery Kansans regarded as a wholesome message of deterrence to the "border ruffians."

The conflict over slavery did not stop with summary executions and vigilante raids but soon escalated into a civil war claiming the lives of more than 600,000 Americans. Abolitionists proved to be wrong in assuming that the end of slavery would also lead to an end of lynching and mob violence. Instead the emancipation of four million black slaves at the end of the Civil War triggered unprecedented levels of racial violence. Yet in the later decades of the nineteenth century, as mob violence against slaves during the antebellum era faded from the memory of white Americans, they became increasingly willing to accept the paternalistic claims of former slaveholders that the peculiar institution had fostered racial harmony and mutual affection.

3

Frontier Justice

ACCORDING TO Frederick Jackson Turner (1861–1932), the great historian of the American West, the frontier experience shaped America's national character and institutions, especially the spirit of individualism and grassroots democracy. During centuries of continuous westward expansion, Turner argued, the struggle for survival in an unforgiving wilderness transformed the settlers into sturdy and self-reliant pioneers who formed tightly knit communities based on the ideals of liberty, equality, and local self-government. Turner did not hesitate to acknowledge that vigilantism and punishment outside the law were cornerstones of frontier culture. In dealing with crime, he wrote, "the frontiersman was impatient of restraints. He knew how to preserve order, even in the absence of legal authority. If there were cattle thieves, lynch-law was sudden and effective." Turner articulated what can be called the frontier theory of lynching. In short, it holds that the practice of lynching in America had its roots in conditions on the frontier and sprang from necessity rather than from a spirit of mob violence. In the absence of an effective government, the people had no choice but to take the law into their own hands. Vigilantism, far from representing lawlessness, was a first and inevitable step toward building a civil society.

The idea of the frontier as the crucible of the American character is among America's oldest and most enduring cultural myths. It has been celebrated ceaselessly by fiction writers, historians, artists, and movie producers. If lynching was an integral part of this formative national experience, perhaps it was not altogether reprehensible. In a long tradition, apologists have defended extralegal punishment on the frontier as wholesome popular justice, to be distinguished from the bloodlust of racist mobs during the Jim Crow era. If the natural and social environment

of the frontier made recourse to lynch law inescapable, it may well be
seen as a necessary transitional phase of American history rather than a
blemish on the nation's soul.

The frontier theory of lynching, however, raises several problems.
To begin with, America has not been the only frontier society in history. But while lynching was not unheard of in other English settler
colonies such as Canada or Australia, it never became as pervasive as
in the nineteenth- and twentieth-century United States. Equally important, it never enjoyed the widespread ideological support that it
did among Americans. Furthermore not all groups who settled on the
American frontier resorted to lynch law. In the colonial era, religious
communities such as the Puritans, the Quakers, and the Mennonites,
who lived for long periods of time under frontier conditions, did not
establish a record of meting out rough justice; nor did the Mormons in
the nineteenth century. On closer inspection the frontier theory of popular justice administered by virtuous pioneer communities gives way
to a much more murky and often sordid picture which includes racial
hostility as well as class conflict. The widespread notion that frontier
vigilantes acted only where efficient law enforcement was nonexistent
does not square with the historical record, which contains numerous
lynchings of criminal suspects who were already in custody. Distrust of
government played as large a role as lack of government.

Like all historical myths, the frontier theory of lynching contains some
elements of truth. During the early decades of the nineteenth century,
when the line of settlement advanced from the Appalachian Mountains
to the Mississippi River, the frontier had not yet acquired notoriety as a
place where unbridled violence and mob rule were the order of the day.
In punishing outlaws, frontier vigilantes made a point of demonstrating
their respect for the spirit of the law, if not the letter. In the early 1820s
an English traveler described how vigilantes on the Kentucky frontier
fought outlaws. "All the quiet and industrious men of a district form
themselves into companies, under the name of 'Regulators.' They appoint officers, put themselves under their orders, and bind themselves to
assist and stand by each other." Before taking action, these Regulators
issued a stern warning to criminals to leave the state as soon as possible.
If their cautions were ignored, they paid a nighttime visit to obstinate
scoundrels who could expect a severe flogging. In the unlikely event that

a follow-up visit became necessary, the Regulators applied enhanced methods of punishment. One notorious robber and thief had his ears cut off. While such practices appeared strange to Europeans, the English observer emphasized that the Regulators themselves lamented the need for their services and looked forward to the day when a formal system of law enforcement would be established.

Regulator companies were customary instruments of popular justice in frontier states such as Missouri, Kentucky, Illinois, and Indiana. Sometimes communities formally selected the members of vigilante groups and commissioned them to drive out felons and preserve order and tranquility. As a rule the regulators agreed to a code of conduct they occasionally put in writing. In one such statement in Illinois, recorded in 1820, the vigilantes vowed to protect their settlement against "all crimes and misdemeanors" and to "punish, according to the code of his honor, Judge Lynch, all violations of the law." While these purposes were to be achieved "as peaceably as possible," the men who signed the compact left no doubt that "we are to accomplish them one way or another." As this document demonstrates, in the early nineteenth century lynching had not yet acquired a bad name on the frontier but was closely associated with the idea that the people had the right and duty to uphold the law if necessity called for action. As long as lynchers observed basic rules of fairness and moderation, they enjoyed widespread support in their communities.

Most of the time frontier vigilantes whipped and evicted those they considered outlaws or threats to public safety. In some cases, however, they also inflicted the death penalty. In 1834 the inhabitants of the mining settlement of Dubuque in present-day Iowa arrested and tried a man named Patrick O'Conner, whom they accused of murder. The trial carefully emulated the procedures of an official criminal court. The defendant was brought before a jury of twelve local residents but given the opportunity to object to individual jurors. He could also name a friend to act as his legal counsel. Witnesses had to testify under oath. The jury delivered a guilty verdict after two hours of deliberation and sentenced the accused to death, claiming this would have been the punishment "in a land of laws." The jurors also determined that the execution be carried out not immediately but after three weeks, giving the condemned time to prepare and, possibly, allowing for a reconsideration of the verdict. Shortly before the execution a committee of citizens appointed a temporary sheriff whom they charged with performing the hanging and promised financial compensation for his service. During the execution, perfect order was maintained among the fifteen hundred people who reportedly watched the spectacle. Most likely, no one deemed the trial and execution of Patrick O'Conner a lynching, including perhaps the condemned man himself, though no formal laws sanctioned the action.

All the same, while they may have accepted its necessity, many contemporary observers realized that frontier justice had its dark side. Because no higher authority oversaw the vigilantes, there was an obvious danger that the regulators might impose high-handed and excessive punishment, ignoring the codes to which they supposedly felt bound. As one critic wrote, even a suspect who had been acquitted by a jury risked being rounded up by vigilantes if "the public voice has proclaimed [him] a thief or a swindler." Moreover, while the regulators invariably claimed that they fought murderers, horse thieves, robbers, counterfeiters, and all other kinds of "desperadoes," such terms could also be used to stigmatize social outcasts or just anyone unpopular among the local community. In 1819 a native New Englander was charged with robbery in Indiana but acquitted for lack of evidence. Sensing that he was no longer safe, the Yankee immediately departed with his family, only to be overtaken and ferociously beaten by a vigilante committee.

On the frontier it was also sometimes difficult to distinguish regulators from outlaws. Whoever had the numbers and the guns could claim to act on behalf of the people. Brutal murders and the settling of old scores might easily be disguised as popular justice. Thus behind the image of virtuous communities establishing law and order by other means there loomed the ugly specter of anarchy and mob violence.

Mobs acting under the guise of law in fact became a hallmark of frontier justice. In 1841 a sheriff from Mississippi led a posse across the Mississippi River into Arkansas to make short work of a band of alleged horse thieves. As soon as the vigilantes had overpowered their unsuspecting targets, the sheriff ordered twenty-two men bound and thrown into the river. Those remaining in the settlement, mostly women and children, were driven away. Later the vigilantes defended the massacre by claiming that they had reluctantly taken the law into their own hands, responding to cries for justice coming from an "outraged and insulted community." As a reward for their heroic exploits, several members of the posse felt entitled to take possession of the property that the supposed criminals had left behind.

In the 1840s the frontier moved westward beyond the Mississippi River. Over the next decades, hundreds of thousands of family farmers, cattle ranchers, miners, railroad workers, land speculators, and adventurers poured into the vast territories of the West where no institutions of law enforcement existed. Yet the popular image of the "Wild West" as a place of unfettered violence and lawlessness needs to be qualified. There was little crime and violence among the settlers who traveled the Overland Trail to Oregon and California, and hence no need to impose harsh communal punishment. The same holds true for ethnically homogeneous farming communities such as the Scandinavian and German settlements of the Dakotas. The "real" Wild West, where brawls, gunfights, robbery, murder, and lynching were indeed rampant, was to be found largely on the mining and cattle frontiers. During the second half of the nineteenth century some towns and counties in Colorado, Arizona, and California experienced homicide rates ten to twenty times higher than those of major cities in the East.

One key factor that contributed to the high levels of crime and violence on the mining and ranching frontiers was gender. Young single males, the most violence-prone group in all known societies, made up a disproportionately large part of the population in the Wild West. Many of these young men believed they needed to be strong and ruthless to exploit the frontier's opportunities. Not unlike the honor code of the Old South, the culture of the West required a man to respond with force to any slight. Strong liquor whipped up tempers, and guns were never in short supply to settle an argument on the spot. Furthermore, in a multiethnic society comprising Anglo-Americans, African Americans, European and Chinese immigrants, Native Americans, and Hispanics, ethnic tensions exacerbated the climate of violence. Both personal and collective violence, including lynchings, often had its roots in racial and ethnic hostility.

Not surprisingly, vigilantism and lynch law became closely associated with life on the Western frontier. People took it for granted that everyone who left the realm of regular governmental institutions tacitly consented to the code of Judge Lynch. Instant and tough punishment of dangerous criminals enjoyed broad support. Without a functioning system of criminal justice, all good citizens had the duty to participate in vigilante

groups and to hunt down, try, and punish outlaws. In essence, vigilantism was seen as local self-government in action. Conviction by a popular
tribunal carried as much legitimacy as the verdict of a legally established
court. For many of its defenders, popular justice had even greater legitimacy. They argued that if the courts did not execute the true will of the
people or, more precisely, of those who claimed to speak for the people,
citizens had a right to take the law into their own hands. But as much as
the vigilantes tried to create the semblance of fair trials, the "defendants"
usually faced the very same people in different roles—as accusers, juries,
witnesses, judges, and, finally, executioners. Guilty verdicts and immediate executions were almost foregone conclusions. The popular story of
the man who was lynched for allegedly stealing a horse that was later
found where its drunken owner had forgotten it probably was a tale of
black humor, but all too often it came close to reality.

   It was no coincidence that vigilante justice soon became known as
"California law." The former Mexican province, which the United States
annexed after the Mexican-American War (1846–1848), was an ideal
breeding ground of frontier violence and lynch law. While formally under Mexican jurisdiction, prewar California had been far removed from
the authority of the central government. The American takeover in
1848 created a power vacuum that would have been difficult to fill even
if no gold had been found earlier that year. Once the Gold Rush took
off, tens of thousands of prospectors from around the world, including
the United States, Mexico and other Latin American countries, Europe,
Australia, and China, flooded into California in search of quick riches.
From an estimated 14,000 non-Indians in 1847, the population of the
state soared to roughly 250,000 in 1852. Many of the newcomers were
transient males determined to strike it big by any means necessary, and
then leave again. In the gold fields of the Sierra Nevada, where virtually
no institutions of law enforcement existed, crime and violent confrontations soon became rampant. Under these circumstances it was perhaps
inevitable that the frontierspeople of California enacted their own brand
of justice. If they apprehended the perpetrator of a crime, they formed
juries, held instant trials, and administered the punishment they saw fit.
In the absence of jails, this usually meant severe whipping or hanging.
Between 1849 and 1853 Californians may have carried out as many as
200 extralegal executions. Few commentators doubted the necessity of

Vigilantes administer "California Law" during the Gold Rush.

lynch law as communal self-defense against a wave of crime committed by the "scum of the earth."

Lynching was also part and parcel of a broader picture of racial and ethnic violence directed primarily against people of Mexican origin and other Latin Americans who were often confused with them. After the annexation of California by the United States and the discovery of gold, native-born Mexican inhabitants quickly became a heavily outnumbered minority in their own land. Although the peace treaty between Mexico and the United States guaranteed equal rights, the protection of property, and even U.S. citizenship to those Mexicans who chose to remain in the annexed territories, many of the Euro-American newcomers considered themselves racially superior conquerors. "The North Americans hate us," a Mexican diplomat remarked, "they consider us unworthy to form with them one nation and one society." The propagandists of "Anglo-Saxonism" despised the "greasers," as they derisively called the Mexicans, as a degenerate race of "mixed bloods" supposedly sprung from the miscegenation between decadent Spaniards and savage Indians. By way of legal deceit or threats of force, many Mexican landowners lost their property. In 1851 the California legislature passed the so-called Foreign Miner's Tax, which imposed a stiff license fee on all foreign-born miners. In reality the tax was levied mostly on nonwhites such as Chinese, Mexicans, and Mexican Americans, even if they were native Californians. Four years later the Anti-Vagrancy Act allowed for the summary arrest of all persons "commonly known as greasers or the issue of Spanish and Indian blood and who are armed and not peaceable and quiet persons."

Apart from its blatantly racist definition of criminality, the Anti-Vagrancy law mirrored the fact that the Mexicans fought back. For Anglos, Mexican "bandits" posed a serious danger to the public safety and needed to be dealt with harshly and swiftly. In the eyes of the Mexicans, the bandits were heroes avenging the outrages perpetrated by the "gringos," and became the subject of song and legend. The most famous or infamous, depending on one's perspective, of these Mexican outlaws during the days of the California Gold Rush was a man known as Joaquín Murrietta. The story goes that he had been forced to watch as Anglo thugs lynched his brother and raped his wife. For the next two years Murrietta and his gang went on a rampage, hunting down the perpetrators and dragging them to death. Eventually, in 1853, a posse confronted and killed the "notorious murderer and robber" in a gun battle. Later a head said to be Murrietta's was placed on public display.

Murrietta may have been an ordinary criminal whom folklore made into a Mexican Robin Hood. Nevertheless there can be no doubt that Mexicans had ample reason to be aggrieved over the discrimination and violence they suffered at the hands of newly dominant Euro-Americans. *El Clamor Público* (*The Public Protest*), a Mexican-American newspaper published in Los Angeles, sarcastically called the California system of government a "linchocracia."

Mexican crime against Anglos, whether trumped up or real, offered welcome opportunities to assert Anglo supremacy. In 1855, for example, a gang of bandits that included several Mexicans murdered five Anglo-Americans, among them a woman, and one American Indian near the towns of Sutter and Rancheria. In the ensuing manhunt, mobs arbitrarily killed between eight and sixteen Mexicans, burned down several homes of Mexican residents, and issued an order for all Mexicans to leave the region at once. One newspaper account described the spirit of raging mob rule, noting that "nearly every man in that region is under arms and ready to level on the first unfortunate greaser that comes across his track." In reality, few of the lynch victims had any connection to the crime. To make matters worse for the Mexican community, local Indians, seeking revenge for the murder of their tribesman, indiscriminately killed Mexican men, women, and children.

Anglo vigilantes, as a rule, did not target women. The only female known to have been killed by a California lynch mob was a young Mexican woman named Josefa who in 1851 had stabbed an Englishman for calling her a whore. Although Josefa seemed to conform to the stereotype of the lewd and cunning Mexican *puta*, she impressed her executioners with calmness and defiance in facing death.

It is impossible to determine how many Mexicans fell victim to Judge Lynch during the rowdy years of the California Gold Rush. A recent conservative estimate puts the number for the period from 1848 to 1860 above 160. In addition to Mexicans, Native Americans and Chinese immigrants also faced mob violence from Euro-American Californians who coveted Indian land and resented the competition of Chinese miners. But both groups account for substantially fewer lynch victims than Mexicans. Military-style assaults and massacres were more common forms of violence in displacing the indigenous Native American population than the lynching of individuals. The Chinese, whose numbers swelled to roughly fifty thousand until 1860, lived in clannish and virtually all-male communities and had few social contacts outside their own ethnic group. Thus lynchings of Chinese were relatively rare. African Americans were few and far between during the days of the California Gold Rush, perhaps no more than fifteen hundred persons. All the same, during the 1850s there were at least three confirmed lynchings of black men in California. Obviously conditions on the frontier were conducive to racial and ethnic violence, but racially motivated lynchings in the West continued long after those conditions had ceased to exist.

Vigilante groups on the frontier argued that extralegal punishment was a legitimate response to crime because the official institutions of law enforcement were inadequate to ensure peace and tranquility. As a vigilance committee in Sonora, California, phrased it in 1851: "We are not opposing ourselves to the courts of justice already organized. We are simply aiding them or doing work which they should do but which under the imperfect laws of the state, they are unable to accomplish." In reality the champions of popular tribunals often inflated both the extent of crime and the ineptitude and corruption of the forces of the law. Rather than establishing law and order in a quasi state of nature, the vigilantes frequently interfered with the operation of the law because they regarded the course of justice as too slow and cumbersome or the prospective outcome as too lenient. In 1854, for example, an interethnic mob of Mexicans and whites stormed a jail in Los Angeles and lynched an Anglo prisoner who had been granted a stay of execution while his Mestizo accomplice was executed. Reportedly the mayor of Los Angeles himself led the lynchers. The incident also demonstrated that the two ethnic groups shared a basic sense of popular justice in spite of their mutual hostility.

Vigilantes commonly tried to present themselves as authentic agents of the people. Yet many vigilante movements of the West in the second half of the nineteenth century were dominated by local elites who pursued their own political and economic agendas along with a call for punishing criminals. The vigilance committees of San Francisco in the 1850s, which many writers have celebrated as the epitome of responsible citizenship, are excellent cases in point. While the "leading citizens" of San Francisco claimed to defend an unprotected city besieged by an army of predatory outlaws, in fact they waged a political campaign against the institutions of criminal justice they considered as irredeemably corrupt. Fighting crime was the keystone of what some historians have called a "businessmen's revolution" to take control of the city government. The men whom the vigilantes executed were indeed criminals, but they were also pawns in a political power struggle.

San Francisco was a rough-and-tumble place in the years of the Gold Rush. Countless adventurers from around the world disembarked in the city's port hoping to get rich quickly. Within a few years the population grew from roughly a thousand in 1847 to as many as fifty thousand. Not surprisingly, crime soared. As robbery and murder appeared to be the order of the day, many people felt that no one's life was safe anymore. Newspaper reports alleged that as many as a thousand murders had been committed in the city between the onset of the Gold Rush in 1848 and the summer of 1851, when the first vigilance committee was formed. Frequent fires, suspected to be the work of arsonists, deepened the general feeling of insecurity. The police, critics charged, were utterly corrupt, and in fact they were often in league with thugs. "Policemen here are quite as much to be feared as the robbers," one foreign visitor noted. And the courts were no better. As a consequence, criminals who ended up in jail had no trouble escaping or buying their freedom. Clearly many citizens deeply distrusted the criminal justice system. Inspired by frequent reports of hangings in the state's mining areas, they warmed to the idea of employing Judge Lynch. Their wrath was not limited to violent criminals. In January 1851 bystanders threatened to string up a pickpocket who had just been arrested by a policeman.

In June that year the patience of the good citizens of San Francisco had ostensibly run out. A group of merchants issued a call for the formation of a vigilance committee, which was instantly heeded by roughly a hundred men considered to be among the most prominent members of the community. Together they wrote a constitution that pledged to observe the laws "when faithfully and properly administered." But they made it known that henceforth villains would no longer "escape punishment either by the quibbles of the law, the insecurity of prisons, the carelessness or corruption of the police or a laxity of those who pretend to administer justice." This proclamation was as much a challenge to the authorities as to the criminals scourging the city. Most local newspapers eagerly supported the appeal to communal self-help.

Yet the vigilantes' claims that violent crime was soaring while the police and the courts were as incompetent as they were crooked, were seriously inflated. Careful research by recent historians has calculated much lower crime rates for San Francisco in the period of the Gold Rush than contemporary accounts allege. This is especially true for the murder rate. On average the city experienced no more than one criminal homicide a month in the early 1850s. Certainly newspaper reports that criminals had committed one hundred murders during the first six months of 1851 were wild exaggerations, as sober observers noted at the time. Nor were transgressions against property out of control. On a per capita basis the incidence of crime in San Francisco was similar to the situation in Eastern cities.

The same may be said about the work of the notoriously underpaid and understaffed police. San Francisco had established a police force in 1849, several years earlier than New Orleans, Boston, Chicago, and Cincinnati. Corruption was endemic in nineteenth-century American law enforcement, but by and large San Francisco's record was no worse than other places experiencing rapid population growth. The fact that the city's police repeatedly protected prisoners from lynch mobs may be seen as evidence of their sense of duty—as in March 1851 when policemen fought off a crowd trying to seize a murder suspect who later turned out to be innocent.

All the same, the vigilance committee was determined to prove that it could do a much better job in making the city safe. It immediately found the perfect culprit to serve as an example. An Australian immigrant, known by the name of John Jenkins, had burglarized the office of a shipping agent but had been apprehended before he could escape. His captors apparently planned to turn him over to the police, but a member of the committee arrived on the scene and persuaded them to surrender their prisoner to the vigilantes instead. The committee lost no time in arranging for an immediate "trial," in which its leader, a wealthy businessman named Samuel Brannan, acted as the "judge" while all other committee members served as "jurors." No one cared to appoint a lawyer for the "defendant." Yet it is doubtful whether California's best lawyer could have saved Jenkins's neck. The "Sydney Ducks," as the ex-convicts from the British penal colonies in Australia were called, had a reputation as hardened, unreformable criminals and could expect no clemency. After the committee had deliberated for two hours in Brannan's warehouse, the "judge" stepped outside to address a large crowd that had gathered in front of the building. Brannan solemnly announced the death sentence for Jenkins and asked the approval of the people, who enthusiastically seconded the verdict. As the committee paraded Jenkins to Portsmouth Square where the hanging would be staged, a police captain and several officers, aided by David Broderick, a prominent Democratic state senator, tried to interfere and seize the prisoner. In the eyes of the vigilantes, this daring attempt to uphold the law once more confirmed that the police, instead of protecting law-abiding citizens, shielded criminals from their just punishment. The lynchers rebuffed the lawmen and strung up Jenkins while the crowd cheered them on.

The lynching of John Jenkins prompted a coroner's inquest, which identified nine mob leaders by name. No indictments were brought, however. Instead more than 180 vigilance committee members, all of them leading and well-to-do citizens, publicly took responsibility for executing Jenkins. The community overwhelmingly supported the extralegal execution; after the hanging, 500 San Francisco residents lined up to join the vigilance committee. Those few dissidents who dared to speak out against lynching faced physical attack and death threats. In order to maintain control, the vigilante leaders formed an executive committee and raised a volunteer police force of 100 men to patrol the streets. For all practical purposes, the vigilance committee took over the adminstration of criminal justice in San Francisco. Most important, in June and July 1851 they pushed a "reform" of the regular police department through the city council. The measure reduced the number of police districts from three to two, cut back the size of the force by a stunning three-quarters, and slashed the pay of police officers. It may appear paradoxical that the same people who complained about inefficient law enforcement now curbed the police, but the reform made perfect sense from the vigilantes' point of view. Curtailing a supposedly corrupt and overstaffed police department not only reflected the fiscal conservatism of businessmen unwilling to pay taxes, it also manifested the deep-seated conviction of many nineteenth-century Americans that law enforcement should not be a government monopoly but a right and duty of the people themselves.

The vigilance committee also ordered the deportation of several Australians suspected as members of the "Sydney Ducks" gang. Then, in early July 1851, the vigilantes got hold of a notorious criminal and alleged murderer named James Stuart, also a former prison inmate from Australia, who willingly implicated a number of accomplices, among them several San Francisco officials. If Stuart had hoped to save his life by cooperating with the vigilantes, he was sadly mistaken. The executive committee recommended a death sentence, which the committee at large confirmed. As in the case of Jenkins, vigilante leaders asked for a voice vote from an assembled crowd. As soon as they were done with the formalities, the lynchers took Stuart to the Market Street wharf where he ended his life before thousands of excited spectators. The city coroner attempted to intervene, only to be pushed brusquely out of the way.

Shortly after Stuart's death, two of his Australian cohorts, Robert McKenzie and Samuel Whittaker, came into the custody of the committee. Meanwhile, however, voices advocating a return to the official courts were growing louder, arguing that the crisis had passed and that the vigilance committee was no longer needed. The committee disagreed, supposedly because it did not believe the courts would convict McKenzie and Whittaker. Then again, there were rumors that the two men knew too much about the criminal involvement of committee members and therefore had to be silenced. Since both had confessed to their crimes, the vigilantes condemned them to die.

At this moment the duly constituted authorities felt they had to react or risk being completely supplanted by the vigilance committee. The governor of California, John McDougal, traveled from Sacramento to San Francisco where he summoned the mayor and the sheriff to prevent the lynching of McKenzie and Whittaker. The three officials led a posse that snatched the prisoners from committee headquarters and shepherded them to the county jail. McDougal called upon the citizens of San Francisco to respect law and order, but the vigilantes were in no mood to admit defeat. A few days later a committee task force, possibly aided by jail guards, seized the condemned men and hurried them back to their headquarters. They were greeted by an agitated crowd of six thousand, impatiently waiting for the hanging to be carried out.

The lynching of the two Australians was another humiliation of the city and state governments which, apart from a few tepid proclamations, had done little to assert their authority. It was not to their credit when the vigilance committee finally ceased to operate in September 1851. After four spectacular public hangings within twelve weeks, excitement peaked and interest in the committee began to wane. The champions of vigilantism claimed that, thanks to the committee, crime was down. Reformers had purged the police department and the courts from corrupt elements. Ironically, the final action of the 1851 vigilance committee was to *prevent* a lynching when in late October a mob of angry sailors tried to hang a captain who had brutalized and killed several of their mates on the high seas. Clearly social class defined the difference between respectable vigilantism and despicable mob rule.

Although the vigilance committee no longer patrolled the streets and held popular tribunals, a small executive committee remained in office with the intent of monitoring public safety. In the eyes of many San Francisco citizens, vigilantism remained a viable option should crime and corruption again encroach on their city. That moment appeared to arrive in late 1855 when Charles Cora, an Italian gambler, shot and killed a federal marshal. Calls for reviving the vigilance committee now appeared throughout the city. Murders and robberies, one pamphlet contended, threatened to plunge San Francisco into a "state of anarchy." To save the community the author called for "the never failing remedy so admirably

laid down in the code of Judge Lynch." The advocates of popular justice
saw their worst fears confirmed when the trial against Cora ended in a
hung jury. Rumors spread that friends of the defendant had bribed the
jurors, but the failure to convict may just as well have resulted from credible evidence that Cora had acted in self-defense. Even so, James King,
editor of the newly founded *San Francisco Daily Evening Bulletin* and a
veteran of the 1851 vigilance committee, continued to whip up passions
over crime in general and the Cora trial in particular. Then, on May 14,
1856, King himself fell victim to homicide when a man named James
Casey, whom the editor had denounced as an ex-convict and a promoter
of crime and vice, shot him to death in the heat of an argument. The killing struck the city like lightning. After Casey had turned himself in to
the police for safekeeping, a large mob gathered in front of the jail. The
leaders demanded the prisoner, shouting, "There is too much law and
too little justice in California." The police barely beat back the assailants.
The next day a new vigilance committee formed under the leadership of
William T. Coleman, one of the wealthiest merchants in San Francisco.

The ranks of the committee quickly swelled as thousands of men
signed up. On May 17 a well-armed crowd confronted the sheriff and
forced him to give up both Cora and Casey. Attempts to summon militia
troops to uphold the authority of the law failed miserably when several
militia companies instead joined the vigilantes. Following the script of
the 1851 events, the committee first "tried" and then publicly hanged the
two prisoners from the front windows of its headquarters. In late July
two other men accused of murder met the same fate.

Like its 1851 predecessor, the 1856 vigilance committee executed
four delinquents and, in addition, banished about thirty alleged criminals from the city. But the newer movement was even less about fighting crime than the one five years earlier, the rhetoric of its proponents
notwithstanding. The 1856 movement may be more properly described
as a political insurgency to take over the city government by force. Many
supporters justified the events in San Francisco as a popular overthrow of
a tyrannical and corrupt government. The immediate target of the vigilantes was the political machine that dominated the city administration,
but they also challenged the state government.

The Democratic party organization of San Francisco was based
largely on Irish immigrants and working-class residents, and had a

EXECUTION OF JAMES P. CASEY AND CHARLES CORA,
BY THE VIGILANCE COMMITTEE, OF SAN FRANCISCO,
On Thursday, May 22d, 1856, from the Windows of their Rooms, in Sacramento Street, between Front and Davis Streets.

JAMES P. CASEY AND CHARLES CORA

Were hung by the Vigilance Committee at precisely twenty minutes after one o'clock—the former for the murder of James King of Wm., and the latter for the murder of Gen. William H. Richardson. Both persons had been tried before the Committee, and found guilty. A promise had been made to Casey that he should have a fair trial, and be permitted to speak ten minutes. These conditions had doubtlessly been observed. Casey was informed on Wednesday afternoon that he had been condemned to be hung. While under the charge of the Vigilance Committee his spirit appeared to be unbroken. Cora attracted less attention, and conducted himself more quietly.

At eight o'clock on Thursday morning, the General Committee was notified that Casey and Cora would be executed at half-past one, and ordered to appear under arms. During the morning preparations were made for the execution. Beams were run out over two of the windows of the Committee Room, and platforms about three feet square extending out under each beam. These platforms were supported next the house by hinges, and outside by ropes, extending up to the beams. Along the streets, for a considerable distance on each side of the place of execution, were ranged the Committee—more than three thousand in number—some on foot with muskets, and others on horseback with sabers.

At a quarter past one o'clock Casey and Cora were brought out upon the platforms. The former was attended by the Rev. Father Gallagher. The arms of both were pinioned at the elbows. The noose was placed around Cora's neck, when he stepped upon the platform and stood firm as a statue, while a white handkerchief being wrapped around his head. The noose was placed around Casey's neck, but at his request removed, while he had some three or four minutes' conversation with his priest. He then came forward and addressed the people. After he had concluded, the noose was again adjusted, his eyes bandaged, and, as he was about to step forward, he faltered, and was about to sink, when the arms of two men were extended and supported him to the fatal spot.

Both prisoners being prepared, the signal was given, and at the same moment, the souls of James P. Casey and Charles Cora were launched into eternity, and their bodies became an inanimate mass of corruption. Neither of them struggled much, Casey showing the most physical suffering.

JAMES P. CASEY,
According to his own account, was born in New York City, in 1827, and at the time of his death was twenty-nine years old; but by Of his early history little is known—the first the Sing Sing Prison certificate and description of his person, he is said to be at that time (1849) thirty-two years old, which would make him thirty-nine at the time of his death; and, as his description is very accurate in other respects, we are inclined to believe it most reliable in this.

CHARLES CORA
Was born in Genoa, in the year 1818, and was forty-three years old at the time of his death. we hear of him was at Natchez, Mississippi, about the year 1845. He was then quite a young man, leading a dissolute life, associating with abandoned characters, and gambling for a livelihood. From there he went to New Orleans, where he took up with Belle Cora, with whom, in 1849 or '50, he came to California.

YANKEE SULLIVAN,
The subject of this sketch was born in Ireland, and at the time of his death was about forty-nine years of age. His vocation is too well known to require mention here. He came to California in 1850, and soon left for New York, from which place he returned to San Francisco in 1854. He was arrested by the Vigilance Committee, and terminated his career by suicide, for fear of being sent to Sydney, where he had been transported for felony, and escaped to the United States in 1839.

EDW. M'GOWAN,
Who was indicted as an accomplice of Casey in the murder of James King of Wm., and who is now a fugitive from justice, has been a prominent politician in San Francisco, and held a responsible office under Gov. Bigler. He has been more or less connected with the leading political events of this city for the last four years. He has thus far eluded the vigilance of the Committee.

Execution of James P. Casey and Charles Cora by the vigilance committee of San Francisco, May 22, 1856.

well-founded reputation of rigging elections and strong-arming its opponents. Its boss, former state senator David Broderick, had received his political education in New York City's Tammany Hall. While San Francisco swiftly grew into a bustling city, the Broderick administration initiated numerous construction projects, collecting handsome kickbacks in the process. As a consequence, the city debt skyrocketed. Taxes soared while public credit plummeted. The businessmen who led the 1856 vigilance committee first of all sought fiscal and municipal reform. When they talked about battling crime they meant crushing the Broderick machine. James Casey, for example, had been a bully for the San Francisco Democrats, and his execution served as a stern warning to the Broderick organization. Almost all the men who were expelled from the city by the committee belonged to the Democratic machine, including Broderick himself.

In August 1856, when the Broderick organization lay in tatters, the ostensibly nonpartisan vigilance committee formally dissolved but immediately reorganized as the People's party and won a sweeping victory in the November elections. The organization subsequently merged with the budding Republican party and controlled San Francisco politics for roughly a decade, making sure that city expenditures were drastically reduced and taxes lowered. These were legitimate political objectives, but whether vigilante tactics and lynching were necessary to break the grip of the Broderick machine is highly questionable. From the point of view of the San Francisco "municipal reformers," though, the ends justified the means. Who cared if cleaning up the city included stringing up a few rogues who only got what they deserved?

In fact some citizens of San Francisco did care. They appealed to California's Governor Neely Johnson to halt arbitrary arrests and executions. The governor declared San Francisco in a state of insurrection and appointed General William T. Sherman (later to be a great figure of the Civil War) to restore law and order. Sherman quickly realized that he lacked a sufficient military force and that public sentiment made the use of military violence against the vigilantes too risky. Desperate for help, Governor Johnson petitioned President Franklin Pierce, asking for federal intervention because the state could "no longer afford protection to its citizens, or punish the lawless acts this body of men [the vigilance committee] have been guilty of." Yet Pierce, well

aware that the San Francisco vigilantes enjoyed broad support throughout the nation, declined the request.

Throughout the United States commentators praised the San Francisco vigilance committee for its apparent restraint and discipline, its
laudable goals, and its broad support among the hardworking, thrifty
classes. One Kansas newspaper cheered San Franciscans on "to slough
off the dead flesh that mars the healthy action of their social system."
In the view of many Americans, the vigilantes represented the power
of the people and set an example of patriotic citizenship. A closer look
at the events of 1856, as well as those of 1851, reveals the hypocrisy and
duplicity employed by the champions of vigilante justice to mask their
hidden agendas and their ruthlessness. The leaders of the committees deliberately inflated the danger of crime and the enormity of corruption.
Their victims were convenient scapegoats and political enemies rather
than dangerous criminals. They sought political and economic power as
much as justice. The vigilantes arrogated themselves the right to overthrow the city government because they disagreed with it and wanted it
gone. Whatever the deficiencies of law enforcement in Gold Rush San
Francisco, neither in 1851 nor in 1856 did they justify vigilantism and
extralegal executions.

After the Gold Rush, California vigilantes continued to lynch—not
because there was no law but because the law did not satisfy their demand for instant revenge. As the record bears out, most lynching victims
had already been taken into custody or even been placed on trial before
mobs took action. In 1860 lynchers seized a murder suspect from a jail
near Downieville, then executed the man by hanging. In 1876 a farmer
in Sonoma County shot a neighbor in an argument over roaming hogs.
Claiming self-defense, he turned himself in and waited for his trial.
When a month had passed without indictment or trial, two hundred
men stormed the jail and lynched the prisoner. Three years later two
brothers in Kern County faced trial for the alleged murder of two men
in the course of a mining dispute. The trial against one of the defendants
produced a hung jury while the second brother was found guilty but successfully appealed to the California Supreme Court for a new trial and a
change of venue. At this point the aggrieved community, weary of legal
hairsplitting, resolved to render the justice that the law obviously could

not provide. Vigilantes, encountering little resistance from jail guards, hanged the two brothers in their cells.

The legacy of popular justice lingered on long after California had ceased to be a frontier state. The last lynchings occurred in the 1930s when Judge Lynch had retired nearly everywhere else outside the Deep South.

California vigilantes established a pattern that typified the West, except that the death toll of the San Francisco vigilance committees was modest compared to what lynchers accomplished elsewhere. In 1864 the Idaho vigilante organization announced that it had executed twenty-seven thieves and murderers during the preceding year. In neighboring Montana a vigilance committee claimed to have uncovered an abominable conspiracy led by Sheriff Henry Plummer, who allegedly headed a gang of bandits responsible for more than a hundred murders and countless robberies in the mining region around Virginia City. Over several weeks the vigilantes hunted down and hanged the entire gang of at least twenty-four men, including the nefarious sheriff who reportedly cried like a child when he faced the stern justice of the people. Then again, the entire conspiracy may well have been a fabrication rooted in a power struggle between pro-Confederate Democrats who backed Plummer and the sheriff's Radical Republican enemies who launched the vigilance committee.

In the remote and mountainous West of the 1860s and 1870s, lynching was a routine way of punishing wrongdoers. While there were certainly many unreported cases, the confirmed numbers of extralegal executions in this thinly populated region appear staggering, especially when considered on a per capita basis. In 1870 eleven persons were lynched in Colorado, amounting to one in every four thousand inhabitants. Clearly the frontier conditions in the West fostered popular justice. From the late 1850s on, tens of thousands of adventurers poured into the Rocky Mountains region where no governmental structures had yet been established. Even discounting the usual exaggerations, serious crime against life and property was the order of the day and made communal self-organization imperative. Upon the founding of Denver in 1858 the residents organized so-called people's courts to provide for some kind of judicial process in dealing with criminals. The first defendant to face such a court was a man named John Stuffle, a German-born miner who was convicted of robbing and murdering his brother-in-law and was sentenced to hang. Although the Denver people's court lacked authorization by federal officials in charge of the Kansas Territory, the trial against Stuffle painstakingly observed the rules of an ordinary criminal court. The judge, who had some legal education, appointed a counsel for the defendant, and a jury of twelve local men rendered the verdict. But when someone suggested bringing Stuffle before the U.S. district court in eastern Kansas for appeal, Denver citizens demurred, pointing out that the delinquent might escape during the trip that would require several weeks. Two days after the murder had been discovered, the people of Denver executed Stuffle in an exercise of what they surely regarded as swift and proper justice.

Indeed, their distrust of the faraway federal court in Leavenworth, Kansas Territory, was not entirely unwarranted. One year later William Middaugh, the sheriff of Denver, arrested a fugitive named James Gordon wanted for homicide. Because he captured the suspect in eastern Kansas, he had to bring him before the Supreme Court for Kansas Territory. In an incomprehensible ruling, the court's chief justice held that the defendant had committed the crime in a place where no official court had jurisdiction, and ordered him released. When a mob in Leavenworth attempted to lynch Gordon on the spot, Middaugh rescued him and brought him before the people's court at home. The case attracted national attention, and Denver citizens went to great lengths to ensure that Gordon received an orderly trial. Eventually he was convicted and executed without benefit of a federal trial, yet few observers found fault with the proceedings. Unlike other popular tribunals, the people's courts in Denver not only prided themselves on conducting fair trials but actually acquitted several defendants for lack of evidence. Other people's courts in Colorado, however, were less scrupulous in complying with basic principles of due process and soon began to practice summary justice.

After the U.S. Congress made Colorado a federal territory in 1861 with its own U.S. marshals and courts, the people's courts could no longer claim to act in lieu of nonexistent official law enforcement. Extralegal executions nevertheless continued, lynchers proudly citing the precedent set by the people's courts. In 1866 mobs in the Denver area lynched eleven people in six weeks; two years later lynchers strung up two robbers within a few days. Although the citizens of Denver resented the reputation of their booming town as a hotbed of mob violence, they generally condoned the lynchings as the quickest and cheapest way to rid the community of unreformable criminals, a task they believed the official courts could not accomplish. Many Westerners had little confidence in the agents of the law, whom they suspected of being incompetent and corrupt. Moreover they complained constantly that the laws were inefficient and too lenient. In 1870 the *Idaho Statesmen* maintained that over the past eight years more than two hundred people had been murdered in the territory while only five murderers had been legally executed. As a consequence, many people concluded they had to dispense justice themselves. When the governor of Idaho commuted the death sentence against a convicted killer to life in prison, a mob overruled the reprieve and hanged the man anyway. Typically, most reported lynchings happened after the victim had come into the custody of the law, reflecting community's mistrust of swift and just retaliation. As one eyewitness of a lynching declared, such rough justice was preferable to the "systematic evasion of justice which is commonly practiced throughout the Western country."

Criminal justice in the West often failed to meet popular expectations of harsh punishment. As a rule, only a minority of defendants charged with a serious crime had to stand trial, and only a minority of those brought to trial were convicted. Lynching seemed to be the inevitable consequence of negligent law enforcement. Between 1863 and 1889 Colorado legally executed fewer than twenty-five criminals, compared to five times as many lynchings. To some extent the often-criticized indulgence of the courts resulted from the unwillingness of the people to fund an efficient system of law enforcement, including adequate prison facilities. As many alleged criminals escaped conviction, angry citizens concluded that they must take the law into their own hands. Thus lynching reflected what one might call the paradox of frontier justice: Westerners complained about the weakness of criminal justice but at the same time refused to accept the need for strong penal institutions, partly because they shied away from the financial burden and partly because they distrusted government in general.

Many Westerners railed particularly against the laxity the courts supposedly showed toward horse and cattle rustlers. Although horse theft was a capital crime in some regions, regular courts were hesitant to impose the death penalty. Lynchers, however, dispatched horse and cattle thieves as readily as murderers or rapists. In 1874 a mob in Bell County, Texas, stormed a jail and shot to death nine alleged horse thieves in one of the deadliest lynchings in Western history. The extralegal executions of alleged horse and cattle rustlers often was the work of vigilante groups connected to large cattle growers who resented that small homesteaders and ranchers supposedly preyed upon their herds. Because juries were generally sympathetic to poor people struggling to make a living on the open range, the big cattlemen resorted to lynching. On occasion, however, class hostility worked against the rich. In 1888 a mob in Colorado lynched a wealthy stockman who had killed his tenant in an argument. The mob feared that a rich man might get away with murder. The charge of cattle stealing also triggered one of the few cases when a Western lynch mob executed a woman. In a notorious incident in 1889, Wyoming vigilantes hanged James Averell and his companion Ellen Watson, known as "Cattle Kate." Because lynching a white woman was out of the ordinary, the pro-vigilante opinion denounced Ellen Watson as a prostitute who reputedly accepted stolen cattle as payment for her services.

Lynchings on the frontier normally followed a uniform ritual. As a rule the vigilantes held some kind of a trial to create an air of legality, then gave the convicted men an opportunity to pray, confess, and sometimes to write a farewell letter. Lynchers rarely inflicted additional torture, though occasionally the hanging went awry and the unfortunate victim suffered terribly. According to numerous eyewitness accounts, many victims accepted their fate as just punishment for their misdeeds. But these reports must be read with caution since most of them were written by people interested in defending the legitimacy of extralegal justice.

As long as popular sentiment condoned lynching as a civic virtue, lynchers had nothing to fear from official investigations. After the so-called Citizens Protective Union of Nevada had broken into a jail and hanged four prisoners for murder in 1864, the grand jury ruled that the vigilantes had acted only in "opposition to the manner in which the law has been administered rather than by any disregard of the law itself." In 1882 a mob in Seattle, Washington, snatched two murderers from a courtroom and hanged them right away. For good measure they also broke into the jail and lynched a third convicted killer who was awaiting his execution. Afterward a coroner's jury declared that "substantial and speedy justice has been served." Clearly many Westerners saw no great difference between lynching and legal executions as long as the rascals received their just deserts.

Still, beginning in the late 1870s, lynchers became more furtive in conducting their ghastly business. Vigilantes increasingly preferred the dead of night and often donned masks. This does not necessarily mean that they feared reproach from their communities, let alone prosecution by the authorities. Usually their identities were well known, and newspapers praised them as "leading citizens" acting on behalf of all law-abiding people. But as frontier conditions faded, the "necessity" argument in defense of lynching began to wear thin. Communities seeking to attract capital and professional elites could no longer afford to be seen as breeding grounds of mob violence. Hence a small masquerade on the part of the lynchers, combined with token resistance by the forces of the law, offered everyone the opportunity to deny knowledge and involvement. Still, while the absolute numbers of lynchings declined in the late nineteenth century, the West, on a per capita basis, matched the lynching rates of the Jim Crow South.

At the same time lynching began to lose credibility in the modernizing West, its legacy became enshrined in the region's folklore. In 1887 the historian Hubert Howe Bancroft (1832–1918), himself a resident of San Francisco during the vigilante days of the 1850s, published his influential two-volume history of the West's *Popular Tribunals*, in which he detailed their supposedly civilizing mission. The author took pains to distinguish vigilance committees from "mobocracy" and lynch law. "Holding brute force and vulgar sentiment in wholesome fear," he believed, was among the foremost tasks of vigilantes. "The vigilance committee will itself break the law," Bancroft reasoned, "but it does not allow others to do so." In his view vigilantes were conservative revolutionaries who defended law and order by resorting to the "right and duty, whenever they see misbehavior on the part of their servants, whenever they see the laws they have made trampled upon, distorted or prostituted, to rise in their sovereign privilege and remove such unfaithful servants, lawfully if possible, arbitrarily if necessary."

Bancroft conveniently ignored the facts of his own materials, which painted a much more squalid picture of Western vigilantism. More often than not, popular tribunals lacked basic procedural safeguards. Conviction and execution were usually foregone conclusions. Even by the standards of the time, punishment appeared excessive. Many innocent people presumably lost their lives, such as the unfortunate man in Oregon who was falsely accused of having poisoned his brother-in-law and quickly hanged—while his putative victim soon recovered. Rather than being inspired by the spirit of the law, many vigilante groups sought personal vengeance, political power, or economic gain. And the self-appointed guardians of the law and protectors of the people could easily become criminal oppressors themselves. Finally, the thin veneer of civic respectability associated with innocuous terms like "vigilance committee" or "people's court" must not obscure the grim reality of Western lynching as the opposite of law and order.

4

Lynching, Riots, and Political Terror in the Civil War Years

THE CIVIL WAR was undoubtedly the most violent period in the history of the United States. Between 1861 and 1865 more than 600,000 Americans died in combat or of war-related causes such as epidemic diseases or malnutrition. Incidents of mob violence and lynching during these years may thus appear as mere footnotes to the carnage of the battlefields. Nevertheless the era of the Civil War and Reconstruction (1861–1877) marks a distinct and crucial phase in the history of lynching in America for two main reasons. First, in a general climate of insecurity and social upheaval, mob violence became more rampant and deadlier than ever before. Second, political terror emerged as a major objective of mobs and vigilante groups and temporarily overshadowed the traditional idea of lynch law as communal punishment for heinous crimes. After the surrender of the Confederacy, many white Southerners concluded they had no choice but to resort to rioting, night riding, and lynching to defend themselves against the dreaded "Negro rule" that they believed vindictive Northerners had foisted upon them. Eventually their continuation of the war by other means proved highly successful. Mob violence, lynching, and vigilante terrorism played a key role in enforcing white supremacy in the postbellum South and in undermining Northern resolve to protect black citizenship rights in the South.

In the 1860s and 1870s Americans used the term lynching mostly to describe extralegal punishment meted out in legitimate communal self-defense, a practice they associated with conditions on the Western frontier. To focus on this narrow usage, however, would obscure much of the mob violence perpetrated during the Civil War and Reconstruction.

Most important were the countless racially and politically motivated murders and massacres in the South during the Reconstruction years, which claimed tens of thousands of lives. Lynching-style executions were part of this larger picture, but few contemporary observers cared to discriminate between different types of mobs and vigilante action. A broader approach would link lynching to other forms of collective violence such as riots, the summary killing of prisoners, and night riding as well as to the dramatic social changes caused by the emancipation of four million black slaves.

The popular view of the Civil War as a military conflict between two unified sections of the country fighting over the right to secession has long obscured the high levels of internal discord and discontent in both the North and the South. Not surprisingly, the hardships of a long and costly war led to class tensions and civil unrest in both sections, exacerbated by conscription laws favoring the rich. As early as the summer of 1861, food riots by the wives and daughters of Confederate soldiers cropped up in New Orleans. Throughout the war similar incidents of unrest continued throughout the South. Although they usually did not result in fatalities, these disturbances threw into sharp relief what disgruntled Southerners dubbed a "rich man's war but a poor man's fight." Wealthy planters not only had enough to eat and profited from soaring prices, they were also exempt from the draft if they had to supervise more than twenty slaves. In the North, inequitable draft laws that allowed the affluent to pay a commutation fee of three hundred dollars or hire a substitute also created nagging resentment and often sparked violent resistance. In October 1862 six hundred troops had to restore order in Port Washington, Wisconsin, where anti-draft protesters had burned the enrollment lists and attacked the homes of draft officials. After Congress passed the Enrollment Act of March 1863, which authorized conscription but exempted the unfit and those wealthy enough to avoid it, major riots swept through Northern cities, including Detroit, Chicago, and, most deadly, New York City.

With an official death toll of 105 and possibly hundreds more, the draft riots that raged through New York City from July 13 to 17, 1863, count as the most devastating civil uprising in American history. Eventually the authorities had to summon regular army units from the Gettysburg battlefield to regain control of public order. The city, in particular

In the New York draft riots of July 1863 white rioters lynched numerous blacks.

its large German and Irish immigrant populations, was a stronghold of the so-called Peace Democrats who advocated a negotiated settlement with the Confederacy and couched their opposition to the war in racist terms. These Copperheads, as their political adversaries contemptuously called them, denounced conscription as a Republican conspiracy to sacrifice white men for the abolition of slavery. Before the outbreak of the riots, New York Copperhead leader Fernando Wood insinuated that the federal government intended to replace drafted white workers with freed slaves from the South. Hence the rioters directed their furor against both the representatives of the Republican government and the black community. The violence involved the wholesale destruction of recruitment offices, police stations, and private homes, including a black orphanage, but also the lynching-style murder of individual victims. For example, the mob tortured to death Colonel Henry O'Brien of the New York Volunteers because he had ordered his soldiers to open fire on the insurgents, killing a woman and her child among other casualties.

African Americans who fell into the hands of the rioters received especially cruel treatment. A black shoemaker who shot an assailant in

self-defense was first savagely beaten and then hanged. Later his murderers dragged his body through the streets and burned it in public. An
elderly black mother had to watch as a mob strung up her disabled son
and afterward mutilated his corpse. One African-American man disguised himself as a woman and tried to escape to Brooklyn along with
his wife, but the rioters exposed his cover. The attackers bludgeoned
him to death and dumped his body into the river. Many more blacks
suffered a similar fate, some being killed on the spot, others succumb-
ing to their injuries over the following days.

Although the mobs that wantonly slaughtered African Americans
on the streets did not claim to punish any particular offenses, their action involved key features commonly associated with racially motivated
lynchings. Destitute white laborers, particularly Irish immigrants, hated
blacks because they were convenient scapegoats for the war and the
draft as well as competitors for menial jobs. By driving blacks from their
neighborhoods, the rioters sought to protect both their economic interests and the ethnic integrity of their local communities. Moreover their
racial hatred expressed itself in sexually charged violence. In at least one
case, mob leaders cut off the genitals of a slain black man to symbolically
deprive the victim of his manhood. The rioters also targeted interracial
couples and families as, for example, William Derrickson, his white wife
Ann, and their son Alfred. The father managed to flee, but assailants
grabbed the son and set out to hang the boy from a lamppost when a
group of neighbors boldly intervened and rescued him. His mother later
died from wounds she had suffered fighting to save her son.

The New York draft riots represented the bloodiest unrest in the
North during the Civil War, but they were not the last incident of this
kind. Following the mayhem in New York City, anti-war protests flared
in Boston, Newark, New Jersey, and Hartford, Connecticut, among
other places. In March 1864 Peace Democrats clashed with U.S. soldiers
in Charleston, Illinois, leaving nine persons dead.

Then again, most Northern civilians lived a relatively tranquil life
during the war years compared to the inhabitants of the border states
and the Confederacy, where most of the fighting took place. In addition
to the military operations of the Union and Confederate armies, guerrilla units in the South engaged in irregular warfare, blurring the line
between military combat and terror against the civilian populations. In

1863, for instance, Confederate guerrillas raided Lawrence, Kansas, and massacred 150 civilians. In guerrilla warfare, both sides practiced summary executions of captured enemies. In areas where the populace was sharply divided between supporters of the Union and the Confederacy, as in the border states of Missouri, Kentucky, and Kansas or in the Appalachian regions of Tennessee, North Carolina, and Alabama, the conflict over secession became a civil war in the literal sense of the phrase.

This kind of situation also existed in Cooke County in northern Texas, which in the fall of 1862 became the scene of a notorious mass lynching known as "The Great Hanging at Gainesville." Most of the county's residents were small farmers and artisans who owned no slaves and had voted against secession. When the Confederacy passed its first conscription law in April 1862, including exemptions for slaveholders and overseers, Cooke County residents drafted a protest petition demanding repeal. Some dissenters, however, went further and formed a clandestine Union League. Its members declared their loyalty to the United States Constitution and organized armed companies that prepared for action in case federal troops should invade northern Texas. But the organization's secrecy was short-lived. In October the Confederates who dominated the militia and the civil government in Cooke County cracked down on the Unionists, arresting more than 150 people, many of whom had no connection to the League.

As the prisoners were brought to Gainesville, the county seat, large crowds of Confederate sympathizers gathered and demanded the immediate execution of the "traitors." To assuage the swelling hysteria, county leaders called a town meeting. The assembly voted to choose a jury of twelve men and hold trials immediately. Although these "citizens' courts" claimed to represent the will of the people, they had no legality under either military or civil law. Nor did they provide the defendants with normal procedural rights and safeguards. Conviction required only a majority vote instead of the usual unanimous verdict. The defendants had no legal counsel, nor could they appeal their sentences. Predictably, the citizens' courts quickly condemned several "conspirators" to death. Public hangings followed a day or two after the trials.

The trials were held in the presence of angry crowds of as many as eight hundred men who had no patience for legal niceties. After some jurors voiced second thoughts about the fairness of the procedure, the court increased the requirement for a guilty verdict to a two-thirds majority and decided to adjourn for one week. But the mob insisted that the hangings continue and singled out fourteen prisoners for instant execution—a clear indication that there were personal scores to be settled. The jury, supposedly to avoid the wholesale slaughter of all prisoners, delivered the fourteen men, who were hanged on the spot without the semblance of a trial. Hopes that this concession would satisfy the bloodlust of the lynchers and calm the situation were soon frustrated, however, when unsubstantiated rumors spread that a band of pro-Union guerrillas from Kansas, known as Jayhawkers, were approaching Cooke County to aid their companions. The Confederates formed a posse which clashed with scattered local Unionists and lost two men in the fighting.

At this point the crowd again descended on the Gainesville jail and demanded that the tribunals against the conspirators be resumed at once. Again the citizens' courts obliged and tried more than seventy men within a period of eighteen hours. Nineteen were found guilty, sentenced to death, and swiftly executed.

Altogether at least forty-four men died in the "The Great Hanging at Gainesville"; roughly half of them did not receive even the paltry privilege of a trial before the citizens' courts. While the Cooke County Confederates justified their action as communal self-defense in the face of mortal danger, critics charged that the alleged conspirators were lynched because they refused to fight for slavery and secession.

The mass executions in Gainesville demonstrated that many Southern slaveholders feared the disloyalty of their nonslaveholding fellow citizens and were willing to use lynch law to ensure conformity. But they were even more afraid of their slaves taking advantage of the wartime absence of white men. Despite the draft exemptions for planters and overseers, the ratio of military-age white males to slaves dropped precipitously in the plantation South, creating a general feeling of vulnerability among the white population. The unceasing nightmare of slave insurrections had been a major source of lynching and mob violence in the antebellum South. During the war, white fears of plots and revolts multiplied and triggered new rashes of brutal suppression against the slave population. In deterring rebellion and escape, and in enforcing the obedience of their increasingly unmanageable "Negroes," slaveholders and Southern authorities accepted fewer legal constraints than ever before. One Louisiana planter boasted that he had shot several of his slaves to force them back to work and that he was fully prepared to shoot more if need be. At the slightest suspicion of insurrection slaveholders reacted with swift and harsh punishment. In 1862 the leaders of an alleged conspiracy to burn down the city of Natchez, Mississippi, were hanged without any legal proceedings and their bodies publicly displayed as a warning to other slaves. Two years later the authorities in Richmond, Virginia, ordered the execution without benefit of trial of two blacks accused of burglary. Wartime anxieties also undermined the limited protections that slaves had enjoyed before the war because of their status as valuable property. In July 1861 an Arkansas mob lynched a slave accused of killing an overseer. When the owner filed a complaint and demanded compensation, the local authorities ignored him.

Despite white fears, no major slave rebellion occurred during the Civil War. Most of the uncovered plots were either the product of slaveholder hysteria or preparations for a group escape when slaves planned to meet advancing Union troops. Nevertheless the planters' mounting complaints about the "insolence" of their slaves were not unwarranted. The bondspeople, quickly sensing that the war was changing their situation, became more assertive. They often refused to work, talked back to their masters, and increasingly resisted corporal punishment. In some cases slaves visited violent revenge upon overseers and masters. One ex-slave from Texas remembered the death of a notorious overseer: "One day de slaves caught him and one held him whilst another knocked him in de head and killed him." A Mississippi slaveholder who returned from service with the Confederate Army determined to inculcate discipline in his slaves was shot dead in an ambush. When the Union Army approached and the authority of the slaveholders collapsed, slaves sometimes reversed their roles, whipping their masters and mistresses or pillaging their personal possessions. Widespread rumors of atrocities notwithstanding, however, the orgy of vengeance that white Southerners had anticipated never occurred. Yankee soldiers were astonished to find little desire for revenge among the slaves.

While the freed people surely did not behave like stereotypical bloodthirsty savages, they nevertheless defied their former owners' illusions about their "faithful Negroes." Taking advantage of their new freedom, the liberated slaves left the plantations in droves, depriving planters of their desperately needed workers. Some of the dispossessed slaveholders did not hesitate to use lethal force to keep and discipline their chattels, regardless of emancipation. When six freedmen left a plantation in South Carolina, planters and overseers formed a posse and hunted them down. Rather than usher them back to the cotton fields, they decided to make an example of their captives. One man who tried to flee they shot dead; the others they hanged along the road. As the war came to an end, planters' quest for a cheap and pliable labor force became a key motive of mob violence and lynchings in the post-emancipation South.

The lynching of Saxe Joiner, a slave living in Unionville, South Carolina, in March 1865, reflected the fierce determination of white Southeners to preserve the racial order in spite of imminent defeat and emancipation. As the arrival of the federal troops neared in early 1865, Joiner, a carpenter in his mid-twenties, wrote a note to his mistress Martha Hix telling her not to worry because he could bring her to a place where she would be safe from the Yankees. Apparently Joiner was literate despite the laws against teaching slaves to read and write. Although it was unsuitable for slaves to address their owners in such a forthright manner, the letter could be interpreted as a token of Joiner's loyalty to his mistress. But Joiner sent a second note to Susan Baldwin, an eighteen-year-old white girl living with the Hix family, offering her protection too. With this message the slave crossed a dangerous line. In the Southern white mind his suggestion surely looked like a devious attempt to exploit a vulnerable white female, possibly with an intent to rape her.

Unfortunately for Joiner, his owner, Dr. James Hix, found the note to Susan Baldwin and had him arrested. The next day the slave stood trial before a justice of the peace. Surprisingly, he was convicted only of a misdemeanor and sentenced to be taken to the Confederate front lines as a laborer—an indication that the authorities wished to downplay the affair and rid themselves of Joiner. Yet the news of Joiner's temerity and his lenient punishment spread fast and infuriated many white men, who set out to storm the jail. A militia officer confronted the mob and killed one of the assailants in self-defense. In order to quiet tempers, the magistrate of Unionville agreed to place Joiner on trial again; but in the general confusion of the last days of the war, the trial never took place. On March 15, about three weeks after the first lynching attempt, a mob of masked men, many of whom donned Confederate uniforms, once again attacked the jail, this time without encountering opposition, grabbed Joiner, and hanged him from a nearby tree.

Before the Civil War, transgressions like the one Saxe Joiner committed would have been treated as serious offenses and resulted in severe punishment such as flogging, but probably the authorities would have tried to avert a lynching had the threat occurred. With impending defeat and emancipation, however, Southern white men were in no mood to tolerate "impudence" from a black man. In their view Joiner's note, whatever his personal intent may have been, portended a radical change in race and gender relations that had to be resisted at all costs. Anticipating his freedom, a young black man who could read and write and who excelled in a skilled trade dared to offer himself as a protector and possibly even as a sexual partner to white women. Such a bold act represented a head-on challenge to the status of white males as patriarchs and members of a superior race, and called for relentless punishment. Defeat on the battlefield might be inescapable, slavery might be doomed, but, as the lynching of Saxe Joiner was meant to show, Southern men were not about to surrender their sense of honor, manhood, and racial supremacy to "Negro rule."

The Confederate surrender at Appomattox in April 1865 brought no peace to the South. Rather, the old planter elites and the rank-and-file believers in white supremacy resorted to large-scale mob violence and lynching to carry on the struggle against Northern "carpetbaggers," traitorous "scalawags," and, most of all, "savage" Africans who, unleashed from the paternalistic controls of slavery, purportedly posed a mortal danger to white "civilization." Many white Southeners whipped themselves into a frenzy with images of black hordes descending on the Southland and a dreadful race war looming on the horizon. Antebellum rhetoric of paternalistic sentimentalism gave way to expressions of hate and fear. Before the war, one Georgian noted, whites had looked upon the black slave as "a gentle animal that they would take care of." After the war the feeling prevailed "that the negro is a sort of instinctive enemy of ours." The racial threat called for ironclad white unity and for an unconditional commitment to white supremacy. "There can," touted the Louisiana Democratic party platform of 1865, "in no event, nor under any circumstances, be any equality between the white and other races."

Following Appomattox, most Southern states passed statutes, known as "black codes," that sought to remake the freed people into a pariah class of serfs. The codes required all former slaves to sign labor contracts; blacks without employment could be arrested for vagrancy and rented out to the highest bidder. Orphans or the children of black paupers were to be given into an "apprenticeship," preferably to their former owners, who had the authority to inflict "moderate corporeal chastisement." The codes also allowed for physical punishments widely practiced under slavery, such as hanging by the thumbs. Although the U.S. Army and the Freedmen's Bureau, a federal agency Congress had established in March 1865 to assist the liberated slaves, quickly shelved the black codes, these laws nevertheless clearly indicated how white Southerners envisioned the postwar racial order. They tenaciously clung to the belief that cruel violence was indispensable to discipline "black brutes," and that all white men had the right and the duty to administer physical violence against blacks with impunity. Apologists for slavery lamented that emancipation had deprived the freed people of all protections and reduced them to the "condition of a stray dog."

Of course this was a glaring distortion of reality. With the shackles of bondage removed, many African Americans were no longer willing to suffer white violence meekly. If the law offered no protection, blacks on occasion turned to retaliatory mob violence. In 1866 a crowd of armed freedmen descended on a Georgia town to demand the punishment of white lynchers who had hanged a black youth for killing a farm animal. In Columbia, South Carolina, a group of "Colored Men" posted a note that they would "have the blood" of the local police chief who had killed a young freedman while trying to arrest him but had been acquitted by a coroner's jury. Black U.S. soldiers, in particular, who in the eyes of white Southerners embodied defeat and humiliation and became the objects of their visceral hatred, did not shy from carrying out such threats. In Victoria, Texas, black occupation troops stormed a jail and lynched a white man accused of murdering an ex-slave. In South Carolina, African-American soldiers staged an extralegal "court-martial" against a Confederate veteran who had slain a black sergeant, condemning the man to death before a firing squad. Black veterans also formed the backbone of local Union Leagues in the South, which Republicans organized for the political mobilization and education of the former slaves as well as for the self-protection of Southern black communities.

Self-defense and acts of vengeance by the freed people, in combination with a perceived wave of black crime, buttressed the feeling among white Southerners that they had no choice but to fight back by all means necessary. Federal troops, they complained, favored blacks and refused to protect white people from constant transgressions by the unbound former slaves. In reality, whites initiated most of the violence while the freed people and white Unionists suffered most of the casualties. In addition to numerous murders of freedmen and veterans of the Union Army, major riots erupted in Southern cities such as Memphis and New Orleans. The New Orleans race riot of July 1866, in particular, made it clear that the key motive of white violence against African Americans was not fear of black crime but political terrorism. When black and white Louisiana Republicans gathered to hold a constitutional convention, white Democrats, aided by the local police, launched a frontal assault on the meeting. According to one eyewitness the mob numbered around two thousand people. The police, instead of enforcing law and order, indiscriminately fired at the Republicans. At least thirty-eight people were killed and hundreds injured.

The incessant violence against the freedmen and white Republicans was a major reason why Congress resolved to overrule President Andrew Johnson's lenient Reconstruction policies. Beginning with the Civil Rights Act of April 1866, the Republican majority enacted a string of legislation and constitutional amendments that nullified the black codes and declared African Americans U.S. citizens entitled to the equal protection of the laws and equal manhood suffrage. Congress dissolved all state governments in the South, save Tennessee, divided the remaining ten states into five military districts, each run by a general of the U.S. Army, and temporarily disfranchised considerable numbers of ex-Confederates. Military commanders and the Freedmen's Bureau received new powers to suspend unfair labor contracts and protect black voters from intimidation. As a consequence, Republicans, based on the ballots of the freedmen and white loyalists, dominated Reconstruction governments in the South until the mid-1870s. Under the new suffrage laws numerous African Americans were elected to public office, including twenty-two to the U.S. Congress. The South Carolina legislature temporarily even had a black majority. From the viewpoint of white supremacists as well as freed people in the South, the world was turned upside down. The specter of "Negro rule" that had haunted Southern whites for so long had finally arrived.

Because of sweeping changes in the status of black Americans, recent historians consider the Civil War and Reconstruction as the "Second American Revolution." Indeed, the leaders of the Radical Republicans, such as Pennsylvania congressman Thaddeus Stevens, openly admitted that their aim was to "revolutionize Southern institutions, habits, and manners" and to break the power of the slaveholding oligarchy. But most white Southerners resisted a revolution they equated with defeat and disgrace. Not surprisingly, the planter class was not prepared to yield to their former chattels. "I am willing to do almost anything and submit to anything in preference to nigger domination," an Alabama planter vowed in 1867. But most lower-class whites who had not owned slaves or benefited from slavery before the war also rejected the idea of a social revolution that made blacks their political and social equals. In the antebellum years, nonslaveholding whites, as slave patrollers or members of posses and mobs, had participated in the defense of slavery because they had feared rebellion and emancipation no less than the planters. During Reconstruction poor white farmers, sharecroppers, and laborers fought "Negro rule" alongside the plantocracy, among other reasons because they feared the freedmen as competitors for land and jobs and because the battle cry of white supremacy reassured them that they too were part of the "ruling race."

Much of the mob violence during Reconstruction was specifically directed against symbols of black upward mobility. Newly established black schools were burned down throughout the South, and freedmen who had acquired land were driven from their farms. One night rider who had participated in a raid to expel black farmers from his home county squarely described the motive of the assailants: "We wanted to let the poor white man have a chance." Racism, first and foremost, became the tie that bound the majority of white Southerners together, regardless of social class.

In response to the racial revolution imposed by Radical Reconstruction, Southern white supremacists waged a protracted campaign of counterrevolutionary terror, seconded by a propaganda battle to depict white Southerners as victims of ruthless oppression who had every right to defend themselves. Of the various vigilante groups that surfaced in the postbellum South, none acquired greater notoriety than the Ku Klux Klan. Named after the Greek word for cycle, *kuklos*, the Klan was founded by Confederate veterans in Pulaski, Tennessee, in early 1866. The clandestine fraternity exuded an aura of male bonding and mystery, including strange rituals and fanciful garbs with distinctive pointed hoods, which attracted especially many younger men who found it difficult to readjust to the less adventurous life of peacetime. Although its founders did not conceive of the Klan as a political organization, it soon became embroiled in battles between Unionists and conservative Democrats in Tennessee. By early 1868 the Ku Klux Klan had spread to all Southern states and, for all practical purposes, developed into the militant branch of the Democratic party in the South. The group's grandiose titles, including Grand Wizard or Grand Cyclops, as well as its purportedly rigid structure, ranging from local dens to statewide realms to the enigmatic "Invisible Empire," suggested a centralized organization that in reality never existed. Nevertheless in the late 1860s the Klan established a daunting reign of terror in large parts of the South, aimed at suppressing Unionism and keeping the freed people in their place.

Klan violence encompassed threats and intimidation, whippings and mutilations, assassinations and lynchings in the dead of night as well as in open daylight. Its leaders fervently denied that the secret association pursued a political agenda or sought to harm the "poor African," but, as one witness testified before a congressional committee investigating the Klan, its main objective was "to use force or violence to prevent certain parties from exerting too great an influence with the colored population." Clearly racial and political terror was the Klan's main objective. Kentucky, a former slave state which had not seceeded and was therefore outside the purview of Reconstruction but firmly within the realm of Klan terror, may serve as a case in point. Within a four-month period in 1871 the Klan murdered nineteen white Union veterans and Republicans in the state. In August 1871 a shoot-out between black Republicans and white Democrats erupted in Frankfort on election day, resulting in the death of two whites and as many as six African Americans. After the confrontation the police arrested two black men who had allegedly started the shooting. During the night a mob of more than 250 men surrounded the jail and took hold of the two prisoners, meeting no resistance. The two victims were later found on the outskirts of town, hanging from a tree.

African Americans known as Republican activists faced a particularly high risk of murderous visits from the Klan. In 1872 Kentucky Klansmen hanged a black man, his wife, and his daughter because they had tried to register black voters and ignored several warnings not to do so. If the targets of the Klan were fortunate they were not murdered on the spot but got away with a ferocious beating and a stern warning. After Klansmen had whipped William Coleman, a black Mississippi Republican, senselessly, they told him, "You are a nigger, and not to be going about like you thought yourself a white man." In 1871 Henry Lowther, a black Republican from Georgia, told a congressional committee how he had suffered sexual mutilation at the hands of the Klan, administered in the most diabolical manner. After having been arrested without any warrant or charges in Wilkinson County, Lowther met with a white vigilante leader who told him that the Klan was coming for him and that he could save his life only by giving up his "stones." Late at night more than a hundred Klansmen abducted Lowther from the jail, brought him to a nearby swamp, and confronted him with the grim choice of being killed or castrated. Understandably he preferred to live. Having carried out their ghastly threat, his tormentors abandoned their victim, who nearly bled to death before finding a doctor. The Klan's message was unmistakable. Black men who claimed political power challenged the principle that citizenship was a privilege of white manhood. By emasculating Lowther, the Klansmen symbolically sought to reduce him again to inferior status.

It is worth noting that the Klansmen castrated Lowther without charging him with a sexual offense. In its propaganda the Ku Klux Klan liked to portray itself as a traditional vigilante group meting out communal justice for odious crimes, including the rape of white women by black men. But the notion that white Southerners became obsessed with the specter of the "black brute" immediately after emancipation and invariably resorted to lynch law whenever rumors of rape surfaced is misleading. Recent historians have shown that antebellum views of race, class, and gender continued to influence white reactions toward freedmen accused of raping white females. If the alleged victims were lower-class women, possibly with a tainted reputation, their accusations created no great excitement in the community. Black defendants whose employers and former masters vouched for their good character had a good chance of receiving relatively light prison sentences or pardons.

Still, even though rape charges did not automatically trigger a lynch mob, many white Southerners became increasingly worried that civil and political equality would lead to the social equality of blacks and ultimately to racial "amalgamation" and the destruction of the white race. Opponents of Reconstruction successfully exploited such fears politically, creating the impression that black-on-white rape had taken on epidemic proportions. "It is vastly more frequent now than it was when he [the black man] was in a state of slavery," Augustus Wright, a former congressman from Georgia, contended before the congressional committee investigating the Ku Klux Klan—albeit without being able to name a single incident. Still, many white Southerners believed that the "black rapist" had become a serious problem and raised no objections when mobs took the law into their own hands. "The community said amen to the act," the Tennessee *Fayetteville Observer* commented on the lynching of an African American accused of rape, "it was just and right. We know not who did it, whether Ku Klux or the immediate neighbors, but we feel that they were only the instruments of Divine vengeance."

Not surprisingly, lynchings to avenge atrocious sexual crimes, such as the rape and murder of children, met with widespread communal approval. But this did not mean that the Ku Klux Klan enjoyed the unanimous support of all white Southeners. Behind the façade of Southern unity, class tensions loomed large. While the old elites were happy to use the Klan to regain power, they found it hard to control the vigilantes, many of whom were rowdy, undisciplined young men from the lower classes. Furthermore, excessive racial violence did not necessarily serve the planters' interest in a submissive black labor force. Surely they did not condone the Klan's efforts to drive out freed people in order to improve the economic fortunes of poor whites, for the planters needed blacks to work the cotton fields. Some Southern critics also cautioned that Klan violence would only prolong military occupation. Finally, not all Southerners who favored white supremacy believed in murdering scores of political opponents, black or white.

It is thus difficult to gauge how many white Southerners backed the Klan. It is even more difficult to determine to what extent this support rested on ideological conformity or simply on fear and intimidation. The conspicuous fact that much of the Klan terror occurred in the dark, with the Klansmen camouflaging their identities behind their hooded guises, suggests a less than perfect consensus. Interestingly, the term "lynching," except in rape cases, rarely surfaced in reference to Klan violence. Because the name of Judge Lynch still commanded the respectability of righteous citizens administering legitimate popular justice, the Klan's Republican foes preferred to speak of "outrages" rather than lynchings.

Desperately trying to hold on to their newly won rights, African Americans fought the Klan in countless instances, sometimes amounting to wholesale battles between heavily armed black and white militias. Sentries of freedmen also protected jails against Klansmen trying to seize and lynch black prisoners. In one 1874 incident in Kentucky, black guards fired at a mob of fifty white men, killing one and driving off the rest. Even so, blacks and their Republican allies fully realized that without the protection provided by federal troops their enemies would eventually prevail. Although by and large the U.S. Army made a good-faith effort to keep the peace and suppress Klan terror, their numbers were far from sufficient to achieve these goals on an enduring basis. For example, by 1870 only about seven hundred federal troops were left in the entire state of Mississippi. And because army commanders lacked the authority to hold military trials, most of the Klansmen they arrested were soon released. The key issue was political, though. How long would the North be willing to maintain a coercive military regime in the South to protect the freed people?

White Northerners were deeply divided over how to deal with the violence perpetrated by the Klan and other white terrorists in the South. Democrats and many conservative Republicans favored swift reconciliation between the sections and deeply resented the expansion of federal powers over those of the states. They dismissed reports of Southern outrages against the freed people as gross exaggerations fabricated by Radical Republicans seeking to cement the rule of their party over the reconstructed South. A Democratic senator from California lambasted the Radicals, charging that disorder and violence were "the natural fruits of the war and of your own misgovernment." Nonetheless between March

1870 and April 1871 the Republican majority in Congress passed three so-called Enforcement Acts. The third one, known as the Ku Klux Klan Act, specifically threatened with fines, imprisonment, or hard labor those individuals who "go in disguise upon the public highway or upon the premises of another," conspiring or using violence to deprive "any person or class of persons" of their constitutional rights. The law also empowered the president to suspend the writ of habeas corpus in areas he declared to be in insurrection. Critics attacked the Ku Klux Klan Act as manifestly unconstitutional because the prosecution of individuals committing violent crimes was a traditional prerogative of the states. Indeed, over the following decades the argument that federal laws against mob violence and lynching violated the Constitution became an insurmountable stumbling block to the passage of such legislation in Congress.

Once they took effect, however, the Enforcement Acts proved highly useful in fighting the Klan. Furnished with new powers and boosted by the shocking testimony of Klan victims before a congressional investigation, the army and federal prosecutors launched a serious effort to apprehend, indict, and convict Klan members. Beginning in mid-1871 federal troops made mass arrests in the Carolinas and in Mississippi, resulting in hundreds of indictments. In North Carolina federal grand juries issued more than seven hundred indictments; in Mississippi the number was well above two hundred. Of course winning convictions was more difficult, but in North Carolina the federal district attorney obtained forty-nine guilty verdicts, with sentences ranging from fines to several years in the federal penitentiary in Albany, New York. In the South Carolina upcountry, where President Ulysses S. Grant suspended habeas corpus, Klan leaders fled the state while hundreds of rank-and-file Klansmen were arrested.

Only a small proportion of the Klan indictments resulted in convictions. The punishments inflicted by the courts were rather light because the defendants could not be charged with murder—which remained a crime punishable under state law—and the offenses detailed in the Enforcement Acts carried a maximum six-year prison term. In fact few Klansmen received a sentence exceeding one year; by mid-1872 there were only sixty-five Klan convicts in the penitentiary at Albany. All the same, the crackdown created enough confusion to upset the Klan and rein in its terror. Where the federal government showed its muscle, night riding and lynchings dropped precipitously. As a consequence, the election campaign in the fall of 1872 was relatively peaceful despite incidents of voter intimidation and abuse.

The suppression of the Ku Klux Klan halted the Southern counter-revolution only temporarily. Eventually most Northern Republicans and their constituencies, plagued by high taxes and economic depression, had no stomach for maintaining "bayonet rule" indefinitely and grew tired of horror stories from the South. The nagging "Negro question," they concluded, must no longer stand in the way of national reconciliation. With political support for Radical Reconstruction waning in Washington, the Enforcement Acts lost their edge. Prosecutions of Klansmen slowed to a trickle while pardons were granted generously. Not unexpectedly, the U.S. Supreme Court, in its 1876 *Cruikshank* decision, denied the consitutional authority of the federal government to prosecute private individuals for committing acts of mob violence. The Court threw out indictments against three white participants in the infamous 1873 Colfax Massacre in Louisiana, when an army of white Democrats overpowered a black militia unit and slaughtered dozens of defenseless prisoners. Congressional amnesties restored the voting rights of former Confederates while many carpetbaggers gave up and returned home, and many scalawags concluded that it was time to switch sides.

With renewed vigor, the old elites proceeded to "redeem" the South. Although the Klan no longer played a major role, mass violence accompanied the Democratic reconquest in all Southern states. Party armies, known as "White Leagues" or "Red Shirts," broke up Republican gatherings, intimidated and harassed voters, and seized polling stations. In December 1874 more than six hundred armed white men attacked the office of Peter Crosby, the black Republican county sheriff of Vicksburg, Mississippi, forcing him to resign. When a black militia approached the town to reinstate the sheriff, Crosby begged them to disperse to avoid bloodshed. On their return home they were nevertheless ambushed by white snipers who killed at least twelve people; late at night rioters rampaged through Vicksburg's black neighbourhood, slaying an unknown number of African Americans.

Although terror and violence against black and white Republicans continued during the the 1870s, the federal government gradually reduced its level of troops in the South. Finally, in the aftermath of the contested presidential election of 1876, the Republicans agreed to end military occupation altogether in exchange for the Southern Democrats' acceptance of Republican candidate Rutherford B. Hayes as the next president. The freedmen felt betrayed. "We had to wade through blood to help place him where he is now," one of them bitterly commented on Hayes's deal with the white South.

The religious overtones of the word notwithstanding, the "redemption" of the South was in essence a terrorist campaign without parallel in American history. No reliable figures exist on the number of people who perished in the violent cataclysms of the Reconstruction years. Contemporary observers were clearly appalled by the frequency of mob violence. The people of Kentucky, a newspaper from neighboring Ohio noted in 1869, were "becoming accustomed to these summary executions by unauthorized bodies of men."

No doubt African Americans suffered by far the greatest number of casualties. According to one estimate, between 1868 and 1871 alone the Klan may have killed as many as twenty thousand freed people. As deadly violence became the order of the day, few chroniclers bothered to distinguish between people who died in large-scale riots, massacres, shoot-outs, from an assassin's bullet, or at the hands of a lynch mob. In fact writers used the term lynching mostly in reference to mobs disposing of "ordinary criminals" without an evident racial motive. Yet while precise numbers are unavailable, historians agree that the total extent of collective violence during the Reconstruction era, including lynching-style executions, exceeded even the levels of the 1890s, which are often considered the heyday of lynching in American history.

Finally, it is impossible to draw a clear line between lynching as punishment for crime and as political terrorism. In August 1874, for example, Trenton, Tennessee, became the scene of an appalling mass lynching when a crowd of as many as one hundred masked night riders descended on the jail and snatched sixteen black prisoners who had been arrested for allegedly plotting an insurrection. The freedmen supposedly had planned to murder all whites in the area and take over their land. The night riders marched their prisoners out of town and shot them dead. From their own point of view, the perpetrators of this massacre were fighting a race war for the survival of their own community, and they were in no mood to give quarter. African Americans, however, fully understood that they

The War of Races. Regulators shooting blacks near Trenton, Tennessee, August 1874.

were scapegoats against whom white Southerners vented their anger to
avenge their defeat in the war. "Our only crime is that we are negroes," a
black journalist who had investigated white terrorist violence in Tennessee exclaimed. "We are outraged by these cowards because we are in the
minority and are loyal to that Government which subdued the rebels and
triumphantly established the nation's flag upon the ruins of the Southern
Confederacy."

Southern blacks, in spite of their dogged resistance and loyalty to the United States government, were powerless to prevent the triumph of the Southern counterrevolution. Although the former Confederates could not reverse the outcome of the war or restore slavery, they succeeded in achieving "home rule" and in enforcing white supremacy. The Reconstruction experiment in interracial democracy, halfhearted as it was, was brutally crushed and replaced by a racist and repressive political and social order that endured until the second half of the twentieth century. Equally important, in the minds of many white Southerners the experience of Reconstruction and "redemption" reinforced the legitimacy of lynching and mob violence, especially in defense of white supremacy. In the ensuing decades Southern propagandists celebrated the Ku Klux Klan and the redeemers as noble defenders of white civilization. In his 1905 apologetic novel *The Clansman*, the author and minister Thomas Dixon of North Carolina enshrined this view of history in the collective memory of the South. Dixon's book provided the script for the startling and widely popular 1915 motion picture *Birth of a Nation*—a glorifying portrayal of the Reconstruction Klan that helped boost the rise of the second Klan movement that flourished in the 1920s.

Perhaps the greatest feat of Southern propaganda was to persuade the rest of the nation, including most white historians, that the black rights revolution of the Civil War years had been vindictive folly that had plunged the South into chaos and mayhem. The responsibility for the excessive violence of the era, according to this perspective, rested with the Radical Republicans and their black minions while white Southerners were simply defending themselves against "Negro domination" and an oppressive federal government. Of course the struggle for white supremacy did not end with Reconstruction. For many decades to come, lynching and mob violence remained readily available weapons of racist terrorism.

5

"Indescribable Barbarism"

The Lynching of African Americans in the Age of Jim Crow

ON JANUARY 31, 1893, a sheriff's posse captured a black man named Henry Smith at Clow, a flag station on the Arkansas & Louisiana Railway in southwestern Arkansas. They arrested the fugitive for the rape and murder of Myrtle Vance, a three-year-old white child and the daughter of the sheriff in Paris, Texas. Smith, a young man with a record of mental problems, had allegedly killed the child to visit revenge upon Sheriff Vance, who had repeatedly brutalized him. When the posse passed through Texarkana on its way back to Paris, an angry crowd awaited Smith and his captors. The leaders of the posse were able to avert a lynching, pleading with the residents of Texarkana to allow them to return the killer to the scene of his crime, where he would be brought to justice. The crowd deferred, but hundreds of people boarded the train to Paris to witness the spectacle that would surely follow. For it was understood that the posse never intended to deliver Smith to the legal authorities for trial.

Meanwhile news of Smith's capture had attracted a gathering of roughly ten thousand people in Paris. Several men had erected a ten-foot-high scaffold furnished with a chair and a small furnace. The word JUSTICE was painted in large white letters on the front side of the scaffold. The "justice" administered to Henry Smith consisted of red-hot irons that Sheriff Vance and several members of his family applied to the victim's body for almost an hour. After Smith's torturers had poked out his eyes and burned his tongue, they doused the platform with kerosene and set it on fire. As soon as the flames had consumed Smith, onlookers began scavenging the ashes for whatever parts remained of the scorched body. Throughout the grisly act, observers had taken photographs, and the next day newspapers on the East Coast featured graphic eyewitness accounts of the lynching in Texas.

In her 1894 pamphlet *A Red Record*, the African-American anti-lynching activist Ida B. Wells (1862–1931) called the torment of Henry Smith an "indescribable barbarism" without precedent in the "history of civilization." Unfortunately the brutality of the lynching at Paris was by no means exceptional. During the decades between the end of Reconstruction and the 1920s, "spectacle lynchings" before large crowds, often involving drawn out torture, mutilation, burning, and the dismemberment of the victim's body, occurred regularly in the New South. Nor did witnesses find such events indescribable; in fact they often indulged in sickening voyeurism. In April 1899, for example, a newspaper depicted the death of Sam Hose, a black farm worker from rural Georgia charged with the murder of Alfred Cranford, his white employer, and the rape of Cranford's wife, in words that are hard to fathom: "Before the torch was applied to the pyre the negro was deprived of his ears, fingers and other portions of his anatomy. The negro pleaded pitifully for his life while the mutilation was going on, but stood the ordeal of fire with surprising fortitude. Before the body was cool it was cut to pieces, the bones were crushed into small bits. . . . The negro's heart was cut into several pieces, as was his liver. Those unable to obtain these ghastly relics directly paid fortunate possessors extravagant sums for them."

Both contemporary opponents of lynching and historians have pondered the nagging question of why "ordinary Americans" who had families, went to church, held steady jobs, and otherwise claimed to be law-abiding citizens were capable of perpetrating such atrocities while showing no signs of shame or remorse. That question, however, is misleading. Most acts of collective violence in history, including mass murder, genocide, and war crimes, have been committed not by perverted aberrants but by "ordinary people" acting in perfectly good conscience because they received orders, believed in noble causes, or simply saw an opportunity to exert power over life and death with impunity. Most participants in lynch mobs viewed themselves as rendering an honorable service to justice and to the safety of their communities. Thus in order

The lynching of Henry Smith in Paris, Texas, 1893.

to understand lynching it is necessary to explore the cultural, social, economic, and political forces that sustained mob violence.

The most salient chapter in the history of lynch law in America was
the lynching of African Americans in the late nineteenth and early twentieth centuries. According to the most conservative estimates, slightly
more than 4,700 persons were lynched in the United States between the
early 1880s and World War II. Seventy-three percent of all victims were
blacks. In the South, where more than 80 percent of all lynchings occurred, black deaths were a staggering 83 percent of the total, representing 3,245 fatalities.

The obvious answer to the question of why white Southerners lynched
African Americans is that lynching was an instrument of racial control.
By the late 1870s the "redeemers" had successfully shaken off the fetters
of Reconstruction, but most white Southerners continued to be deeply
troubled by the fact that they found themselves living amidst a large
black population no longer restrained by the institution of slavery. The
answer to their predicament was to impose a racial caste system of white
supremacy, popularly known as the Jim Crow system, designed to reduce
African Americans to a pariah class without meaningful rights. To this

end, white Southerners introduced rigid racial segregation along with "electoral reforms" such as literacy tests and poll taxes to disenfranchise nearly all black voters.

In the last resort, however, white supremacy depended on the ability of whites to inflict violent repression on blacks with impunity. Racial violence in the age of Jim Crow ran a broad gamut, from individual bullying to wholesale pogroms with dozens of black victims. The so-called race riots in Wilmington, North Carolina (1898), New Orleans (1900), and Atlanta (1906) were the most conspicuous events of this type, but many lesser-known incidents could be added. In 1920, for instance, a confrontation in the township of Ocoee in Orange County, Florida, in which a black farmer killed two attackers in self-defense, resulted in a three-day orgy of mob violence that left scores of African Americans dead and the entire village destroyed. Thus the lynching of individuals or small groups of blacks was only one manifestation of the racist violence that pervaded life in the Jim Crow South. But lynching was highly visible and effective.

Lynchings did not have to happen every day to fill black communities with fear and horror. As with all forms of terror, the ever-present threat sent a powerful message of intimidation. Even slight transgressions of racial etiquette or misunderstandings might trigger fateful consequences. When Sandy Reeves, a black youth from rural Georgia, accidentally dropped a five cent piece in front of his employer's three-year-old daughter in September 1918, he should have let the girl keep the nickel instead of wresting it back from her hands. The child ran home, frantically crying that Reeves had harmed her. Her parents assumed that the young man had sexually assaulted their daughter; Reeves was lynched the following night. His fate may appear extreme, but Southern blacks knew that such incidents could happen to them too.

Lynchers made every effort to ensure that the black community got their message. They left the bodies of their victims on display for hours, sometimes even for days, and attached signs warning that future offenders would meet the same fate. Spectacle lynchings, such as the burnings of Henry Smith or Sam Hose described earlier, were frightening reminders that there were virtually no limits to what whites could do to blacks. Although only about one-tenth of all mob killings were mass spectacles, they nevertheless epitomized the meaning of lynching as racist terror staged as communal ritual. Mock trials and confessions,

even if obtained under torture, were essential to underscore the legitimacy of the punishment and to create the impression that the lynching
was tantamount to a legal execution. Extreme cruelty like mutilation
and burning satisfied the popular desire for retribution that fit the
enormity of the crime. The practice of bystanders riddling dead lynch
victims with bullets emphasized community approval. The public exhibition of body parts as trophies symbolized the triumph over a common
enemy. Because the excessive violence of spectacle lynchings was rarely
applied to white victims, no one could miss the point that the cruelty
served the purpose of dehumanizing African Americans. Replicating
a pattern that had been established during two centuries of slavery,
lynchers treated blacks as inferior "brutes" who were insensitive to any
but the most horrible physical pain.

But why did so many white Southerners believe they had to go to such
extremes in order "to keep the Negro in his place"? After all, whites
were a substantial majority of the population in most regions of the
South. They held all positions of political power and owned nearly all the
wealth. Certainly whites had absolute control of the criminal justice system and could make sure that blacks who were accused of crimes against
whites faced severe punishment. There was also no need to use violence
in order to keep the races separate. Although African Americans wanted
political and civic equality, they had very little interest in social involvement with white people because interracial contacts only reinforced their
subordinate status. At closer look it becomes clear that, in addition to intimidating blacks, racist mob violence in the South helped restore racial
solidarity among Southern whites.

During Reconstruction most white Southerners, regardless of social
class, had supported the struggle against "Negro rule" by all means necessary. But once redemption was complete, class tensions within the white
South reemerged. A key reason was the decline of cotton prices. Many
small farmers went into debt, lost their farms, and became tenants or
sharecroppers. The agrarian crisis sparked a powerful protest movement,
known as populism, which challenged the dominance of the Southern
planter and business elites. The Populists were willing to forge interracial alliances based on the common economic interests of lower-class
whites and blacks. The ruling conservative Democrats, used to manipu-
lating the black vote in their own favor, responded by waging a ruthless

campaign for white supremacy that once again employed lynching and vigilantism as instruments of political terrorism. Lynching peaked in the early 1890s, at the height of the Populist revolt and its conservative backlash. In the election year of 1892, at least 161 blacks were lynched, many of whom were involved in the Populist movement.

Attempts to lynch black Populists sometimes led to amazing consequences. In late October 1892 H. S. Doyle, an African-American Populist leader from Georgia, received threats to his life and fled to the home of Thomas Watson, the most prominent white Populist in the state. Watson immediately summoned an army of two thousand white supporters for Doyle's protection. In the end, however, the divide-and-conquer strategy of the conservative elites succeeded in driving a wedge into the fledgling interracial alliance. The Southern Democrats first adopted key items of the Populist program, then persuaded the white majority that "the Negro" was the source of all Southern troubles and had to be disfranchised, segregated, and forcibly kept in his place if tranquility was to return. As the historian C. Vann Woodward put it, the black man became "the scapegoat in the reconciliation of estranged white classes." Indeed, some scholars have argued that the role of blacks as scapegoats goes a long way in explaining Southern lynchings, pointing out that whenever cotton prices fell, mob violence increased. Lynching, they have concluded, was most of all a way for lower-class whites to vent their economic frustration against their black competitors. The failure of interracial solidarity in the Populist movement showed that for most white Southerners race came before class. Poor whites, a disillusioned Tom Watson noted, "would joyously hug the chains of wretchedness rather than do any experimenting on the race question." For his part, Watson decided to stake his political fortunes on white supremacy. He turned into a race-baiting demagogue and a vociferous apologist of lynching.

The appeal to the joint class interests of poor whites and blacks foundered on a powerful cultural legacy that demanded conformity on racial issues from all Southern whites. The institution of slavery had accustomed whites to the ideas that blacks stood outside the ordinary law and that all whites were responsible for controlling a potentially rebellious population of outcasts. It was no coincidence that some mob killings of African Americans in the New South resembled the insurrection scares of the antebellum days. In 1901, for example, a mob of

two hundred white men hunted down and hanged two blacks in Boss-
ier Parish, Louisiana, for allegedly slaying a local white man. The two
killers, the local newspaper insinuated, had been members of a conspiracy ring responsible for the recent murder of several whites. Hence the
lynching was a "necessary precaution" to protect the white community
from a black uprising.

Slavery as a legal and social institution had provided white Southerners with a sense of unquestionable superiority and relative safety vis-à-vis
black slaves. Emancipation had not only ended human bondage but had
made blacks equal citizens before the law. In the eyes of many whites,
this was an insult and a threat to their own status, and they made every effort to undermine the political and civic advancement of the freed
people. Nevertheless blacks in the South now struggled steadfastly to ac-
quire a modicum of education and economic independence, challenging
the racist dogma that they were fit only for menial agricultural labor under white supervision. Moreover younger African Americans who had
no personal recollection of slavery refused to wear the mask of subservi-
ence that their enslaved parents had been forced to adopt. Many whites
were deeply disturbed by what they perceived as a new black assertive-
ness. "Too many negroes," the *Atlanta Constitution* warned in 1889, "are
either mad or bad, and they are increasing in number." Supposedly these
"bad niggers" were responsible for the crime wave that seemed to plague
the South in the late nineteenth century. Black men who tried to make
a living as migrant workers faced the highest risk of incurring mob violence. The notorious black "floater," whites complained, was roaming
the roads day and night, looking for an opportunity to steal and making
it unsafe for women to leave home without male protection.

White supremacists concluded that the "impudence" of the first gen-
eration of freeborn African Americans proved that blacks were relaps-
ing into savagery, now that the civilizing institution of slavery had been
unwisely abolished. In their rhetoric, white racism knew no limits.
James K. Vardaman, a leading politician from Mississippi, characterized "the Negro" as a "lazy, lying, lustful animal which no conceiv-
able amount of training can transform into a tolerable citizen." Works
of fiction and pseudoscientific tracts, with such titles as *The Negro: a
Beast* or *The Negro: A Menace to American Civilization*, endlessly be-
labored the purported racial deterioration of African Americans and

their mortal threat to white Americans in general and white Southerners in particular. Freedom, the proponents of this ideology contended, had unleashed the supposedly insatiable sexual appetite of black males, driving them to rape white women at every opportunity. Thus lynching was essential for the protection of white women because only the sight of instant and merciless revenge could impress potential black rapists with sufficient terror. Furthermore no true white man could resist the impulse to avenge outrages against helpless women, regardless of legal constraints. "Whenever the Constitution comes between me and the virtue of white women," South Carolina governor Coleman Blease boasted, "I say to hell with the Constitution."

It is difficult to exaggerate the pervasiveness of the "Negro-as-savage-rapist" theme in debates over lynching in the age of Jim Crow. To be sure, these notions of uncontrollable black male sexuality and the need to preserve the "purity of the white race" were not new. In the late nineteenth century, however, black-on-white rape became an obsession. The historian Jacquelyn Dowd Hall has called it "a kind of acceptable folk pornography," which the white Southern press circulated with great relish. Some scholars have speculated that the fascination with the black rapist mirrored the repressed sexual fantasies of white men who vicariously punished black men for their own secret desires. The specter of the black rapist also helped cement the patriarchical dominance of white men over their wives and daughters at a time when traditional family life on the farm was giving way to a situation of more and more white women seeking wage labor outside the home. To gain protection against the menace of rape, women had to yield to male authority and accept strict limitations of what they could do and where they could go.

The idea that white women might voluntarily agree to sexual relations with black men was anathema to white men. To maintain the pretense of white racial and moral supremacy over black depravity, any sexual contact between a black man and a white woman had to be rape. For white men who discovered a female family member having a consensual affair with a black man, the obvious way to protect the honor of the family was to lynch the black "rapist." For white women who had engaged in interracial sex, sacrificing their lovers by bringing rape charges could be a way to escape shame and ostracism. Sometimes women were left with no other choice. In her 1892 anti-lynching treatise

Southern Horrors, Ida B. Wells reported the harrowing story of a mob in Texarkana that forced a white woman to accuse her lover of rape before the man was burned to death.

In addition to denying the possibility of consensual sex between a white woman and a black man, many white Southerners entertained paranoid notions of what constituted sexual assault. Because black men were said to be constantly lusting after white females of any age, there could be no innocuous situations. In 1917 an illiterate black man in Georgia was lynched because he had asked a little white girl to read a letter to him.

Black men occasionally did rape white women. But most certainly the wave of black-on-white rape that the apologists of lynching claimed threatened the white womanhood of the South was a racist fantasy, albeit a powerful one. Therefore anti-lynching activists worked hard to discredit the argument that rape was the root cause of lynching. According to various statistics they collected for the decades between the 1880s and World War II, in roughly 75 percent of all lynching cases sexual assault was not even alleged, let alone affirmed. All the same, rape dominated the public perception of lynching. Not surprisingly, Southern race baiters ignored the evidence that most lynchings had nothing to do with sexual crimes. Yet the rape myth also found widespread acceptance among white mainstream Americans outside the South.

Typically, Northern opinion leaders condemned lynching as unacceptable lawlessness. But they conceded that rape was its main cause and called upon the black community to curb sexual crime. In 1904 President Theodore Roosevelt, in a speech in Little Rock, Arkansas, pontificated that "the worst enemy of the Negro race is the Negro criminal of that type . . . and every reputable colored man owes it as his first duty to himself to hunt down that criminal with all his soul and strength." Even prominent supporters of black civil rights joined the chorus. In 1901 the influential white social reformer Jane Addams, who eight years later helped found the interracial National Association for the Advancement of Colored People (NAACP), declared that she was willing "to give the Southern citizens the full benefit of their position" on the rape issue. Most academic works on lynching, either explicitly or implicitly, accepted the causal link between rape and mob violence. As late as 1933 the sociologist Arthur Raper (ironically named in this instance), in his study *The Tragedy of Lynching,* alluded to the rape myth

when he suggested that "Negroes can contribute much to the eridica-
tion of lynching, by demonstrating the ability, character, and good citizenship of the race." Thus white mainstream opinion placed African
Americans in a double bind by blaming lynching on black rapists and
at the same time burdening the black community with the responsibility for eliminating its alleged cause.

The discrepancy between the popular obsession with rape on the one
hand and the claim of anti-lynching groups that charges of sexual crime
played a role in only one of four lynchings requires a closer look. The
available numbers on the precipitating events of lynchings provide the
following picture: Charges of homicide were by far the single most important trigger, accounting for 41 percent of all incidents, followed by
rape and attempted rape (25.3 percent), robbery and theft (4.9 percent),
felonious assault (4.3 percent), and insult to a white person (1.8 percent).
More than one in five lynchings (22.7 percent) fell into the category of
"other reasons." The overriding significance of murder is not a surprise
given that the Southern states in the late nineteenth century had by far the
highest homicide rates in the country, exceeding those of New England
by ten to thirty times. Contemporary observers blamed the high level of
personal violence on the traditional Southern code of honor that led to
countless violent confrontations with a fatal ending. Because many white
Southerners saw their criminal justice system as weak and inefficient,
they believed they had no alternative to taking the law into their own
hands, either by seeking individual revenge or by meting out communal
punishment. Blacks who killed whites almost invariably provoked community outrage and became likely targets of mob violence.

Yet the story of black-on-white murder as a cause of lynching requires
no less critical scrutiny than the rape myth. African Americans killing or
assaulting whites represented but a tiny fraction of all violent crime, if
only for the fact that most acts of personal violence occur among friends
and family members. Still, whenever a black person committed homicide
or assault against a white person—or was suspected to have done so—
mob violence became highly likely regardless of whether the suspect had
already been taken into custody. Given the racist prejudice of the times,
blacks accused of violent crimes against white people had little chance of
receiving a fair trial. In many cases public rage against the black murderer obscured the evidence of what had actually happened. Numerous

blacks who were lynched for murdering a white person may have been perfectly innocent of any crime or acted in legitimate self-defense.

In 1903 a mob lynched Jennie Steers, a black domestic, for poisoning the daughter of her employer, a wealthy Louisiana planter. Whether the girl had died as a result of natural causes or a devious crime remained unclear. But the traditional fears of Southern planters that their black servants were constantly plotting to poison them made Jennie Steers an expedient scapegoat for the unexpected loss of a loved family member. Accusing an African American could also be a convenient way to cover up a crime. In 1918 James Cobb, a black man from Cordelle, Georgia, was lynched for the murder of Mrs. Simmons, a white woman, though the victim's father suspected his son-in-law to be the real culprit. Of course Cobb's demise precluded further investigation.

Other murder charges grew out of interracial confrontations in which blacks often acted in self-defense. In the case of Sam Hose, the black farm worker burned to death in Georgia in 1899, private investigators hired by anti-lynching groups contested the widely publicized reports that Hose had crushed Alfred Cranford's head while the unsuspecting man was eating his supper, and then raped Mrs. Cranford. According to their findings, Hose and his boss had been arguing over the worker's request for an advance. When Cranford grew angry and drew his pistol, Hose flung his axe at him, killing him on the spot. Sensationalist newspaper stories, however, quickly portrayed the black man as a monstrous killer and sexual predator for whom only the most gruesome torture was fitting retribution.

It is impossible to determine if Hose killed Cranford in self-defense. Obviously the opponents of lynch law had a stake in claiming that the victims of mob killings either were innocent or had acted under mitigating circumstances. In contrast, white Southerners who cherished their own right to self-defense would not countenance the idea that blacks also had a right to protect themselves, their families, their property, and their honor against provocations from whites. Southern planters, in particular, took black deference for granted and continued to assume that they had a right to discipline their "insolent" black laborers and sharecroppers. Whenever blacks defied the authority of white employers or fought back, the situation was bound to escalate. In 1904 a black tenant farmer in Georgia killed his landlord in an altercation that resulted from the tenant insisting on his right to sell his crop to a merchant of his own choice. A mob promptly lynched the black "murderer."

Many historians have argued that lynching in the New South served the interests of the planter class. The reliance on extralegal punishment preserved part of the unfettered personal power the planter aristocracy had enjoyed in the days of slavery. Rural elites could easily instigate mob violence against "bad niggers" but could also protect their black clients if they saw fit. In 1894 a white mob pretending to act as a posse hunting down black criminals went on a lynching spree in Brooks County, Georgia, and massacred five African Americans. When the lynchers began molesting the black tenants of Mitchell Brice, one of the leading planters in the area, Brice halted the mob by threatening retaliation and prosecution. In addition to their traditional paternalism and the desire to maintain their personal authority, wealthy landowners occasionally took steps to curtail mob violence because they were afraid that their black workers would leave the area if life became intolerable. Ironically, though lynching was an instrument of racial terror that helped sustain the status quo in favor of the old elites, the frequency of mob violence was relatively low in many of the rural black belt counties of the Deep South where wealthy landlords exerted their paternalistic rule over a majority population of poor blacks.

In contrast, small towns where African Americans comprised about one quarter of the population had the highest incidence of lynchings. As both black and white Southerners moved to urbanizing areas in search of industrial work, the competition between the races for jobs intensified while anonymous interracial social encounters heightened the risk of violent clashes. As African Americans sought more personal freedom in towns and cities, whites saw the need to reassert white supremacy, insisting on strict racial segregation in the public sphere and on preferential treatment in the labor markets. Characteristically, lynching in Louisiana was most prevalent not in the northern rural black belt of the state but in the parishes neighboring on the city of New Orleans, which in the late nineteenth century underwent rapid industrialization and black and white in-migration.

One of the most spectacular lynchings in the urban South occurred in Waco, Texas, in the spring of 1916. In many ways this city of more than thirty thousand, including almost ten thousand African Americans, epitomized the vision of the modernizing New South. Waco was a major railway hub and had a thriving industrial sector, notably a bottling plant for the Dr Pepper soft drink. It boasted the tallest building in Texas, a skyscraper owned by the Amicable Life Insurance Company. Its residents enjoyed the benefits of electricity, streetcars, telephones, and public libraries. In fact Waco was particularly proud of its vibrant cultural and educational life, calling itself the "Athens of Texas." Not all citizens, however, appreciated the opportunities for base amusements, such as saloons and brothels, that the city also offered and that many whites associated with "Negro crime." Under the surface of Waco's bustling New South image, racial tensions simmered and from time to time boiled over. In 1905 a mob had lynched a black man charged with raping a white woman, hanging him from a bridge over the Brazos River. The confluence of a vigilante tradition, racism, and the ferment of brisk social change created a climate in Waco that was highly conducive to racist mob violence.

The moment arrived when on May 8, 1916, the dead body of Lucy Fryer, a fifty-three-year-old mother and immigrant from England, was discovered on the farm of her family in Robinson, a small village about eight miles outside Waco. The investigation quickly concentrated on Jesse Washington, a seventeen-year-old black youth who worked on the Fryer farm. After Sheriff Samuel Fleming arrested the teenager at his home, he brought him to the jail in Waco. At first Washington, who was illiterate and possibly mentally retarded, denied the charges, but later he confessed to having slain Lucy Fryer following an argument over his treatment of a team of mules that belonged to the Fryers. Possibly his interrogators forced a confession from the black youth, but there was nevertheless strong evidence against the suspect. His clothes were stained with blood, and he led the police to the place where he had concealed the hammer he had used to crush his victim's head. It is thus quite likely that Washington killed Mrs. Fryer, though the black press later insinuated that her husband George Fryer had either committed the murder himself or incited his worker to do the job for him. It remained unclear if the black man had also raped his victim, which the Waco newspapers reported in lurid detail.

Anticipating mob action, Sheriff Fleming had the prisoner transported to Dallas County for safekeeping. Predictably, as soon as news of the murder spread, a mob took control of Fleming's jail and left only after learning that Washington was not there. The sheriff assured mob leaders that the culprit would be put on trial in Waco as soon as possible. Indeed, the trial commenced just one week after the murder, on May 15, before a crowd of fifteen hundred spectators who raucously voiced their opinion that no court was needed. At least the judge managed to retain a façade of due process until the jury, after deliberating for fewer than five minutes, rendered a guilty verdict. At this point the mob grabbed the defendant and began driving him toward the bridge where the 1905 lynching had been carried out. But several men insisted that burning was the appropriate method of execution and built a pyre in front of the city hall. With a mesmerized crowd of ten thousand gaping at events, the lynchers tied their victim to a chain they tossed over the branch of a tree. They then lit a fire under his feet, repeatedly pulling him up and down to prolong his suffering. Shortly before Washington died, his tormentors cut off his fingers, toes, and genitals. Finally a man on horseback dragged the corpse through the streets of Waco, followed by a throng of young boys. Some of the body parts were sold to onlookers, others ended up on display in Robinson, the scene of Washington's crime.

Although the risk of mob violence had been evident for days before the trial, the Waco police department took no precautions to prevent the lynching. On the contrary, Sheriff Fleming, who faced reelection in the fall, ordered his men not to resist the mob and himself watched the spectacle alongside the mayor of Waco. The sheriff also allowed a local photographer to take pictures from a window of the city hall; the photographs subsequently became coveted souvenir items. But the appalling image of Jesse Washington's charred body chained to a tree, one of the most infamous visual documents of American history, also ensured that the "Waco Horror" received nationwide attention and condemnation. The lynching, commented the *New York Times*, brought "disgrace and humiliation" on the entire country, for in no other civilized nation "could a man be burned to death in the streets of a considerable city amid the savage exultation of its inhabitants." The NAACP sent Elizabeth Freeman, a white suffragist, to investigate the Waco affair and later published a special edition of its monthly magazine *Crisis*, featuring a photograph of Jesse Washington's disfigured corpse on the cover. To make sure that white Americans took note, the organization sent copies to hundreds of newspapers and to every member of Congress.

Jesse Washington's charred corpse after the infamous 1916 lynching in Waco, Texas

Facing strong criticism from around the country, the white leaders of Waco mounted the usual defense. The lynch mob had been much smaller than the estimated ten thousand, they claimed, even though the pictures left little doubt about the enormous size of the gathering. The photographs also would have made possible the identification of the mob leaders, but no one was ever prosecuted for participation in the public murder. In as much as Waco leaders talked about the ghastly incident at all, they agreed that the lynching had been the deed of madmen coming from "the lowest order of society." Of course this was a blatant distortion of the facts. Not only had the crowd included men and women from all walks of life, but, as Freeman found, the mob leaders were solid working-class and middle-class men who had every reason to believe they were acting with the full approval of Waco's white citizenry. In this respect the "Waco Horror" of 1916 was not different from many other lynchings in the New South. As countless photographs document, neither active perpetrators nor onlookers made any effort to conceal their identity because they had no reason to fear criminal prosecution. Even when lynchers had their pictures taken with dangling and disfigured bodies, the coroners would later declare that the victims had suffered "death at the hands of parties unknown."

Not all lynchings were the work of mass mobs carrying out sadistic rituals. There were also smaller mobs, ranging from a handful of participants to perhaps two or three dozen, that acted furtively, killing their victims in remote places at night without further ado. Like mass mobs that staged spectacle lynchings, small mobs claimed to avenge crimes for which the law allegedly offered no adequate punishment. Unlike mass mobs, however, small mobs often sought secrecy because they could not be sure of widespread support from the larger community. Typically this was the case when the lynchers sought personal revenge for offenses that had not triggered much public outrage. For instance, in 1912 members of a white family in Columbus, Georgia, lynched a young black man who had accidentally shot one of their own and was later convicted of manslaughter. Apparently the local white community had been satisfied with this outcome, but no one questioned the family's desire for harsher retribution. Lynchings by private mobs may have accounted for roughly one-third of all lynchings. They were especially common in cases when whites or blacks executed members of their own race outside the law. As demonstrations of white supremacy and communal justice, however, they were of minor importance compared to the spectacle lynchings by mass mobs.

Most of the participants in lynching parties were members of the white rural and urban working classes—small farmers, sharecroppers, construction workers, or saloonkeepers. Nevertheless mass mobs usually included people of all social backgrounds and certainly were not confined to the proverbial "riffraff." On the contrary, the legitimacy of popular justice depended on the involvement of "respectable citizens." Southern newspapers often rejected lynching in the abstract but cited the presence of the "best citizens" of the community—without providing specific names—in order to justify a particular lynching. Local luminaries supposedly ensured order and embodied the consent of the people. In combination with the rape myth, the participation of Southern elites helped make Northern opinion receptive to the apology for extralegal executions. In 1901 the Harvard University scientist Nathaniel Southgate Shaler published the essay "American Quality," in which he condemned mob rule but insisted that most lynchings were carried out by "decent men of American, law-abiding type." Such lynchings, Shaler suggested, were the equivalent of legal executions, not "a sign of real lawlessness, nor of a people given to savage outbursts of fury."

Approval from elected officials lent added respectability to mobs. Southern demagogues such as James Vardaman, Tom Watson, and Coleman Blease were notorious for their defense of lynching as legitimate popular justice. Sometimes public officeholders even participated in lynchings. In 1911, for example, Joshua W. Ashley, a member of the South Carolina state legislature, led a mob in Anderson County that hunted down Willis Jackson, a black man accused of attacking a white child. The lynchers hanged Jackson by his feet and then riddled him with bullets. Governor Blease not only refused to prosecute the mob leaders but declared that, rather than sending the militia to protect the alleged child rapist, he would have resigned his office and come to Anderson County and led the mob himself. For public officials to take a determined stand against lynching carried the risk of alienating voters. In 1926 a Florida judge who had presided over a lynching investigation lost his bid for reelection.

As a rule the execution of popular justice was the domain of men. But if black-on-white rape was the alleged offense, women could become key players in lynchings. To begin with, women provided their men with moral support. As one of the vigilantes who set out to hunt down Jesse Washington phrased it: "When we left home tonight our wives, daughters and sisters kissed us good bye and told us to do our duty, and we're trying to do it as citizens." Yet, far from being limited to the role of passive objects of male chivalry, women participated in manifold ways. In most cases women had to report the initial crime of rape. Although false accusations were sometimes made, especially to cover up a consensual affair, for a Southern white woman to admit publicly that she had been sexually abused by a black man was no easy step. Even though no one was likely to question the veracity of her charges, rape, also known as "the fate worse than death," always left a stain of shame on the victim. Moreover every white woman who accused a black man of sexual assault knew that he was doomed.

If the identity of the rapist was in doubt, identification by the victim became a centerpiece of the mock trials that often preceded the execution. The defenders of lynch law insisted that the crime of rape did not belong in regular courts because no white woman should have to suffer the ordeal of having to confront her attacker face-to-face. Nevertheless positive identification by the rape victim lent a legitimacy to mob executions that few dared to question. In 1885 a Georgia mob brought a suspect before a young wife and mother, repeatedly admonishing her that the man's life depended on her word. After she had confidently recognized him as the culprit, the leaders suggested she choose the mode of execution. Although some men called for a burning, the woman wanted the man hanged, and got her will. Of course, most lynchers considered identification a mere formality and were perfectly satisfied if the outraged woman declared that the man they dragged before her *could have been* the rapist.

Some white women who joined lynch mobs inflicted physical violence on the victims voluntarily and eagerly. They cheered on others, brought ropes or fuel, ignited torches, or pumped bullets into bodies, dead or alive. The desire to take an active part in lynchings was by no means limited to women who had been raped or otherwise suffered personal injury. In 1916 an Oklahoma sheriff who prevented the lynching of two black men accused of murder testified "that there were women in the crowd and that they were no less eager for the blood of the negroes than the men." Women too scavenged for body parts and wanted their pictures taken with the victim's body. In mass mobs it was not uncommon to see mothers with their children. At the burning of the alleged black rapist Lloyd Clay in Vicksburg, Mississippi, in 1919, eyewitnesses observed a woman and several children pouring gasoline over the man.

Black critics of Southern lynch law condemned the participation of white women in mob violence as the epitome of depravity and hypocrisy, belying the adulation of white women as torchbearers of Christian civilization. Then again, most Southern white women believed in the myths and privileges of white supremacy, especially in their right to protection from sexual assault. In contrast to the antebellum era, when the worship of white Southern womanhood had been confined to ladies of social standing, the white supremacist ideology of the late nineteenth and early twentieth centuries also incorporated poor white women into the "ruling race." Furthermore, inflicting violence on a perceived enemy of the community could be an empowering experience for women no less than for men. In a perverse and sordid manner, the assertive roles that women played in lynch mobs may have mirrored the efforts of Southern women to carve out a larger degree of power and independence for themselves.

The most prominent and articulate white Southern woman defender of lynch law was Rebecca Latimer Felton (1835–1930) of Georgia. An advocate of women's suffrage and temperance and a reform-minded supporter of the Populist movement, Felton, like her fellow Georgian Tom Watson, initially denounced lynching and backed political rights for blacks. She switched sides after many Populist candidates, including her husband, lost to the white supremacy campaign waged by Southern Democrats in 1894. Three years later Felton's speech on the "Needs of Farmers' Wives and Daughters," in which she blamed white men for failing to protect their female family members from black rapists, gained national notoriety. For the most part her speech was a harsh critique of the corruption of male-dominated Southern politics. By courting the black voter on election day and befuddling him with liquor, she explained, white politicians "make him think he is a man and a brother," thus encouraging sexual assaults on white women.

Felton called for moral and educational reforms that would benefit poor rural girls and women. Yet, as long as political and moral corruption exposed hapless females to shame and fear, extralegal justice must continue: "If it needs lynching to protect woman's dearest possession from the ravenous human beasts, then I say lynch a thousand times a week, if necessary." White supremacist opinion leaders in the South celebrated Felton as a "true southern woman" while conveniently ignoring the feminist aspects of her speech. At the same time Northern criticism prompted Felton to close ranks with Southern white men and radicalize her statements. When a Georgia mob lynched Sam Hose in April 1899, Felton commented that a mad dog being shot was "more worthy of sympathy." The same year, lynching in Georgia reached its peak. Of course not all white women of the South approved of lynching, and only a small minority participated in mobs. But it was extremely diffcult for white women to speak out against racial violence. Those who did so inevitably faced reproach for betraying their race and depriving helpless and innocent girls of male protection.

The specter of the black rapist did not offer a plausible excuse for the lynching of black women. Mob executions of black females enjoyed much less popular support than those of men, and they occurred much less frequently. Still, they were not rare exceptions. Estimates vary from at least 75 to 130 African-American women who fell victim to lynch law between the 1880s and the 1920s. The use of brutal violence to discipline black women had been commonplace under slavery, regardless of the sentimental images white slaveholders held of their black "mammies." When black women, like men, claimed freedom and independence from white control in the decades after the Civil War, they appeared increasingly defiant and aggressive in the eyes of Southern whites. Thus when black women were accused of especially shocking offenses, white lynchers insisted that they deserved the same rough justice as black men.

Most African-American women were lynched for the crime of murder, and many of them were killed in summary executions along with male family members. Typically such multiple killings resulted from confrontations with police officers. In 1911 Laura Nelson and her son were hanged from a bridge in Okemah, Oklahoma, because she had shot and killed a deputy sheriff who had intruded into her home. In 1918 a mob, acting as a posse, shot down the entire Cabiness family in Walker County, Texas, including the mother and one daughter. According to an affidavit sworn by a surviving daughter, the Cabiness family was unarmed when the posse began firing. Press reports, however, depicted them as a dangerous gang of criminals staging a deadly shoot-out with the forces of the law. In 1926 a mob seized eighteen-year-old Bertha Lowman, along with her brother Demon and her cousin Clarence Lowman, from a jail in Aiken, South Carolina, and shot them "like rats," as one newspaper report put it. Earlier the Lowman family had killed a sheriff in self-defense.

When a black woman was lynched, the white press usually assumed her guilt and defamed her character, similar to its reporting on black male lynch victims. Even anti-lynching activists sometimes hesitated to protest mob violence against women who were known for their "bad character" and had a reputation for lewdness. When Marie Scott, a seventeen-year-old black woman living in Wagoner, Oklahoma, was charged with stabbing to death a young white man named Lemuel Pearce in March 1914, newspapers immediately concluded that she was guilty of murder. Supposedly Scott had attacked Pearce for no apparent reason. Hours after she had been arrested, a mob of about a hundred men overpowered the jailer in the middle of the night and hung

Scott—who desperately fought for her life—from a telephone pole. When the NAACP inquired into the circumstances, a local attorney indicated that Scott had been a resident of the "red light district." But he refused to give the "revolting and shocking" details of Pearce's death to the NAACP's white secretary May Childs Nerney because he would not discuss them with a lady. NAACP leaders concluded that Marie Scott was a prostitute and therefore that her lynching would not arouse public sympathy. Several weeks later, however, the NAACP obtained a letter from a black informant telling a different story. Two white men, including Lemuel Pearce, were roaming the neighborhood, the letter reported, and spotted Marie Scott alone in her room. They broke into the family's home and raped her. Scott's brother came to her rescue and killed Pearce with a knife. The young man then ran away and was smuggled by black sleeping-car porters to Mexico. His sister remained as the obvious murder suspect and suffered the wrath of the mob.

The lynching of four young African Americans between the ages of fifteen and twenty, two men and two women, in Shubuta, Mississippi, in December 1918 also prompted very different accounts of what had happened. Indisputably the four youngsters had killed their employer, a retired dentist and farmer named Dr. E. L. Johnston. One white Mississippi newspaper related that the four had ambushed and murdered Johnston because he had discharged them from his farm. In contrast, an investigator for the NAACP claimed that Johnston had sexually abused the two sisters, Alma and Maggie Howze. When Maggie Howze and Major Clark, who was working on Johnston's farm along with his brother Andrew, disclosed their desire to marry, Johnston told the young man to leave "his woman" alone. A scuffle ensued, and Major Clark accidentally shot his employer, according to the NAACP report. Although the dentist, a notorious drunkard, was not popular in the white community, a mob seized the four young blacks from jail and hanged them from a bridge across the Chickasawhay River. Reportedly the two women were visibly pregnant at the time of their deaths.

Mary Turner, the victim of one of the most brutal lynchings involving a black woman, was also pregnant when she and her husband became caught up in what the NAACP aptly called a "lynching orgy," which occurred in Brooks and Lowndes counties, Georgia, in May 1918. The murder of Hampton Smith, a white farmer, sparked hysteria among the white population of the area. Within a week mobs and posses killed up to eleven African Americans believed to have been involved in the slaying. Among the victims was Hayes Turner, a black farm laborer who had worked for Smith. When his wife Mary announced that she would press for the prosecution of her husband's murderers, she herself became the target of the mob. Walter White, the NAACP field secretary who personally investigated the events, reported that the eight-months-pregnant woman was hanged with her head downward, doused with gasoline and set on fire. While she was still alive, one of the lynchers grabbed a knife and cut the unborn infant from her womb. Another man then crushed the baby's head with the heels of his boots. Finally the mob unloaded their guns into the dead woman's body.

The lynching frenzy in Georgia provoked condemnation throughout the United States. As American soldiers were fighting German "Huns" to make the world safe for democracy, observers emphasized, lynching did enormous harm to the war effort. President Woodrow Wilson, who held profound sympathies for white Southern views on race, admonished his countrymen that "every mob contributes to German lies about the United States." Southern apologists responded that German spies had caused the trouble in the first place by fomenting insurrection among the black population of southwestern Georgia. But even in the hysterical climate of World War I, few people outside the Deep South took such ridiculous excuses seriously.

In the early twentieth century many Americans came to see lynching as a peculiar Southern problem. They viewed the region as painfully backward and isolated, and populated largely by semi-literate "rednecks" whose favorite pastimes were to guzzle moonshine liquor, engage in brawls, and abuse black people. In 1917 Baltimore's acerbic journalist H. L. Mencken spurned the South as "almost as sterile, artistically, intellectually, culturally, as the Sahara Desert." Lynching, Mencken thought, was a "popular sport . . . because the backward culture of the region denied the populace more seemly recreations" such as brass bands, symphony orchestras, or athletic contests.

Critics of the South tended to ignore that lynchings also occurred in other parts of the country. Northern mobs, too, killed African Americans, and they targeted them for the same reasons as Southern whites. One incident of particular callousness occurred in Coatesville, Pennsylvania, in

August 1912, after a black man named Zachariah Walker had killed a white police officer in a saloon scuffle. While a posse was pursuing Walker, the fugitive tried to shoot himself but merely injured his jaw. The police brought him to a hospital where, the following night, a mob seized him. Although the black man desperately pleaded that he had shot the policeman in self-defense, his abductors burned him alive before a crowd of five thousand men, women, and children. In similar fashion a mass mob overpowered police headquarters in Duluth, Minnesota, in June 1920 to seize three young black men held for the alleged rape of an eighteen-year-old white woman. The lynchers then stripped their victims to their waists and hanged them from a lamppost in the city center. A newspaper from Valdosta, Georgia, the scene of the Mary Turner lynching two years earlier, gloatingly pointed out that the incident had taken place in a state that prided itself on "its great love for the poor friendless colored man and has criticized the Southern people for not living on terms of social equality with the blacks."

In these episodes there were nevertheless significant differences between North and South: the lynchings in Pennsylvania and Minnesota resulted in serious efforts to bring the perpetrators to justice. In the Coatesville affair, officials launched a thorough investigation and were able to obtain indictments against eight men, including the police chief and his deputy, for neglecting their duty to uphold the law. Eventually a local jury acquitted all defendants. Incensed by this mockery of justice, the governor of Pennsylvania threatened to revoke the town charter of Coatesville, though he never followed through with his announcement. Prosecution in the Duluth case was more successful. The governor of Minnesota immediately dispatched the National Guard to the city, and the commanding general began a preliminary investigation. A photographer who had displayed images of the lynching was charged with exhibiting "indiscreet and obscene pictures." Ultimately more than a dozen of the lynchers were indicted. In September 1920 a jury convicted two men for rioting and sentenced them to up to five years in prison. A juvenile defendant served time in the state reformatory. The authorities also prosecuted thirteen black men for their alleged involvement in the gang rape of the young white woman. But lawyers hired by the NAACP obtained releases or acquittals for all but one of the defendants, who was sentenced to thirty years in prison but paroled in 1925. In fact there was considerable doubt that a rape had occurred at all. A medical examination was inconclusive, and suspicion surfaced that the young woman and her boyfriend may have made up the rape story to conceal a sexual liaison.

In both these cases the outcomes of the criminal prosecutions were disappointing. Yet they compared favorably to situations in most Southern states where lynchers had virtually nothing to fear from the authorities. When in 1918 NAACP representatives called upon Mississippi governor Theodore Bilbo to take action against the lynchers of the four black youngsters in Shubuta, Bilbo responded they should "go to hell." Because African Americans could not expect protection from law enforcement or political leadership in the South, they had to wage their own struggle against lynching. But what could people who personally encountered racial violence do to fight lynching?

Despite black poverty and powerlessness, racist terror did not cow all African Americans into silence and submission. Resistance encompassed a broad spectrum of behavior ranging from gestures of defiance to armed self-defense. One conspicuous way blacks demonstrated their opposition was to refuse responsibility for burying the victims. Following the Shubuta murders, local blacks reportedly declared that "the white folks lynched them and they can cut them down." To express their protest, African Americans also boycotted the businesses of lynchers or refused to work for them. Sometimes mob violence triggered a black exodus. In the aftermath of a triple lynching in Memphis, Tennessee, in 1892, the city's black population fell by two thousand. Following the Georgia lynching spree of 1918, observers warned that the South was driving its black labor force northward. If fear or protest caused blacks to leave, lynching was perhaps one of the "push factors" in the Great Migration north that began during World War I.

Blacks also found other ways to resist mob violence. These included hiding a fugitive from a mob or perhaps setting fire to the property of lynchers. Such forms of resistance were extremely dangerous because they invited instant retaliation if discovered. Clearly the most confrontational way to stand up to lynching was armed self-defense. African American leaders unanimously insisted that blacks had not only a right but a duty to fight back when attacked by a mob. "A Winchester rifle should have a place of honor in every black home," Ida B. Wells famously proclaimed, "and it should be used for that protection which the law refuses to give."

Many blacks who faced a mob put up a last-ditch fight. Perhaps the most legendary of these stands occurred in New Orleans in July 1900 after Robert Charles, a black worker in his mid-thirties, had wounded a police officer in self-defense and then fled the scene. When the police, accompanied by a swelling mob of several thousand whites, found his hiding place, he barricaded himself behind a window and took aim at his pursuers with his rapid-firing rifle. In a gun battle lasting several hours, the injured fugitive supposedly killed seven whites and wounded twenty more before he was smoked out and felled by volleys from policemen and vigilantes. Enraged by the death toll Charles had exacted among his opponents, white mobs staged a major riot that claimed the lives of more than a dozen African-American residents of the Crescent City.

The incident demonstrated that armed self-defense carried a high risk of provoking massive retaliation against the larger black community. The black press nonetheless celebrated African Americans who fought back as heroes. "May his ashes rest in peace for protecting his manhood," the *Chicago Defender* eulogized Tom Brooks of Sommerville, Tennessee, who in May 1915 killed two white lynchers before he was hanged.

In contrast to individual acts of valor, collective armed self-defense had a greater chance of success. In 1911 rumors in Stanford, Kentucky, indicated that whites planned to seize two African Americans from the local jail. This prompted leaders of the black community to organize an armed sentinel to guard the prisoners. When the would-be lynchers spotted the patrol, they dispersed. Twelve years earlier a similar event in Darien, Georgia, had led to what local whites perceived as a "Negro insurrection." When a black man accused of raping a white woman was arrested, a large group of armed black men rushed to the jail for his protection. Evidently deterred by the presence of the sentry, no mob showed up. But the picket remained watchful and refused to allow the sheriff to remove the prisoner, fearing he would surrender him to a lynching party. Whites became so frightened by the apparent black takeover of the town that they called in the militia. The black guards agreed to hand over the prisoner to the militia but resisted the arrest of their leaders, wounding two white men. A major confrontation was barely avoided. Eventually the alleged rapist was acquitted while twenty-three of the so-called "insurrectionists" went to prison for "rioting."

Although they often were outgunned, outmanned, and risked harsh retribution, African Americans, no less than whites, cherished the ethics of self-defense, honor, and vengeance. After the Shubata lynching, the *Baltimore Daily Herald*, a black newspaper, defended Major Clark for killing Dr. Johnston because the latter had abused two young black women. Noting correctly that African-American women lacked legal protection from white aggressors, the paper criticized the youngster only for ambushing Johnston—as the white press had reported—rather than confronting him "in an open and manly fashion" and then fighting him to the death. Such conduct would have made Clark "a martyr to the cause of Negro womanhood."

Reared in a culture of violence, many blacks were not opposed to lynching in principle. Primarily they resented its racist thrust. Even Ida B. Wells admitted that she had condoned mob violence in reaction to rape before she became an anti-lynching campaigner. If Judge Lynch acted in an ostensibly color-blind fashion, blacks found reasons to applaud his work. In 1919 a mass meeting of the black community in Lexington, Georgia, endorsed the action of whites who had lynched "Obe" Cox, an infamous black criminal, for assaulting and murdering a white woman. Allegedly Cox had earlier raped a black woman too.

Between the 1880s and the late 1920s roughly 150 African Americans fell victim to lynch mobs that were either racially integrated or all-black. In many ways black-on-black lynching mirrored the general trends of mob violence in the age of Jim Crow. It peaked in the 1890s and gradually declined afterward, and it was most prevalent in the states of the Deep South. Moreover nearly three-fourths of all blacks executed by mobs of their own race were accused of murder and rape. Often the crime had been of a particularly heinous nature. In 1885 a group of black vigilantes dispatched a man from Jones County, Mississippi, for murdering a black woman and her two children to whom the killer was a half-brother. He had also allegedly raped his half-sister before slaying her. Although less frequently than white mobs, black lynchers occasionally displayed extreme cruelty, burning their victims or throwing them into boiling water.

While the rationale of white supremacists that lynching was necessary because the law treated black-on-white crime too softly was patently absurd, black Southerners indeed had reason to complain about law enforcement. The authorities not only refused to protect them against white mob violence but also cared little about black-on-black crime. According to a late-nineteenth-century remark attributed to a Southern police chief, there were three types of homicides: "If a nigger kills a white man, that's murder. If a white man kills a nigger, that's justifiable homicide. If a nigger kills a nigger, that's one less nigger." Punishment often depended on white interests. When labor was scarce, planters were inclined to intervene on behalf of workers charged with a crime against another black person in order to keep them out of prison. Because many white men regarded black women as fair game, the white-dominated criminal justice system paid little attention to black-on-black rape. Moreover if black men lynched other black men for raping black women, such acts merely confirmed for whites their view that the menace of the "black brute" had become intolerable even to his own people.

Although racial hatred obviously played no role in black-on-black lynchings, participants in black mobs shared with white supremacists some of the key beliefs in popular justice. Most important, lynchers maintained they were agents of communal self-defense necessitated by a weak system of official criminal justice. Southern racism in the age of Jim Crow radicalized these ideas by creating the specter of the black rapist. But in principle, popular justice had never been limited to the purpose of racial terror. Its adherents continued to mete out extralegal punishment to other groups as well.

6

Popular Justice Beyond Black and White

TODAY MOST AMERICANS associate the term "lynching" with racist mob violence directed against African Americans during the age of Jim Crow. Indisputably a sizable majority of lynching victims were blacks. Anti-black racism, especially hysterical fears of the "Negro rapist," played a key role in the defense of lynch law and found many supporters far beyond the Mason-Dixon line. Still, this story is incomplete and obscures other important facets of lynching in America.

First, at least one-quarter of all persons lynched between the 1880s and World War II were not African Americans. By the most cautious tallies, the total adds up to twelve hundred, but, as in the case of black victims, probably there were many more unreported casualties. The fact that nonblacks were lynched in significant numbers in itself warrants a closer look. The classification "nonblack" is accurate here because it is a mistake to assume that all victims who were not African American must have been white, meaning of Euro-American descent. Statistics compiled by contemporaneous opponents of lynching, including researchers at the Tuskegee Institute and the NAACP, understandably concentrated on black suffering and often used "white" as a residual category. It is thus reasonable to assume that this category also comprised victims of Mexican, Native American, and Asian descent.

Moreover the traditional black-and-white picture is misleading because it cements the notion that lynchings were of two distinct varieties: the white supremacist type aimed at terrorizing African Americans, and the popular justice variety that targeted white criminals. In these latter incidents race supposedly did not matter. But racial and ethnic hatred not only played a role in the lynching of Mexicans, Mexican Americans, Native Americans, and Asians. Even so-called white victims sometimes belonged to ethnic groups whose "whiteness," measured by the dominant Anglo-Saxon Protestant standard, seemed in doubt. In the late nineteenth century, for example, Italian immigrants fell into this category.

Although popular justice gradually lost support in the Western states as frontier conditions receded in the late nineteenth century, lynching continued. While absolute numbers were much higher in the Deep South, per capita rates of lynching put the West almost on a par with the South. For example, with sixty-four lynchings during the last two decades of the nineteenth century, Colorado matched the total head count for North Carolina. But its per capita rate stood more than four times higher and exceeded even that of Alabama. In the late nineteenth and early twentieth centuries, the West and the South remained the two regional strongholds of popular justice in the United States.

Persons of Mexican ethnic background, irrespective of whether they held Mexican or U.S. citizenship, represent the largest group of neglected lynch victims. While the Tuskegee Institute's statistics list only 50 Mexicans lynched for the period from 1880 to 1930, recent research has identified more than 200. A conservative estimate of the number of Mexicans lynched in the southwestern United States includes roughly 600 dead for the eight decades from the end of the Mexican-American War in 1848 until 1928, when the last known extralegal execution of Mexicans occurred in New Mexico. According to the historians William Carrigan and Clive Webb, on a per capita basis Mexicans in the Southwest faced as great a risk of being murdered by lynch mobs as African Americans in the South.

Mexicans who came under U.S. sovereignty in 1848 had a right to American citizenship and received guarantees of their property. But they soon encountered a swelling majority of Euro-Americans, commonly referred to as Anglos, who coveted their land and were not inclined to accept them as fellow Americans. During the turbulent 1850s, when Anglo miners, ranchers, and farmers poured into the Southwest and California, interethnic violence soared. At least 160 Mexicans were lynched during this decade. Mexicans, resentful of widespread de facto discrimination and Anglo contempt, fought back and sometimes resorted to lynch law themselves.

Although Euro-Americans swiftly established their demographic, political, and economic dominance in the annexed territories, anti-Mexican mob violence and extralegal executions of Mexicans persisted until the 1920s. Similar to the situation in the South, lynching served as an instrument to terrorize the Mexican minority into accepting Anglo supremacy. But added wellsprings of mob violence surfaced in the Southwest. Because the border between the United States and Mexico remained contested and volatile, Mexican raiders continually ventured into American territory to steal cattle and horses. In response, American posses relentlessly pursued the brigands, often far into Mexico. Suspicious of all Mexicans, the Anglos showed little interest in distinguishing between intruding outlaws and resident Mexican settlers. In the mid-1870s, when the border skirmishes assumed warlike proportions, raids on Mexican homes and execution-style murders by posses went unchecked. One U.S. Army officer observed that many Anglos in Texas "think the killing of a Mexican no crime."

The Texas Rangers, a paramilitary force founded in 1835, acted with a ruthlessness that has prompted historians to compare them to the Ku Klux Klan. Although bound to uphold the law, they were notorious for torturing prisoners and executing them on the spot. And if they did not do the killing themselves, they might well cooperate with a mob. In 1881 Rangers illegally hunted down a Mexican murder suspect on Mexican soil and returned him to Texas. Rather than delivering the suspect to the authorities for arraignment and trial, they handed their prisoner over to lynchers who had been waiting for their return.

Mexicans did not hesitate to retaliate in kind if they could get hold of their Anglo enemies. During the so-called El Paso Salt War of 1877, Anglo political leaders and businessmen tried to establish commercial control over the salt lakes in West Texas that the Mexican community had used for many years. In the fall of that year the conflict escalated into a full-fledged uprising by the Mexican population. After a Mexican mob had overpowered a detachment of Texas Rangers in San Elizaro in early December, the Mexicans immediately executed three of the Anglo leaders, including a judge named Charles Howard, who had led the effort to seize the salt beds.

Many Anglos residing along the Mexican border believed they had no choice but to wage a permanent struggle against predatory bandits. As a rule, American opinion found no fault with meting out summary justice to so-called "desperados." Lynchings that occurred in the pursuit of cattle rustlers, in particular, had a ring of rough frontier justice trig-gered by the heat of the moment. Yet the excuse that the region had no functioning system of criminal justice was no more warranted in the case of Mexican "bandits" than in the case of black "rapists." Of course the raids threatened the safety of Anglo settlers. But, typically, the mobs that claimed to exercise communal self-defense against dangerous criminals killed people already in custody.

An incident in La Salle County, Texas, in October 1895 illustrates this point. A cattleman, U. T. Saul, accompanied by his foreman, a deputy sheriff, and a state Ranger, confronted a group of five Mexicans, includ-ing two men, a woman, a little girl, and a young boy, and accused them of stealing and slaughtering a calf. A shooting ensued in which Saul, one Mexican man, and the boy were killed. The sheriff arrested the surviving Mexicans, all of them wounded, and took them to the jail in the town of Cotulla, where they awaited charges. Responding to rumors of an im-pending lynching, authorities stationed Texas Rangers in front of the jail but withdrew them after three days. As soon as the guards left, a mob overpowered the jailer, grabbed the male prisoner, Florentino Suaste, and hanged him. An inquest following the murder found that Suaste's death was caused by "parties unknown."

The Mexican government officially protested to Washington and de-manded an indemnity from the United States government. In 1897 fed-eral officials conducted an investigation of the affair which determined that the Mexicans had indeed committed the crime of cattle stealing and had opened fire to resist their arrest. Nevertheless the report, written by a representative of the State Department, was remarkably outspoken in its findings about the lynching. Most Anglos in La Salle County condoned the killing because, they told the investigator, it merely anticipated the verdict in a court of law and saved the state the costs of the trial and ex-ecution. The government report also suggested that Cotulla authorities had been seriously negligent. They had known about the threats to the prisoners but had removed the guards all the same. After the lynching, Cotulla authorities made no proper efforts to apprehend the perpetra-tors. The U.S. account emphasized that the October 1895 events reflected a shocking pattern of mob violence. Twice before mobs had seized pris-oners from the same jail and lynched them afterward, but local grand ju-ries had returned no indictments for the crimes. The justice of the peace responsible for the inquest in the Suaste affair was widely known as the mob leader in an earlier lynching. Pursuant to the investigation, Congress appropriated a $2,000 indemnity to the family of the lynch victim.

Diplomatic protests were not the only fallout from the lynchings of Mexicans. After a mob in Rock Springs, Texas, burned alive a Mexican murder suspect in November 1910, anti-American riots broke out in the Mexican capital and several other major cities. Angry demonstrators ransacked American-owned businesses and accosted Anglos on the streets, sending the message that the "gringos" had no monopoly on mob violence. Relations between the United States and Mexico became so tense that many Texans feared a Mexican invasion. In retrospect the incident signified a prelude to a tumultuous decade in U.S.-Mexican relations during the years of the Mexican Revolution. Between 1914 and 1919 the Wilson administration repeatedly sent troops into Mexico to secure American interests and pursue Mexican raiders led by the violently anti-American revolutionary Pancho Villa. Separatist sentiment thrived among Mexicans living in Texas, and would-be insurrectionists raided ranches owned by Anglos. In this atmosphere of mutual violence and suspicion, lynching once again soared. Between 1910 and 1920 Judge Lynch claimed the lives of an estimated 124 Mexicans in the United States as opposed to merely eight victims during the preceding decade. In response, Mexican Americans intensified their protests and formed organizations to protect themselves against discrimination and lawlessness—such as La Liga Protectora Latina, founded in Phoenix, Arizona, in 1915. Radical voices called for violent retaliation instead of peaceful remonstrations. "Force against force. Against armed crime, armed justice," demanded a Mexican newspaper in Los Angeles. "The day will come when the bodies of white bandits will hang from the mezquite groves of the state." As the political situation in Mexico calmed and border clashes ceased, lynching also abated. Still, between 1920 and 1928 another ten Mexicans fell victim to mob killings north of the Rio Grande.

After the lynching of two Mexican suspects accused of having murdered a patrolman in Pueblo, Colorado, in 1919, a local newspaper argued that the victims' nationality did not matter and that American citizens would have been lynched for the same crime. In contrast, Mexican observers insisted that racial contempt made them favorite targets of mob violence. Anglo lynchers, a Mexican activist from Texas declared, "believe themselves better than the Mexicans because of the magic that surrounds the word *white*." True enough, the proponents of Anglo-Saxon supremacy routinely maligned Mexicans as an inferior hybrid race produced by the miscegenation of Spaniards and Indians. Nevertheless there were marked differences from the anti-black racism that inspired the lynching of African Americans in the South, especially with regard to social class and gender.

While white supremacy in the South required that even the lowest white person enjoy a higher social status than the most prosperous and educated black or mulatto, Anglos in the Southwest considered the light-skinned Mexican elite as descendants of the Spanish conquerors and thus as part of the "white race." Intermarriage between Anglo men and Mexican elite women was not uncommon. Because of their relatively privileged status, higher-class Mexicans rarely suffered mob violence. In contrast, most Anglos despised the masses of poor Mexicans as racially inferior. But the racist stereotypes differed from those used against blacks. While Anglo racists slandered Mexican men as filthy, lazy, cowardly, cunning, and innately criminal, whites usually did not view them as sexual predators. Instead whites considered Mexicans a distinctly "effeminate" race as opposed to supposedly manly Anglo-Saxons. Hence in the arsenal of stereotypes there was no Mexican equivalent to the "black brute." Rape charges played a negligible role as a precipitating event to or in the public defense of lynching. Accusations of murder, robbery, and theft accounted for 75 percent of all lynching cases involving Mexican victims, whereas rape appeared as a motive in fewer than 1 percent.

The absence of an obsession with rape may also be one reason why spectacle lynchings that included prolonged torture and burning, a salient feature of anti-black mob violence in the South, were relatively rare in anti-Mexican violence. Nearly five in six Mexican victims were either hanged or shot to death. Of course it makes no sense to debate which victim group suffered the worst abuse. What matters is that racism shaped the character of lynching in different historical circumstances and affected the various racial and ethnic populations in the United States in different ways.

Throughout the nineteenth century, Native Americans suffered large-scale violence in lopsided wars and massacres which sometimes approached genocidal proportions. Indian haters demonized them as bloodthirsty savages while many anthropologists considered them a "doomed race" that would eventually become extinct. Indeed, by 1900 the U.S. Bureau of the Census found that the total Indian population had declined to a nadir of fewer than 250,000. Yet while there was no lack of anti-Indian violence and racism, Native Americans seldom fell victim to individual lynchings as punishment for crime. In the late nineteenth century most Indians lived on tribal lands or reservations and had no continuing contact with potentially hostile white populations. If conflicts emerged, they were likely to result in collective fighting instead of mob violence against individual offenders. When Indians lived and moved in predominantly white areas, however, they were looked upon as suspicious strangers and, when accused of a crime, faced the risk of being lynched. In 1889 a man described as an "Indian tramp" allegedly raped the wife of a farmer in Taylor County, Iowa. After the arrest of the suspect, a mob forced its way into the jail, seized the prisoner, and lynched him in the courthouse yard before a crowd of several hundred onlookers. Eleven years later, lynchers killed two Indians in Oklahoma charged with the murder of a white woman. Such incidents were relatively rare. Because they supposedly were a "dying race," most white Americans no longer perceived Native Americans as a serious threat to "white civilization." Still, future research may uncover more lynchings of Indians than have been acknowledged so far.

In contrast, the horrendous mob violence directed against Chinese immigrants in the second half of the nineteenth century is well established. Anti-Chinese violence thrived on a highly explosive concoction of job competition, racial animus, and cultural contempt, and its brutality resembled what African Americans had to endure. Like blacks, the Chinese became the targets of large-scale riots as well as individual lynchings. According to one estimate, roughly 150 major incidents of anti-Chinese violence occurred during the second half of the nineteenth century, most of them in the states and territories of the West.

Pushed by abject poverty and political turmoil at home and lured by the onset of the Gold Rush, the first Chinese arrived in California in 1848. By 1852, twenty thousand Chinese immigrants had come to California, and their numbers continued to grow. In 1880 the Chinese population in the United States amounted to roughly 100,000 people, nearly all of them on the West Coast or in the Rocky Mountains region. Although Chinese immigrants made up only a miniscule 0.002 percent of the United States population, they attracted racial hatred and violent hostility far out of proportion to their tiny share of the overall immigration. More than any other immigrant group in American history, the Chinese came to epitomize the undesirable "other" who supposedly could not be assimilated into the mainstream of American society. An 1878 congressional report recommended that Chinese not be admitted to the United States because "mentally, morally, physically, and politically they have remained a distinct and antagonistic race." In 1882 the Chinese Exclusion Act barred all Chinese laborers from entering the country for a period of ten years; restrictions remained in effect until the act was repealed in 1943.

Racism and economic competition coalesced in fueling anti-Chinese resentment among Euro-Americans in the West. Like Mexicans, Chinese miners who came to California during the Gold Rush had to pay the "foreign miners tax," which imposed a stiff license fee on all foreign-born miners. Euro-American workers resented Chinese immigrants because employers welcomed them as a cheap, pliable, and hardworking labor force which they could use to break strikes and keep wages down. Chinese workers built the western leg of the Transcontinental Railroad and toiled in the vineyards and orchards of California. As a consequence the labor movement, demanding the protection of "free white labor" from the "unfair" competition of Chinese "coolies," spearheaded anti-Chinese agitation. In 1877 Denis Kearney, leader of the California Workingmen's party and himself an Irish immigrant, minced no words about the party's goals: "We intend to try and vote the Chinaman out, to frighten him out, and if this won't do, to kill him out. . . . The heathen slaves must leave this coast, if it costs 10,000 lives." Shortly thereafter the Workingmen's party made good on its promises and staged a riot in San Francisco, killing dozens of Chinese, setting fire to their homes and shops, and driving thousands out of town.

In addition to Chinese labor competition, Euro-Americans resented the growth of "Chinatowns," which they viewed as holes of vice, disease, and filth. Because most Chinese men did not plan to stay in America, they did not bring spouses but hoped to get married once they returned home. The result was an extreme gender imbalance exacerbated by U.S. restrictions on the immigration of Chinese women, who presumably were brought into the country as sex slaves. As late as 1880 on the West

Coast there were still twenty males for every Chinese female. Not surprisingly, the Chinatowns became nearly all-male ghettos where gangs and secret societies, known as Tongs, controlled much of the social life, and where gambling, opium consumption, and prostitution thrived. In 1871 a fight between two rival Chinese gangs sparked an orgy of mob violence and lynching in Los Angeles.

The trouble started when Chinese gunmen began exchanging fire in a neighborhood of the Los Angeles Chinatown. A police officer summoned a posse of armed white men and rushed to the scene. A shoot-out followed in which one of the posse members was killed and two others wounded. The news of the Chinese killing of white men triggered hysteria among the white population. An armed mob descended on the scene of the shooting, where frightened residents locked themselves in their homes. According to the *Los Angeles Daily News*, the mob turned the area into a "pandemonium," shooting Chinese men and boys at random, looting buildings and trying to set them on fire. The mob executed most of the murders in lynching style, hanging at least fourteen men from improvised gallows. All in all, the massacre left more than twenty Chinese dead. Many more would have lost their lives had they not fled.

Anti-Chinese riots were not confined to California. In November 1880 a mob raged through Denver, Colorado, after a brawl in a poolhall precipitated false rumors that two Chinese had killed a white man. One Chinese was killed and many more were injured while property damage amounted to $50,000. Perhaps the most notorious incident of anti-Chinese mob violence occurred in Rock Springs, Wyoming, where the Union Pacific Coal Department employed Chinese workers as strikebreakers. In September 1885 a mob of white workers killed nearly thirty Chinese and tried to expel those who remained. Because Wyoming was still a federal territory, the federal government sent troops to restore order, not necessarily out of sympathy for the victims but because the mining company had requested protection. In the aftermath of the Rock Springs Massacre, the Chinese government demanded the punishment of the rioters and an indemnity, which Congress fixed at about $150,000. Money, however, could not quiet popular anger in China, where nationalists called for a boycott of American goods and rioters destroyed an American Protestant mission in Peking. This time the Chinese government had to pay compensation and make promises that it would protect American citizens and property.

The main purpose of anti-Chinese mob violence was to drive unwelcome economic competitors and "undesirable" residents out of town. "Chinatown no longer exists," Denver's *Rocky Mountain News* proclaimed triumphantly after riots errupted in the city in 1880. "Washee, washee is all cleaned out in Denver"—referring to the Chinese domination of the laundry business. But many white citizens condemned the riots, and some even sheltered fugitives from the raging mob. Although racial and cultural prejudice against the Chinese was widespread, their advocates praised them as hardworking and inoffensive people who only wished to be left alone. Indeed, because they mostly stayed within the confines of their ethnic ghettos and rarely mingled with whites in social situations, Chinese immigrants committed few crimes outside their own communities. They were notorious for fighting and killing among themselves, but clan solidarity and the Tongs ensured that most disputes were settled within the walls of the Chinatowns.

The fact that the Chinese rarely committed violent crimes or murder against whites helps explain why there were relatively few lynchings of individuals charged with specific offenses. And although whites often berated the suspected immorality of the Chinatowns, there was no pronounced image of the Chinese as a sexual threat to white women. Thus rape charges seldom surfaced in connection with anti-Chinese mob violence. The 1891 lynching of a laundryman in Ouray, Colorado, who had allegedly molested a small child, was an exception. Of course white racists reviled the Chinese as an alien and inferior race and insisted on strict sexual isolation. In 1880 California passed an anti-miscegenation law, prohibiting intermarriage between a white person and "a negro, mulatto, or Mongolian."

Anti-Chinese racism did not simply mirror anti-black racism. Again, as in the case of Mexicans, gender stereotypes of Chinese males differed from those ascribed to black men. Because many Chinese men, for want of other job opportunities, opened restaurants and laundries and thus performed labor usually associated with women, Euro-Americans tended to view them as a "feminine" and therefore as a "degenerate" race. The long braid that Chinese men had to wear due to an ordinance of the Manchu dynasty reinforced this impression. Mobs as well as government officials often took a fiendish pleasure in pulling and cutting the "pigtails," ignoring that Chinese men who returned home without this distinctive hairstyle could be executed as rebels.

If Chinese killed or injured white females, though, lynch law might follow. On April 7, 1887, Hong Di, a Chinese cook in Colusa, California, fired several shots at Julia Billiou, the wife of his employer, and William Weaver, another Billiou employee, killing the former and wounding the latter. After his arrest, Hong Di explained his deed, claiming that he had witnessed Weaver and Mrs. Billiou engaging in sexual conduct and that Weaver had threatened to kill him lest he reveal his discovery to Mr. Billiou. Hong Di insisted he had intended to kill Weaver, not his employer's wife. Surprisingly, the trial jury did not sentence the defendant to death but to life in prison, causing immediate outrage among the citizens of Colusa. A crowd of two thousand people stormed the jail and lynched Hong Di. Before they hanged their prisoner they made him confess that he had lied about Mrs. Billiou being unfaithful to her husband and that he had begun shooting because he was drunk. In addition to correcting the failure of the law, as they saw it, the lynchers considered it a point of honor to restore the moral reputation of a respectable white woman. "All men who respect womanly virtue and rebuke the defamation of the dead will uphold the course of the grand County of Colusa," one California newspaper wrote in applauding the lynching.

It is impossible to say whether Hong Di was lynched because of his race. Had a white man killed Julia Billiou and then accused her of adultery, he might have suffered the same fate as the Chinese cook. Still, it is noteworthy that the most ardent apologists for the lynching were also the most vocal opponents of Chinese immigration.

Although they came from Europe and therefore ostensibly belonged to the white race, Italian immigrants to the West also experienced vicious hostility from those whites who considered themselves members of the putatively superior Anglo-Saxon civilization. Certainly mob action aimed at Italians was much less frequent than violence against the Chinese, but its underlying motives were similar. Italians were unwanted competitors for jobs who worked for low wages and lived on the margins of society. They spoke a strange language and practiced a religion, Roman Catholicism, that many American Protestants viewed with contempt and suspicion. Clearly the Italians represented an alien culture and a distinct ethnic group, and many nativists found the "dagos"—a slur derived, curiously enough, from the Spanish name Diego—scarcely more acceptable than the "Orientals."

Some opponents of Italian immigration also challenged their white-ness. Because southern Italians, in particular, often had a dark complex-ion and shiny black hair, many Anglos questioned their membership in the "white race." According to prevailing ideas of "racial purity," their ambiguous skin color signaled a sinister character and a proclivity for crime. After lynchers had hanged an Italian railroad worker charged with murdering a supervisor in Gunnison, Colorado, in 1881, the local newspaper portrayed the victim as a "swarthy skinned assassin" who, had he worn his hair in a braid, "might have been mistaken for a China-man." His eyes, the article continued, were "almond-shape and cunning and malicious in expression." In 1893 an Italian hotel manager in Den-ver killed an army veteran in a drunken brawl. Shortly after his arrest, a mass mob of approximately ten thousand broke into the jail, dragged the prisoner out on the streets, and hanged him from a telegraph pole. Although the mob had shouted "Give us the Dago!" local observers fer-vently denied that the victim's Italian origins played any role in his fate at the hands of Judge Lynch.

Mob violence against Italian immigrants was most salient in the Deep South. There between 1886 and 1910 lynchers executed at least twenty-nine Italian men, with Louisiana alone accounting for twenty-one vic-tims. All these men died in multiple lynchings. In fact the 1891 lynching of eleven Italians in New Orleans constitutes the most murderous inci-dent of its kind in American history. Because New Orleans was the major Southern port of entry for immigrants who sought work on plantations, in railroad construction, and in lumbering, Louisiana had by far the largest Italian population among the Southern states. In 1890 some nine thousand Italians lived in the state; by 1910 their number had increased to twenty thousand. Most Italians in Louisiana came from Sicily and other parts of southern Italy via a long-standing sailing route between Palermo and New Orleans. In contrast to the supposedly light-skinned and cultured northern Italians, Sicilians were viewed by many Ameri-cans as culturally backward and racially suspect. In some parts of Louisi-ana and Mississippi their children had to attend black schools. Moreover, many of the Sicilian newcomers, unaccustomed to the "racial etiquette" of the South, mingled freely with African Americans. Thus many white Southerners looked down on these Italians as "white Negroes."

Sicilians also had a reputation for being irascible, treacherous, and brutal. Their innate criminality and contempt for the rule of law, the common stereotype held, had given rise to the Mafia which, late nineteenth-century nativists feared, would sink its tentacles into American soil. As a consequence *Sicilian* and *Mafia* became almost synonymous, and guilt by association could be taken for granted. When in August 1896 a mob in Hahnville, Louisiana, broke into the local jail to seize a Sicilian awaiting trial for murder, the intruders found two other Sicilians held on unrelated charges. Concluding that they had uncovered a Mafia ring, the lynchers murdered all three prisoners. Sicilian immigrants also encountered violent hostility in labor disputes. In 1910 striking cigar factory workers in Tampa, Florida, clashed with the company. After a bookkeeper was killed, the police detained two Sicilian workers in connection with the homicide. Their guilt or innocence was never decided in court since a mob snatched the men from the sheriff and sent them immediately to their deaths.

The 1891 lynching of eleven Sicilian immigrants in New Orleans was spectacular, and not only because of the number of victims. The affair began on October 15, 1890, when unknown killers assassinated the city's police chief, David Hennessy. Before he died, Hennessy, who had been investigating crimes in connection with Mafia activities in New Orleans, reportedly muttered, "The dagos shot me." The mayor immediately ordered the police to hunt down the killers and apprehend the entire Italian population of New Orleans if need be. In February 1891 a murder trial commenced against nine Sicilian defendants. The prosecution summoned no fewer than sixty witnesses but still could not make a persuasive case. On March 13, 1891, the jury acquitted all nine men.

Anger and outrage boiled over in the Crescent City. Many citizens took the verdict as proof that the Mafia had already corrupted the criminal justice system. On the morning after the acquittal, a crowd of six thousand people moved against the jail and, after overwhelming the token resistance of the prison guards, lynched eleven Sicilian inmates. Nine were shot to death in their cells, two others were pushed outside and hanged from a lamppost. There was no hard evidence that any of the men were members of the Mafia or had anything to do with the Hennessy murder. Even so, public opinion almost unanimously condoned the mass lynching.

A few weeks later the mob leader, a well-known lawyer named William Parkerson, granted an interview to the New York magazine *Illustrated American,* in which he revealed details of the event and defended the lynching as democracy in action. Parkerson denied that he had personally killed any of the Sicilians but was immensely proud of his leadership role. The lawyer admitted that he had gladly accepted the chairmanship of a committee that had met on the evening of March 13, after the jury's verdict. This committee issued a call for a mass protest, featured by all morning papers. Before the crowd marched on the jail, Parkerson admonished them that they had a "terrible duty" to perform. The citizens—"lawyers, doctors, bankers"—rose to the occasion, acting with perfect determination and order, according to Parkerson's account—which, however, generously ignored that the furious mob had riddled the victims' bodies with bullets. When asked whether he regretted his part in the lynching, Parkerson delivered an eloquent lecture on popular sovereignty. The people had acted in self-defense, he argued, because the killing of Chief Hennessy and the corruption of the law showed that the Mafia was destroying American institutions. In this situation the people had a right to act: "I recognize no power above the people. Under our constitution the people are the sovereign authority, and when the courts, the agents, fail to carry out the law the authority is relegated back to the people." Of course it was understood that the "people" did not include the "dagos." A report on the lynchings in New Orleans, published by a citizens committee in May 1891, unequivocally stated that Sicilians were "undesirable as citizens." All the same, the governor of Louisiana insisted that race or nationality had nothing to do with the incident.

The Italian government disagreed, however, and demanded an investigation, the punishment of the culprits, and an indemnity. When a grand jury investigation produced no indictments, the government in Rome recalled its ambassador from Washington. And although Sicilians were not popular in Italy, many Italians fumed at American mobs killing and abusing their compatriots with impunity. On the streets of Rome, ruffians harassed Americans. For a time, war between the two nations looked possible. Eventually the U.S. government agreed to pay an indemnity of $25,000. This concession, in turn, infuriated many whites in Louisiana, who considered it a disgrace to yield to the demands of a nation that seemingly dumped its criminals on America. To assuage the diplomatic fallout, the U.S. government nonetheless continued to pay compensation to the families of Italian lynch victims. After the lynching of five Sicilians in Tallulah, Louisiana, in 1899, Washington disbursed $46,000 to their families, albeit without recognizing any legal obligation.

The lynching of foreign nationals placed the federal government in an awkward position. Certainly Washington did not appreciate the anti-American resentment and diplomatic conflicts such incidents triggered. Under international law and comity, the United States had an obligation to protect foreign citizens on American soil. But it was also true that in the late nineteenth century the federal government had no legal authority to prosecute and punish lynchers because criminal justice was—and for the most part remains—a prerogative of state law and the local courts. Local juries often sympathized with the executioners of popular justice and hardly cared about foreign opinion or U.S. diplomatic relations. Historians have nevertheless argued that the diplomatic protests raised by China, Mexico, and Italy provided some measure of protection and compensatory justice for their citizens. African-American anti-lynching activists often complained that blacks lacked such protectors because their plight was a purely domestic affair.

Italians made up the largest group among the so-called "New Immigration" during the late nineteenth and early twentieth centuries, when millions of immigrants arrived from southern and eastern Europe and profoundly alarmed native-born Anglo-Protestants. Eastern European Jews were the second major group of newcomers. Their growing numbers swiftly surpassed the Jews from central Europe who had lived in North America from colonial times. In 1870 the Jewish population in the United States stood at 200,000; in 1900 it had already passed the one million mark. During the same period "scientific racism" transformed the traditional religious hatred of Jews into virulent anti-Semitism, claiming that Jews represented a distinct "race." Thus one might expect that Jewish immigrants experienced a vicious nativist backlash in America. And indeed, Americans discriminated against Jews in manifold ways. Upwardly mobile Jews encountered informal quotas in elite educational institutions. Lower-class Jews met keen hostility from competing immigrant groups and nativists that occasionally turned violent. As a rule, white supremacists also harbored anti-Semitic prejudices.

Nevertheless most Jewish immigrants considered the United States a haven from the persecution and discrimination they had suffered in Europe for centuries. The pogroms that swept Russia in the 1890s were a main factor in pushing Jews to emigrate to America, where they had equal access to citizenship and could practice their religion freely. Political freedom allowed Jewish organizations such as the Anti-Defamation League to fight anti-Semitism in the courts and in the public sphere. While interethnic violence was part of immigrant life in the big cities of the Northeast, Jews experienced neither pogrom-style mob violence nor popular justice–style lynchings. Still, anti-Semitic attacks claimed some lives. On Christmas Day 1905, for example, a group of young thugs beat up several Jewish laborers in Denver, Colorado, presumably because they worked on a Christian holiday. One victim later died of his injuries. Incidents of this kind were exceptional. Yet a Jewish American did fall victim to one of the most publicized lynchings of the early twentieth century. The Leo Frank case that unfolded in Georgia between 1913 and 1915 not only revealed the hidden virulence of anti-Semitism but developed into an open contest between the rule of law and popular justice, in which the latter triumphed. The affair mirrored the anxieties of modern life in the New South and also seemed to defy the racial certainties of the era.

On April 27, 1915, the night watchman of the National Pencil Factory in Atlanta found the bloodstained body of Mary Phagan, a thirteen-year-old white laborer, in the plant's basement. Although there was no clear evidence of rape, rumors spread that the victim had died fighting to preserve her virginity. At first the investigation focused on the black watchman who had found the body and on a caretaker named James Conley, also a black man. But two days after the murder the police arrested the factory superintendent, Leo Frank, a twenty-nine-year-old Jewish American who had grown up in New York and had earned a degree from Cornell University.

Frank had moved to Atlanta to work in his uncle's factory. He was married, well-to-do, and a respected member of the city's Jewish community. Given his social status and the white Southern fixation on the black rapist, it was startling that the police detained him on the testimony of Conley, the only other suspect and a man with a long criminal record. While Frank had no watertight alibi and made several contradictory statements, the circumstantial evidence against him was so flimsy that many observers were stunned when in late May 1913 a grand jury indicted him for murder.

Leo Frank had the misfortune of getting caught in a fateful tangle of prejudice, class hatred, personal ambition, yellow-press sensationalism, and Southern politics. From the start, the fate of Mary Phagan aroused enormous sympathy and outrage. The youthful murder victim became a symbol for the plight of countless rural whites forced by poverty to send their children to toil in the factories of the urban New South, where they were exposed to the hardships of industrial work and the lures and perils of city life. In glaring contrast to Phagan's angelic image, Frank's detractors conjured up the anti-Semitic stereotype of the "rich Jew" who thrived on exploiting the labor of honest Gentiles and lusted after their daughters. To make things worse for Frank, the tabloid-style *Atlanta Georgian*, a paper owned by the press tycoon William Randolph Hearst, jumped on the case as it waged an aggressive circulation campaign, prompting many of its competitors to emulate its sensationalism. Too, the veteran Populist champion Tom Watson cannily sensed an opportunity to revive his political fortunes by vindicating the "people" against a vile conspiracy of Jews and corrupt officials. In the same vein the Atlanta solicitor-general, Hugh Dorsey, who prosecuted Frank, figured that the conviction of a wealthy Jew for a spectacular crime could help his political career. As it turned out, both Watson and Dorsey reaped a rich political harvest from the case.

On August 26, 1913, the jury found Frank guilty and sentenced him to death. The trial had taken place in a highly charged atmosphere that seriously impaired the defendant's right to a fair hearing. During the proceedings Dorsey smeared Frank as a sexual degenerate who regularly molested young girls and boys. Crucially, the prosecution rested its case on Conley's testimony that Frank had paid him for helping to get rid of Mary Phagan's body. Still, few observers anticipated that an all-white jury in the Jim Crow South would send a white man to the gallows based on the word of a black man who had every reason to pin the murder on the superintendent. Caught off guard by the unexpected verdict, the Jewish community of Atlanta, aided by prominent Jewish lawyers from the North, began waging a legal campaign for a new trial. Their efforts lasted until April 1915, when the U.S. Supreme Court finally rejected

Frank's appeal. Only a pardon could now save his life, but the Georgia Prison Commission denied a recommendation of clemency. It was then up to the outgoing governor, John M. Slaton, to commute Frank's sentence to life in prison or sign his execution warrant.

The campaign to rescue Frank from the hangman had been accompanied by bitter controversy. Observers throughout the United States denounced his trial and conviction as a travesty of justice rooted in prejudice. In Georgia too, petitioners warned against committing "judicial murder," in the words of the *Atlanta Journal*. But the anti-Frank party in the state, led by Watson, was both more numerous and more vociferous. In rhetoric that was heavily suffused with anti-Semitic venom, Watson framed the Frank case as a struggle between ordinary Georgians, who demanded justice for the ruthless murder of a "daughter of the people," and a clamorous minority that considered itself above the law. No matter what evidence Frank's lawyers presented in his favor, it was dismissed as a Jewish conspiracy to thwart the verdict of the people. Whoever expressed doubts about the fairness of the trial must have been bought by "Jew money." Before the governor's decision, Watson made unveiled threats that a commutation would result in a lynching. All the same, fully aware that he would destroy his political future, Slaton commuted Frank's sentence on June 21, 1915, one day before the scheduled execution. He explained to his wife that he would not bear responsibility for the death of an innocent man. As a precautionary measure, he ordered Frank's removal to the state prison farm in Milledgeville, in central Georgia.

The governor himself became the first target of mob action. For days angry demonstrators raged through downtown Atlanta. Throngs of heavily armed men besieged Slaton's home, which had to be guarded by the state militia. Slaton's courage, however, could not save Leo Frank. On August 16, 1915, a vigilante group of about twenty-five men, calling themselves the "Knights of Mary Phagan," staged a carefully planned attack on the state prison farm where they easily overpowered the small detachment of guards. In the middle of the night the kidnappers hauled their prisoner to Mary Phagan's home town of Marietta. According to eyewitnesses, Frank remained steadfast in protesting his innocence. Reputedly he was so convincing that some of his abductors pleaded to let him go. But the majority insisted on following through with their plan.

The lynching of Leo Frank in Marietta, Georgia, 1915.

To underscore their self-image as executioners of true justice, the lynchers painstakingly mimicked the rituals of a legal hanging. Their victim, anonymous reports conceded, met his death with remarkable composure.

Reactions to the lynching of Leo Frank reflected the polarization that had characterized the entire affair. Whereas critics expressed their indignation that the forces of the law had been unwilling to protect the prominent prisoner, Tom Watson celebrated the murder as a triumph of the people. "Democracy means," he explained, "that all power is in the people." Because the governor, by granting clemency to Frank, had betrayed his constituents, "the people may ignore the act of a recreant agent, and do for themselves what the agent failed to do." Indeed, many people were thrilled. Thousands traveled to the site of the lynching. Photographs of Frank's dangling body became coveted souvenir items. An Atlanta crowd forced a public display of the corpse before it could be carried away for burial. Frank's killers, widely hailed as virtuous American citizens, never were brought to justice.

In the aftermath of the Leo Frank lynching, the pastor of the Phagan family invoked the biblical metaphor of the scapegoat to account for the

startling fact that the Southern judicial system as well as the advocates
of popular justice had blamed the murder and possible sexual assault of
a young white girl on a white man, even though two black suspects had
been readily available. A black man, the minister mused, would have
been "poor atonement for the life of this innocent girl," while "a Jew, and
a Yankee Jew at that . . . would be a victim worthy to pay for the crime."
Other observers insisted that Frank's Jewish defenders provoked the
anti-Semitic backlash by depicting him as a victim of prejudice. Apart
from blaming anti-Semitism on the Jews, this contention ignored the obvious: If Leo Frank had been a Gentile, all other things being equal, he
would most likely never have been arrested, let alone indicted and convicted. Probably the authorities would have railroaded James Conley to
the gallows or a mob would have lynched him. That scenario, however,
would not have aroused much public interest.

Leo Frank became a victim of anti-Semitic prejudice because of highly
adverse circumstances. The same may be said about the lynching of a
German immigrant named Robert Paul Prager in Collinsville, Illinois,
on April 4, 1918. Surely Germans did not belong among the usual targets
of lynch mobs. While there had been conflicts between Anglo-Protestant
nativists and German immigrants throughout the nineteenth century,
Germans generally enjoyed a favorable reputation as orderly and hardworking people. By the early twentieth century most German Americans had integrated themselves nicely into American society. World War
I, however, placed them in a precarious situation. As tensions grew between Germany and the United States, many Anglo-Americans began
questioning German-American loyalty.

After the U.S. declaration of war against the German Empire in April
1917, anti-German sentiment escalated into all-out hysteria. The kaiser's
spies supposedly lurked behind every corner. Superpatriots banned German culture and language from public life. The German-American
National Alliance was forced to disband, beer halls were closed, and sauer-
kraut became "liberty cabbage." German Americans came under immense
pressure to demonstrate their loyalty by purchasing war bonds and making
public shows of patriotism such as saluting the flag at every opportunity. In
this excited climate, mob violence seemed to be only a matter of time.

Twenty-nine-year-old Robert Prager, born in Dresden, Germany, had
immigrated to the United States in 1905. He worked as a baker and a

miner in Illinois and, like many German workers, sympathized with so-
cialist ideas. It remains unclear whether he acquired U.S. citizenship, as
he insisted. After his death, the press almost uniformly referred to him
as an "alien enemy." In the early spring of 1918 Prager looked for work
in the mining town of Collinsville in southern Illinois. He aroused the
ire of local residents by allegedly "talking socialism" and making "dis-
loyal remarks." A mob grabbed him, wrapped him in an American flag,
and paraded him down main street, seemingly unsure about what to do
with their prisoner. At this point the police intervened and took Prager
into custody. Later in the evening, though, a mob of roughly 350 people,
many of them miners, stormed the jail, pushed Prager to the outskirts of
town, and hanged him. Before he died he was allowed to pray and forced
to kiss the Stars and Stripes.

Public opinion throughout the country divided sharply over the incident. The defenders of vigilantism blamed the lynching on the federal
government which, they said, took too soft a position on spies and sabo-
teurs. Some voices even applauded the mob for teaching a wholesome
lesson to potential traitors. On the other hand, critics condemned the attack on Prager as an act of shocking lawlessness that threatened to drag
the United States down to the morally depraved level of the "Huns" and
damage the American war effort. The governor of Illinois quickly promised to prosecute the lynchers. One week after the murder, the police
made the first arrests. On April 25 a grand jury indicted sixteen men,
including four policemen charged with negligence. The trial commenced
speedily but ended on June 1 with the acquittal of all defendants, even
though their participation in the lynching was not in doubt. In his plea
the defense lawyer cited a "new unwritten law" against traitors in wartime that presumably justified the Prager killing. Apparently that was
enough to sway the jury.

Through the Swiss embassy in Washington, Germany called upon
the U.S. government to protect the rights and liberties of Germans in
America. Although the federal government lacked the practical means to
safeguard one of the largest ethnic groups in the country, the Prager case
remained an isolated event. Many German Americans experienced humiliation and discrimination during the war years, but anti-German resentment generally stopped short of inflicting deadly violence. There was
not enough deep-seated hatred against German Americans as a group

to fuel a widespread approval of lynching and mob violence as instruments of systematic terror. Unlike blacks or Chinese immigrants, German Americans had never been an insulated and ostracized minority, viewed as unfit for full participation in American life. That the war hysteria dealt a devastating blow to the ethnic pride and identity of German Americans is a different matter.

Undeniably, racial and ethnic animosity figured in a large number of those lynchings that departed from the familiar pattern of white mobs killing black victims. Still, in many cases whites lynched whites without any connection to race and ethnicity. For contemporaries, these incidents reflected the lingering spirit of the frontier and the claim of the people that lawbreakers must receive their just deserts. Yet in the late nineteenth century the classic defense of frontier justice—that the absence of effective government forced people to take the law into their own hands— had lost much of its earlier credibility. After all, the United States was no longer a frontier society—in 1890 the Bureau of the Census officially declared the closing of the frontier—but a leading industrial economy and a modern state.

Apologists for popular justice nonetheless continued to complain about what they viewed as the glaring inefficiency of the criminal justice system and of the jury trial in particular, which purportedly allowed too many criminals to get away with their misdeeds. Disenchantment with the law was especially pervasive in the South and the West, where homicides occurred much more often while an extremely broad understanding of legitimate self-defense shielded many killers from prosecution. If a white man of social standing shot another man and then claimed to have defended his honor, he had a good chance of being exonerated. In central Texas, where the traditions of the South and the West meshed, more than half of all murder trials held before 1890 ended in acquittal.

Distrust of the law therefore played a key role in white-on-white lynching. In late 1891 citizens in Choctaw County, Alabama, resolved to ban a notorious group of outlaws who had terrorized the region for months. After the arrest of the leader and four members of the gang, a mob snatched the prisoners on their way to jail and lynched them. The next day the vigilantes tracked down two other members of the ring and hanged them too. Ostensibly the lynchers did not trust the courts to deal swiftly and harshly with these dangerous criminals. In May 1906, when a jury in Wadesboro, North Carolina, failed to reach a unanimous guilty verdict against a man charged with murdering his brother-in-law, a group of masked men abducted and hanged the defendant in the middle of the night. In this and other cases, friends and family of victims of crime may have sought the retribution that the legal process had failed to provide.

A desire for personal vengeance was not, however, a widely appealing defense of lynch law. In order to explain why ordinary, law-abiding Americans resorted to mob action against criminals, newspaper accounts, often for self-serving reasons, highlighted the cruelty of the crime that had triggered the lynching. Some misdeeds, journalists suggested, were so monstrous that they sparked an unstoppable drive for retribution among shocked communities. White mobs preferably lynched those white criminals who had allegedly committed offenses of a particularly callous and perverted nature and thus had placed themselves outside the law designed for ordinary offenders. Not surprisingly, sexual crimes were a salient example. In 1896 lynchers in Alabama executed a white man charged with raping his own daughter.

Waco, Texas, was notorious for its history of mob violence. In 1916 Waco attracted national attention with the lynching of Jesse Washington, the young black man burned alive in the city center. Five years later Waco vigilantes demonstrated some measure of color-blind popular justice when they lynched Curley Hackney, a white man in his twenties. After an eight-year-old girl had accused the former circus performer of rape, police immediately arrested the suspect and, anticipating trouble, concealed him in the cell usually reserved for black prisoners. Undeterred, a mob of several hundred armed men stormed the jail and hauled Hackney to a nearby forest where they hanged him from a tree and riddled his dead body with bullets. Compared to the public burning of Jesse Washington, Hackney died a benign death. The lynchers offered him a last cigarette; they even followed his instructions when he showed them how to fasten the rope around his neck to spare himself unnecessary suffering. Even for sexual miscreants, white skin had its privileges. Still, Hackney's status as an unwelcome social outsider made him a "typical" victim. He had come to town with a circus but stayed on because of a gunshot wound that forced him to walk on crutches. The man had no job and no friends who might have spoken in his favor. After the lynching, public opinion took his guilt for granted, though the rape charges never were investigated. As usual, the official inquest concluded that "parties unknown" had caused Curley Hackney's death.

Most white victims of mob violence lived on the fringes of society and were charged with heinous crimes that incited outrage among the larger community. This combination of circumstances occasionally exposed white women to mob violence, even though lynching apologists endlessly dwelt on the need to protect vulnerable white females from sexual predators. But women who violated the norms of proper "womanly" conduct and became implicated in serious crime faced the risk of being excluded from the community of "true" women who deserved special protection and consideration. To be sure, lynchings of white women were rare exceptions. A recent estimate concludes that there were twenty-six confirmed cases between 1880 and 1930. Most of them happened in the West and the South before the turn of the century, and nearly all victims were lynched alongside men.

In January 1884 the sheriff of Ouray, Colorado, arrested Michael Cuddigan and his pregnant wife Margaret, along with her brother James Carroll, in connection with the death of Mary Rose Mathews, a ten-year-old orphan living with the Cuddigans as a foster child. When a neighbor observed the Cuddigans burying the child, he alerted the authorities. An investigation found that the body showed bruises and wounds indicating violent abuse. As soon as the news of the arrests broke, tempers ran high, fanned by a local newspaper that openly called for Judge Lynch to do his duty. The sheriff announced that he would defend his prisoners and locked them in a hotel that appeared to be safer than the town's makeshift wooden jail. But after days of mounting tension, the mob had little difficulty overpowering the guards. The lynchers ushered the three prisoners to the edge of town where they forced Michael Cuddigan to confess that his wife had beaten Mary Rose and left her to die in the Colorado winter. The mob then hanged both husband and wife but spared James Carroll, who convinced the lynchers that he had been away from Ouray at the time of Mary Rose's death.

Many Coloradians considered child murder a horrible crime that warranted rough popular justice. Yet the execution of a pregnant woman was unsettling. Strangling a "weak defenseless woman" who had already been taken into custody, critics pointed out, could hardly be justified as a courageous act of public-minded citizens. In response, pro-lynching voices cited the usual excuses: a trial would have cost too much money and might not have resulted in a conviction. They also insisted that Margaret Cuddigan, by killing a child, had forfeited all the privileges of her sex. Her crime proved that she was not a woman and mother but rather a ghastly brute. It mattered little that she was pregnant. The *Denver Tribune* reasoned that her death saved her unborn child the misery of being raised by a cruel and heartless mother. Other apologists insinuated that the Cuddigans had sexually abused their ward.

In addition to accusing their female victims of horrendous crimes, lynchers also depicted them as moral outcasts who engaged in improper sexual behavior. When ranchers in Wyoming summarily executed James Averell and his companion Ellen Watson for cattle stealing in July 1889, their defenders portrayed "Cattle Kate," as Watson was known, as a "prostitute of the lowest type," who was "common property of the cowboys for miles around" and who accepted stolen cattle in exchange for sex. In reality, the most likely cause of the murder may have been that the couple had antagonized the wealthy cattlemen who were waging all-out war against homesteaders and small ranchers to enforce their dominance over the Wyoming range.

Adultery could also be used as an excuse for mob violence against white women. In 1895 Mrs. T. J. West, a forty-year-old married woman and mother living in Marion County, Kentucky, began a love affair with her neighbor William Dever, a white man. When her husband confronted his rival, Dever killed him in self-defense, according to the jurors who acquitted him of murder charges. Following the trial, Dever and West not only defied the moral sentiment of the local community by openly living together; they also ignored threats to leave the county. Before long a mob appeared at their home and demanded that the couple appear. When they refused, the assailants set the house on fire. Dever then attacked the lynchers but was immediately killed. Mrs. West perished in the blaze.

After the turn of the century the annual toll of white persons lynched dropped into the single digits, with the exception of three years when the body count again rose to fifteen. Although lynchings of African Americans also declined, they outnumbered white victims by a ratio of five to twenty times, depending on the year. During several years in the 1920s,

lynch law claimed the lives of no whites at all. In November 1933, however, a spectacular murder in San Jose, California, briefly revived the
ghost of Judge Lynch. On November 9 Brooke Hart, the twenty-two-
year-old son of a local department store owner, disappeared. His parents found a note demanding ransom for the release of their son, though
without precise directions for handing over the money. One week later
the police detained two suspects, John M. Holmes and Thomas H. Thurmond. The men confessed to the kidnapping of Brooke Hart but would
not say where they kept their hostage. On November 26 Hart's body was
discovered on the shores of San Francisco Bay. Evidently the kidnappers
had drowned their victim immediately after abducting him and intended
to collect the ransom without leaving a witness.

News of the crime instantaneously aroused excitement in San Jose.
Hinting that they might be able to watch a lynching, a local radio station
called upon its listeners to gather that evening at Saint James Park, opposite the Santa Clara County jail. By nightfall a crowd of fifteen thousand had arrived and began moving toward the jail. Guards fought back
with tear gas and billy clubs but were unable to halt the onslaught. Several police officers suffered injuries. After smashing the jail doors with a
huge metal pipe, the lynchers quickly identified Thurmond and Holmes
among the inmates and jubilantly carried them to Saint James Park. The
mob leaders stripped the two men naked and hanged them from two
separate sycamore trees.

This outbreak of frenzied lawlessness was shocking enough. But the
most troubling aspect of the incident was the reaction by California governor James Rolph, Jr., who openly condoned the lynching and promised
to pardon everyone who might be prosecuted for participating in the mob.
Rolph reportedly had declined requests to dispatch the National Guard
to quell the unrest in San Jose. Observers in California and throughout
the country excoriated both the mob violence and the governor's political
opportunism. Even white newspapers in the South expressed their indignation, though some white supremacists gloated over the fact that Californians seemed to share their own notions of popular justice. Clearly
Governor Rolph had not misread the public sentiment. His constituents
showered his office with telegrams and letters commending him for his
stand, which, many writers claimed, echoed the state's great traditions of
vigilantism during the days of the Gold Rush.

In the aftermath of the San Jose lynchings, Walter Lippmann, a prominent liberal journalist and astute scholar of public opinion, published a commentary in which he pondered the roots of lawlessness. Lippmann chided the governor for betraying his office, but he also conceded that "multitudes of people" agreed with Rolph. The concerns of these people, Lippmann insisted, had to be taken seriously, especially their belief that the law did not work properly. Hence the spirit of lynching could only be eradicated by "a reform of the administration of criminal justice that is sufficiently drastic to impress the criminal with its power and the community with its efficiency." In many ways Lippmann's views mirrored the ambivalence of many mainstream Americans about lynch law. They abhorred mob violence as a blot on civilization and a disgrace to their nation, but they agreed that lynching was a response to crime and weak institutions. More than that, lynching seemed to be related to primordial features of human life, what Lippmann termed "the persistently primitive nature of men, their greed and lust and animal violence." For the sake of civilization, these impulses had to be resisted, but it was also impossible and dangerous to ignore them. The struggle against lynching thus could succeed only if legal remedies satisfied the people's desire for rough justice.

7

The Struggle Against Lynching

HISTORIANS CONSIDER the late nineteenth century as the "lynching era" of American history. According to statistics the *Chicago Tribune* began to compile in 1882, mob killings crested during the 1880s and 1890s when the yearly death toll fluctuated between 100 and 200. In the election year 1892, when the power struggle between Populists and conservative Democrats triggered countless acts of political violence in the South, lynching reached its peak with a staggering 230 casualties, including 161 African Americans. After the turn of the century the numbers dropped into the double digits and continued to decline gradually, from 99 in 1903 to 38 in 1917. Racial tensions elicited by the upheavals of World War I sparked a brief rebound. In 1919, 83 Americans died at the hands of lynch mobs. But in the 1920s Judge Lynch finally seemed on his way out. At the end of the decade the number of lynchings had fallen to ten. Again, the anxieties of the Great Depression temporarily reversed this trend. In 1933 mobs executed 28 people outside the law. Between 1936 and 1940, however, there were fewer than ten incidents each year, amounting to a total of 30 mob killings, all of which occurred in the Deep South. By 1940 even some anti-lynching groups believed that the problem of lynching had at long last been solved.

What accounts for the slow but steady decline of lynching in the first half of the twentieth century? Unlike other major civil rights achievements in American history, including securing the right to vote for blacks and abolishing racial segregation, the end of lynching was not connected to momentous laws or court rulings. No conspicuous event or political decision could be credited with turning the tide against mob violence. Yet neither did lynching fade quietly. As late as 1934 a mob from Marianna, Florida, abducted Claude Neal, a black man accused of raping and murdering a young white woman. The Florida authorities had brought Neal to Brewton, Alabama, for safekeeping, but lynchers seized him from the Alabama jail and drove him back two hundred miles to Marianna, the scene of his alleged crime. After their return, Neal's captors tortured their victim for hours, reportedly forcing the black man to swallow his own genitals. Eventually they shot Neal dead, tied his body to a car, dragged it through the streets, and then hanged it from a tree opposite the courthouse. After the lynching, a raging mob attacked African Americans on the streets of Marianna until the National Guard halted the rioters.

Claude Neal's lynching reminded Americans that Judge Lynch died hard, especially in the rural South. Although the United States had become a modern society, traditions of popular justice persevered and continued to confound the principles of due process. In their struggle against lynching, the advocates of law and order faced a dual challenge. First, they had to discredit the legitimacy of lynch law among the American public at large; second, they needed to pressure authorities to curb mob violence and uphold the law.

Judge Lynch's antagonists did not form a homogeneous movement unified by common beliefs and objectives. Their ranks included courageous activists and social reformers who called for sweeping legislation and drastic executive action but also many lukewarm public officials and politicians who hesitated to defy their constituents. Many "moderates" made far-reaching concessions to popular expectations of rough justice. In 1903, for example, David Brewer, an associate justice of the U.S. Supreme Court, proposed to rein in lynching by abolishing the right of appeal in criminal cases, a cornerstone of due process. Most important, persuading the people to refrain from lynching implied that the death penalty had to be inflicted more frequently and executions carried out more speedily. As a consequence, the line between legal executions and lynchings became increasingly blurred.

The burden of carrying forward the organized struggle against lynch law largely fell on African Americans and their white allies, for in the public mind lynching seemed inextricably linked to the so-called "Negro problem." After 1900 mob killings outside the South became rare. Statistically, more than four of five lynchings occurred in the South, and the overwhelming majority of the victims, about 90 percent, were black.

Thus most mainstream white Americans who lived in the North and the West believed that lynching was not their problem but rather a phenomenon that reflected the backwardness of the rural South. Many Americans nevertheless sympathized with the view of white Southerners that lynching often was an instinctive response to the omnipresent menace of the "black brute." For decades after the end of Reconstruction, national reconciliation hinged on an understanding that the North would not interfere with Southern race relations. Only a tiny minority of Northern whites was willing to question this compromise.

Because lynching seemed to affect primarily blacks, many whites considered the demand for special protection from state and federal governments as "favoritism." Special protection for African Americans had been a hallmark of Reconstruction, which was widely regarded as a tragic mistake. In 1883 the U.S. Supreme Court struck down a federal law that prohibited racial segregation in public accommodations, holding that the former slaves must cease to be "the special favorite of the law." African Americans who protested lynching therefore found it necessary to emphasize that they asked "for no special immunity on account of race," as the New York journalist T. Thomas Fortune insisted in 1884. "Let us agitate!" Fortune implored the black community, "until the protest shall awake the nation from its indifference!"

While agitation usually met with little concern in the North, it often provoked violent hostility in the South, especially if the agitators openly challenged the myth that black-on-white rape was the root cause of lynching. In 1892 the African-American journalist Ida B. Wells from Memphis, Tennessee, wrote a scathing article in her newspaper *Free Speech* to condemn the lynching of three of her friends. The men, who ran a thriving grocery store, had aroused the envy of a white competitor. Because the lynchers did not even claim that their victims were guilty of a sexual offense, Wells boldy exposed "the old thread bare lie that Negro men rape white women." In a calculated provocation she insinuated that a closer inspection of the rape craze would be "very damaging to the moral reputation of [white] women."

For a Southern black paper to assert that rape charges against black men frequently had their origins in illicit consensual relationships bordered on the foolhardy. White editors in Memphis openly called for lynching the author of the article, and a furious mob leveled the offices of *Free Speech*. Luckily Wells had ventured north when the attack took place. Because returning to Memphis proved unwise, she moved to New York and continued to write for T. Thomas Fortune's newspaper, the *New York Age*. From her new base, Wells continued her anti-lynching battle. In 1893 and 1894 she toured Great Britain, publicly chastising lynching in the United States as a menace to human civilization.

In contrast to the militancy of black leaders in the North, Booker T. Washington, principal of the black Normal and Industrial Institute in Tuskegee, Alabama, and the most influential African American at the turn of the twentieth century, believed it unwise to denounce lynching openly and in ways that would offend Southern white sensibilities. Washington blamed mob violence on poor whites and suggested that lynching could be stopped if black southerners followed the lead of paternalistic white elites and otherwise focused on self-improvement through hard work and thrift. His message of accommodation and racial harmony stood blatantly at odds with the experiences of most Southern blacks who encountered segregation, discrimination, and violent repression daily. When, therefore, in 1909 black civil rights activists, led by the sociologist and historian W. E. B. Du Bois, joined forces with white social reformers to form the National Association for the Advancement of Colored People, the new organization openly challenged Washington's strategy.

The NAACP's founding was a direct response to the bloody "race riot" in Springfield, Illinois, in the summer of 1908, an event that began with the attempt of a mob to lynch a black man charged with raping a white woman. Finding that the sheriff had already rushed their targeted victim out of town, the crowd went on a rampage through Springfield's black community, killing two innocent men and leaving behind a path of devastation. The riot in Springfield in many ways exemplified patterns of collective racial violence in early twentieth-century America, but the incident stood out in one important symbolic respect: Americans recognized Springfield as the longtime residence and burial site of Abraham Lincoln, the Great Emancipator. The riot demonstrated that racial hatred was not a Southern but a national problem. It prompted a call by leading black and white advocates of minority rights "to all believers in democracy" to renew the struggle for civil and political rights.

Once the NAACP gained momentum in the early 1910s, it made lynch law one of its key targets. The organization meticulously documented

Flag, announcing lynching, flown from the window of the NAACP headquarters.

incidents of mob violence and launched campaigns of public protest. Its investigators visited lynching sites at considerable personal risk to determine the facts and, possibly, the identity of the guilty parties. The NAACP petitioned state and federal governments to take action and lobbied for legislation that would ensure the prosecution of both lynchers and negligent law officers.

Walter White, an NAACP field worker who later became the group's national leader, acquired legendary recognition for his bold undercover investigations and his skillful and persistent lobbying efforts. A former insurance agent, whose light complexion, blond hair, and blue eyes allowed him to approach whites without being identified as an African American, White had a knack for getting lynchers to boast freely about their exploits. The NAACP made sure that his discoveries, written in dramatic prose, received the greatest possible publicity. In addition to publication in its magazine *Crisis*, the NAACP sent copies of White's reports to newspapers and lawmakers nationwide. As the NAACP's influence grew, its leaders took every opportunity to expose mob violence against African Americans before Congress and in the White House. Walter White made every effort to gain access to the white power elite. During the presidency of Franklin D. Roosevelt, the NAACP leader managed to cultivate the support of First Lady Eleanor Roosevelt, who genuinely sympathized with the plight of African Americans. Even the racially liberal first lady, however, once complained about Walter White's "obsession on the lynching question."

African American anti-lynching activists knew they needed white allies who were able and willing to contribute money, prestige, and political connections to their cause. In the North the NAACP successfully attracted support from liberal white philanthropists and from politicians seeking the votes of Northern blacks. White supremacists naturally reviled the organization as a cabal of radical "outside agitators"; even those white Southerners who opposed lynching often made a point of keeping a distance from the NAACP. Nevertheless in the 1920s and 1930s a growing number of Southern whites, concerned that lynching damaged the region's image and economic progress, began efforts to combat mob violence.

In 1919 blacks and whites founded the Commission on Interracial Cooperation (CIC) in Atlanta, dedicated to assuaging racial tensions and rooting out lynching. Eleven years later the CIC helped found the all-white Association of Southern Women for the Prevention of Lynching (ASWPL), led by the resourceful Texan Jesse Daniel Ames, a social reformer and former suffragist. The ASWPL relied on moral appeals as well as on political tactics. Women, as wives, mothers, daughters, and sisters, might be able reach the conscience of lynchers, the ASWPL hoped. But the group also put peace officers and politicians on notice that women would vote only for candidates who pledged themselves to upholding the law. By 1940 the ASWPL boasted almost forty thousand supporters, many of whom worked in local church groups. To be sure, the membership of the ASWPL consisted of respectable Southern ladies who never questioned white supremacy and segregation. But Ames and her followers took exception to Southern men using the protection of white women as an excuse for mob rule and lawlessness. White racists, including women, attacked the organization for "defending criminal negro men at the expense of innocent white girls."

In spite of their diverse backgrounds and approaches, all anti-lynching groups and activists shared one basic conviction: the key to eradicating mob violence was to enlighten the American people about its causes and consequences. Collecting and publicizing the facts about lynching, most anti-lynching activists believed, had to be the first step toward devising effective remedies. If the overwhelming majority of decent Americans only knew the truth, they would support laws and executive measures to suppress lynch law. Compiling statistical information on lynchings as well as establishing the facts of particular incidents thus became a vital part of the anti-lynching struggle. Following the *Chicago Tribune,* which had kept a record of all known lynchings since 1882, the Tuskegee Institute began publishing the *Negro Yearbook* in 1912, a comprehensive documentation of black life in America which also tallied mob killings. The NAACP and the ASWPL also gathered and published their own data. Moreover the NAACP and the CIC sponsored several major studies of the economic and social factors that appeared to have an impact on the frequency of lynching. Most important, scholars registered the race of lynch victims, the presumed causes of mob killings, and regional patterns. They calculated, for example, whether lynching rose or declined in relation to cotton prices and to the percentage of the black population in a given county. Although the contemporary statistics probably overlooked many mob killings, these materials laid the groundwork on which later historians have built.

The opponents of lynching hoped that accurate facts and statistical methods would provide their cause with an air of scientific objectivity that compared favorably to the rabble-rousing demagoguery of white supremacists. Whether this educational work had the desired effect is difficult to say. The effort to refute the rape myth is a case in point. In the 1890s Ida B. Wells dedicated her investigative journalism to the goal of proving that charges of rape against black men were mostly a pretext for economic jealousy or other reasons that had nothing to do with sexual transgressions. Anti-lynching groups unflaggingly advertised their findings that in three of four lynchings, accusations of rape played no role. All the same, the specter of the "black rapist" retained its rhetorical power as a "knockout argument" to silence all discussion among the larger American public about the causes of lynch law.

In a speech he delivered on the U.S. Senate floor in 1907, South Carolina senator Benjamin Tillman provided a typical example of how Southern demagogues suceeded in shaping the debates on lynching.

Tillman invited his Northern colleagues to send their own daughters to the "backwoods of South Carolina" and see them ravished by "lurking demons." "Is there a man here with red blood in his veins who doubts what impulses the father would feel?" Tillman asked smugly. Anti-lynching activists and scholars were aware that they faced a tough uphill battle in their efforts to counter with facts and reason such deep-seated hatred, fear, and prejudice. Still, many of them remained remarkably optimistic that progress and education would ultimately prevail. In his important *The Tragedy of Lynching*, published in 1933, the sociologist Arthur Raper voiced a widespread expectation when he wrote: "Mobs and lynchings eventually can be eliminated if the irresponsive and irresponsible population elements can be raised into a more abundant economic and cultural life."

Shaming the American people was an important feature of anti-lynching educational strategy. Whereas lynchers claimed to defend white civilization against black savages, their opponents condemned mob violence as a disgrace to American civilization. Investigators deliberately shocked their readers with excruciating details of torture and burning, which they likened to medieval practices. With such a record, how could America claim to be a paragon of progress and civilization? they asked. After a mob had burned a black man in Nodena, Arkansas, in 1921, the NAACP leader and black writer James Weldon Johnson bitterly pointed out that such crimes were not "the deeds of the so-called savages in the dark places of the earth. They are the deeds of so-called superior white men, and women too, in a so-called Christian and civilized State of the so-called great American Democracy." Anti-lynching campaigners incessantly reminded their fellow citizens that mob violence set the United States apart from the civilized world and tarnished their nation's honor. Even in times of war and international tension they did not avoid unfavorable references to denounce the barbarism of lynchers. During World War I black newspapers routinely compared lynching to the war atrocities allegedly perpetrated by the German "Huns," who at that time symbolized the depths of civilized sociery. In a similar vein, black civil rights leaders later exploited the comparison with Nazi Germany in order to expose American "hypocrisy." In 1938 NAACP assistant secretary Roy Wilkins commented on the double standard many Americans evidently applied in condemning Nazi violence against German Jews: "[U]ntil we stamp out the rope and the faggot . . . we cannot make a good case against the cruelties of storm troopers." Certainly Americans found it embarrassing when Nazi newspapers featured stories and grisly images of lynchings in America in response to U.S. protests against the maltreatment of German minorities under Hitler.

The national interest, anti-lynching campaigners insisted, demanded the elimination of mob violence. Such appeals to patriotism, however, were not confined to foreign relations. White Americans, the anti-lynching crusaders suggested, failed to understand the damage mob violence inflicted on the country's psyche and social fabric. In 1935 an NAACP fund-raising flyer featured a photograph of the lynching of Rubin Stacey in Fort Lauderdale, Florida, showing a group of white men and women, including small children, staring at the victim's dangling body. "Do not look at the Negro," the caption read. "Instead look at the seven WHITE children who gaze at this gruesome spectacle. . . . What psychological havoc is being wrought in the minds of the white children? Into what kinds of citizens will they grow up? What kind of America will they help to make after being familiarized with such an inhuman, law-destroying practice as lynching?" The flyer also illustrated how anti-lynching activists used shocking photographs, taken by voyeuristic onlookers, to shame white Southerners.

In exposing the inhumanity of lynching, civil rights activists also enlisted the support of the fine arts. In 1935 the NAACP and a coalition of leftist groups each organized exhibitions of anti-lynching art, including paintings, drawings, and sculptures, in New York City. Apart from their propagandistic purpose, these exhibitions documented the deep impact of racism and violence on modern American artists. The same may be said of American literature. Both black and white American authors, such as Mark Twain, Theodore Dreiser, John Steinbeck, Richard Wright, and Claude McKay, to name only a few, engaged mob violence and lynching in their writing, confronting their readers with gripping depictions of violence and a scathing social critique. Black music also mirrored the horrors of lynching. But when in 1939 the black singer Billie Holiday recorded "Strange Fruit," later to become an anti-lynching classic, she soon found out that many white radio stations and audiences did not appreciate the song. Like anti-lynching protest in general, pointed works of art reached mostly those who already supported the cause.

Anti-lynching campaigners did not expect that education and propaganda alone would suffice to end lynching. The NAACP's propaganda efforts primarily served to muster political support for coercive legislation. As a special type of murder, lynching was theoretically punishable under the criminal laws of the states. But as long as lynch law enjoyed widespread popular backing, the criminal justice system remained virtually paralyzed. As a rule, coroners' inquests concluded that "persons unknown" had caused the death of a victim. Prosecutors did not bring charges, and, if they did, grand juries rarely issued indictments. In those extraordinary cases where lynchers actually faced trial, juries usually acquitted them. After all, the jurors as well as the official representatives of the law were part of the local communities and often shared the lynchers' values and viewpoints, or at least were unwilling to defy them openly. Fewer than 1 percent of all lynchings that occurred after 1900 resulted in convictions; punishment was usually limited to fines or suspended sentences for offenses such as rioting and disorderly conduct.

Because of the difficulties of prosecuting perpetrators of mob violence, advocates of law and order called for special anti-lynching legislation. Typically their bills defined mobs as assemblages of three or more persons, declared murder by mobs a statutory crime, threatened counties and municipalities where lynchings occurred with fines and indemnity payments to the victim's family, and allowed for the removal of negligent law officers. Anti-lynching statutes also strengthened the authority of the governor to employ the state militia to guard prisoners and repress mobs. In response to the wave of mob violence in the 1890s and early 1900s, about a dozen state legislatures passed laws of this nature, including Georgia, Texas, Alabama, and the Carolinas, states with high lynching rates. The laws, however, proved largely ineffective and did not lead to a significant increase in criminal convictions. Skeptics concluded that as long as lynching mirrored the will of the people, legislation would be powerless.

In contrast, proponents of tough anti-lynching bills argued that the states were simply not interested in enforcing the law. As a consequence, they demanded federal legislation. In 1901 U.S. Senator George F. Hoar of Massachusetts, a Republican and a well-known champion of minority rights, introduced a "Bill to protect citizens of the United States against lynching in default of protection by the States." The Hoar Bill echoed

most features of state anti-lynching legislation but differed in two crucial respects. It stipulated that all participants in a mob killing "shall be
deemed guilty of murder," and it shifted the jurisdiction to the federal
circuit courts where presumably convictions could be won more easily.

Not unexpectedly, critics raised constitutional objections to the Hoar
Bill. Even after the Civil War and Reconstruction, most Americans conceived of federalism as a system that strictly separated the powers of the
states and the national government. Clearly criminal justice, including
the prosecution of murderers, fell under the jurisdiction of the states and
the local courts. According to the dominant view among contemporary
legal scholars and the public at large, the Constitution did not authorize
Congress to legislate on the criminal prosecution of lynchers. The spon-
sors of the Hoar Bill claimed this authority could be found in the Fourteenth Amendment: states that failed to protect their citizens from mob
violence denied them the equal protection of the laws. This right Congress had the power to enforce through appropriate legislation. Regardless, the states' right argument carried great weight. Even George Hoar
himself had qualms about the constitutionality of his bill. In May 1902
the Senate Judiciary Committee, headed by Hoar, sensed little support
and voted to postpone the anti-lynching bill indefinitely.

Undaunted, the advocates of federal anti-lynching legislation continued
their struggle for another five decades, hoping their reading of the Constitution would eventually prevail. In 1918 the NAACP launched a new attempt
when it lobbied for a bill sponsored by Republican congressman Leoni-
das Dyer of Missouri, which featured sanctions against delinquent public
officials rather than the prosecution of lynchers for murder. It was more
than three years before the bill came to a vote on the House floor, where it
was passed with the votes of the Republican majority. Senate opponents of
the Dyer Bill, however, succeeded in preventing a vote indefinitely. Other
anti-lynching measures promoted by the NAACP in the 1930s suffered the
same fate. Although by then most Americans had come to support federal laws against lynching, and New Deal Democrats in Congress had
made anti-lynching legislation a cornerstone of their civil rights agenda,
Southern senators successfully obstructed all bills until their adversaries
gave in. A 1938 filibuster lasted for more than a month and featured racist diatribes similar to those of the late nineteenth century. The promoters
of the anti-lynching bill, Mississippi senator Theodore Bilbo warned, bore
responsibility for the "blood of the raped and outraged daughters of Dixie,

as well as the blood of the perpetrators of these crimes that the red-blooded Anglo-Saxon white men will not tolerate." Surely many moderate white Southerners detested race baiters like Bilbo, but they were reluctant to support federal legislation lest they be branded as traitors to the South. ASWPL leader Jesse Daniel Ames, for example, opposed federal bills, fearful that they would offend ordinary Southern whites.

Although the crusade to pass federal anti-lynching laws was ultimately unsuccessful, it should not be dismissed as an outright failure. The struggle against lynching helped mobilize African Americans like no other civil rights issue. Moreover the threat of federal intervention may have played a role in persuading Southern authorities to take a tougher position on mob violence. Defenders of states' rights liked to point to the declining numbers of lynching incidents as evidence that a federal law was not only unconstitutional but also unnecessary because the states were perfectly capable of dealing with the problem. To demonstrate that he could maintain law and order, Mississippi governor James K. Vardaman, a race baiter and apologist for popular justice, repeatedly mobilized his state's National Guard to quell mob violence in the years from 1904 to 1908. For decades, however, neither the states nor local authorities in the South made a credible effort to rein in lynching. Local sheriffs, in particular, notoriously retreated from or actively colluded with the mobs. After the lynching of a black farm worker in Honey Grove, Texas, in May 1930, the sheriff declared proudly: "I handled the thing the best I knew how, and undoubtedly it suited the people of the county. . . . Not a dollar's worth of property was destroyed . . . no innocent people were hurt." A few months later voters reelected the sheriff, rewarding him for splendid discharge of duty.

Most anti-lynching activists agreed that the local sheriffs' indifference to or even complicity in mob violence posed a key problem. Sheriffs were elected by the community and shared the mentality and prejudices of their constituents. Few were willing to risk their popularity by protecting a black prisoner and incur a reputation as a "nigger lover." And collusion with the mob carried little risk. Sheriffs stood almost immune from federal or state interference and could count on the refusal of all-white local juries in the South to convict officers for aiding a lynch mob. The higher courts also showed little resolve. When in 1937 the attorney general of Alabama attempted to impeach a sheriff charged with negligence in protecting a prisoner, the state supreme court dismissed the case. Even a leading white Southern newspaper acknowledged that "if sufficient pressure were placed on the sheriffs . . . much of the lynching would cease."

The Association of Southern Women to Prevent Lynching made pressure on police officers its main objective. "Conscientious sheriffs," the ASWPL declared, "determined to guard their prisoners at all costs, can do more to stop lynching than any other one factor." The organization worked hard to obtain pledges from law enforcement officials to uphold the law and initiated letter-writing campaigns to commend sheriffs who protected their prisoners. Conversely the ASWPL publicly accused officers who neglected their duties of cowardice and stupidity. By the early 1940s, when the ASWPL dissolved, it had obtained 1,355 pledges from Southern sheriffs. Apparently the efforts of the organization accelerated a trend toward more resolute law enforcement that had been under way for a decade before the founding of the ASWPL in 1930. According to data for the period from 1915 to 1941, gathered by the ASWPL from a meticulous study of newspaper reports, the tide began to turn around 1920, when the numbers of prevented lynchings for the first time exceeded those of completed mob killings. In 1914 lynch mobs carried out almost three times as many lynchings as were prevented. In 1936 only one of ten threatened lynchings resulted in the death of the targeted victim.

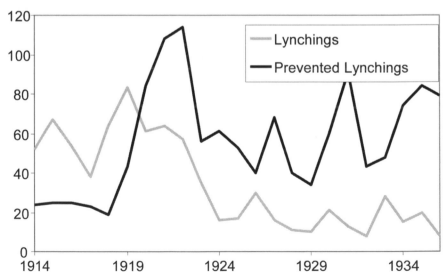

Ratio of Lynchings and Prevented Lynchings, 1914–1934
Source: Jesse Daniel Ames, *The Changing Character of Lynching: Review of Lynching, 1931–1941* (New York: 1973; orig. 1942), 11.

How could sheriffs prevent lynchings? It is important to note that mobs seized most of their victims from jails or police cars and that most lynchings were preceded by periods of rising community tensions, sometimes lasting for days. Meanwhile the sheriff had an opportunity to take countervailing measures, depending on the circumstances. Given enough time, he could remove prisoners to another county or town for safekeeping. If it was too late for removal, he could augment the jail guards. In case local forces were insufficient, the sheriff could call the governor to send reinforcements. When push came to shove, the lawman had to threaten the use of force and make good on that threat if necessary.

In some cases police officers fought pitched battles with mobs, some of which lasted for hours. Audacious sheriffs confronted lynchers head-on, sometimes even unarmed, daring them to get the prisoner "over my dead body." In August 1921 Sheriff W. T. Cate of Knox County, Tennessee, faced a mob in front of his jail and drew a line in the sand. As soon as the would-be lynchers surged forward and began throwing rocks, Cate fired a warning shot over their heads. When some of the men returned the fire, Cate's deputies answered with a volley sufficiently intimidating to disperse the mob. In another incident the wife of a sheriff distinguished herself in battling mob violence. In 1931 the Commission on Interracial Cooperation commended Mrs. J. H. Butler, wife of a Tennessee sheriff, who had single-handedly protected a black prisoner while her husband was out of town. Evidently the lynchers feared risking the consequences of harming a well-respected white lady.

Yet most sheriffs did not respond to the threat of a lynching by standing in front of the jail with a loaded shotgun. Reports collected by the AWSPL confirm that in most prevented lynchings, law officials removed the prisoner to a safe place. After 1930 the use of force against mobs became exceptional, though such incidents received much public attention. Then again, removing a prisoner from the grasp of a mob was by no means risk-free. The records tell numerous stories of dramatic car chases and cunning lawmen eluding their pursuers for hours at a time. Sometimes these chases ended in accidents with the officers and the prisoners badly injured. For example, in 1918 an Alabama sheriff, his deputies, and their black detainee suffered life-threatening injuries on their way to Selma, trying to shake off several cars manned with heavily armed vigilantes.

Mobs attacked sheriffs in order to wrest their prisoners from them but never deliberately killed law officials, even when they easily could have

done so. Unlike the lynching of a black suspect, the murder of a police officer would have resulted in criminal prosecution and severe punishment.
Although it certainly took great personal courage to confront a mob, sheriffs and other representatives of the law commanded an aura of authority
that lynchers were reluctant to challenge head-on. In one 1936 incident in
Danielsville, Georgia, a judge dispersed a furious mob by declaring them
all deputized officers, thereby formally binding them to maintain law and
order. Baffled by the judge's nerve, the lynchers complied with his order.
Unfortunately the black prisoner, whom the judge had saved, later was
kidnapped from an Atlanta hospital and lynched all the same.

It is difficult to explain why sheriffs in the 1920s and 1930s became
more willing to prevent lynchings. Their comments emphasized their
oaths to uphold the law. Obviously public pressure played a role in reminding sheriffs to do their duty. Governors and anti-lynching groups,
such as the ASWPL, awarded honorable citations and medals to men
who had distinguished themselves in standing up to mob violence; the
national and the regional press also lauded courageous officers. In rural areas, sheriffs may have responded to the demands from influential
planters who were afraid of losing their cheap labor force to the Great
Migration north and insisted on better protection for their black workers. Moreover as public support for lynching began to dwindle, the size of
the mobs declined accordingly, thereby reducing the risk for law officers
in confronting them. But the advance of modern technology may have
played a crucial role. Radio communication allowed sheriffs to call in
help quickly and to gather information on where lynchers had set up an
ambush. Automobiles, in particular, enabled the police to remove prisoners much more quickly than in the age of horse carriages. Yet the lynchers also took advantage of modernity's blessings, using their own cars to
pursue the sheriffs.

The fact that throughout the 1920s and 1930s a growing number
of Southern police officers no longer tolerated a free reign of the mob
seemed to signal the "progress" for which many anti-lynching activists
had worked long and hard. But the decline of lynching should not be
mistaken for a radical change in race relations. White supremacists had
not surrendered their goal of maintaining racial control over the black
population but had merely renounced the extreme and increasingly embarrassing instrument of lynching.

While many liberal anti-lynching campaigners hoped that education and cultural uplift would gradually undermine the legitimacy of mob violence, moderates and conservatives stressed the need for swift and harsh criminal justice to satisfy popular expectations. They agreed with the defenders of popular justice that lynching had its roots in ineffective law enforcement and lenient punishment. This sentiment was not confined to the South. After the lynching of a black man in Cairo, Illinois, in 1909, the mayor of the town complained: "There has not been an official execution in Cairo for 10 or 15 years, and yet the city has had its share of murders." In this view the death penalty appeared to be the appropriate cure for lynching. If the people could be certain that murderers and rapists would end up promptly on the gallows, they would no longer see the need to take the law into their own hands.

Evidence thus suggests that capital punishment administered by the state played an important role in the demise of Judge Lynch. In the late nineteenth-century West, executions increased as lynchings declined. In the South this development occurred with some delay. Although no perfect statistical proof exists that the death penalty became a substitute for lynch law, a look at how capital punishment affected African Americans indicates a close connection. In Kentucky, for example, mobs killed 40 blacks in the first decade of the twentieth century, out of a total of 43 lynchings. In the 1930s only two persons were lynched in Kentucky, one white and one black. During the same period legal executions of blacks more than doubled, from 13 in the 1900s to 27 in the 1930s. True, overall the number of legally executed African Americans did not rise in proportion to the decline in lynching. In the 1890s about 1,300 blacks were lynched compared to 608 legal executions; in the 1920s Judge Lynch claimed roughly 250 blacks while state executioners put 567 African Americans to death. Nevertheless the precipitous decline in the ratio of lynchings to legal executions—from 2.1 in the 1890s to 0.4 in the 1920s—suggests that during these decades capital punishment gradually replaced lynching as the key instrument employed by American society in suppressing the perceived threat of black crime.

The 1930s and 1940s were crucial years in this process of substitution. In the 1930s about 100 African Americans were lynched, nearly 60 percent fewer than in the 1920s. In the same period legal executions soared to more than 800, a 44 percent increase over the preceding decade. In the

1940s lynch mobs killed fewer than 30 blacks while the state executed 781, accounting for a staggering 61 percent share among all persons legally put to death in the United States.

Considering executions of convicted rapists, the crime most closely linked to the public perception of lynching, the relationship between the death penalty and the decline in mob violence becomes even more manifest. In the 1930s the states executed 115 blacks convicted of rape. Over the next decade this number jumped to 179, representing 90 percent of all persons executed in the United States for rape, a percentage that remained constant until 1965. These figures reflect the continuing obsession with the specter of the black rapist, especially in the South, where black men charged with raping a white woman faced almost certain conviction and execution, provided they received a trial at all.

How the Southern criminal justice system imposed the death penalty on black defendants often amounted to what has been aptly called "legal lynching." In many trials against accused black murderers or rapists, the threat of mob violence dominated the legal proceedings. In response, law officials made every effort to dissuade would-be lynchers from lawlessness, promising a speedy trial and certain conviction followed by instant execution. For example, in July 1906 an African-American man named Allen Mathias was arrested on rape charges in Mayfield, Kentucky, and brought to Louisville for safekeeping. The white people of Mayfield angrily demanded his return and quick punishment. One week after his arrest, state police escorted Mathias back to Mayfield, where citizens had already erected a scaffold. As soon as the defendant arrived, he was ushered into the courtroom where he pleaded guilty immediately. The jury then deliberated for fewer than fifteen minutes and sentenced Mathias to death. The judge ordered his instant execution. Less than an hour after Mathias had entered the courtroom, the sheriff cut the condemned man's body down from the gallows. For the official record, this mockery of justice counted as a legal execution.

Allen Mathias may have pleaded guilty because he was resigned to his fate and chose a hanging administered by the sheriff over a lynching at the hands of a frenzied mob. It is not known whether he was aware of the fate that another black man had suffered in the neighboring state of Tennessee earlier the same year. After a court in Chattanooga had sentenced Edward Johnson to death for the rape of a young white woman, his white defense lawyers beseeched their client to accept the verdict and forgo an appeal. Although the evidence was thin and Johnson maintained his innocence, his attorneys told him that he had the choice of either dying "in an orderly, lawful manner" or "horribly by the hands of the mob" that would drag him through the streets, beat him ferociously, and display his body in front of a howling crowd. Johnson at first acquiesced, but his father initiated an appeal that succeeded in obtaining an order from the U.S. Supreme Court for a stay of execution. Only hours after the Court had issued its decision, a mob broke into the Chattanooga jail and lynched Edward Johnson. Sheriff Joseph Shipp, who had defied the Court's decree to protect his prisoner, had to stand trial and served a short prison sentence. After his release, a crowd in Chattanooga welcomed Shipp as a hero.

Because the authorities, for obvious reasons, preferred "orderly" executions over mob violence, they were willing to go to great lengths to acknowledge popular calls for quick vengeance. In 1920 a judge in Macon, Georgia, prevented the lynching of an eighteen-year-old black male accused of an attack upon a white woman by hastily convening a special court term. Before the trial began, the judge exacted a promise from the audience to remain calm and let the law take its course. The court proceedings took only a few minutes and ended with a death sentence, which was carried out three weeks later. Another case from 1937, exemplifying the close connection between the prevention of lynchings and subsequent legal executions, occurred in Burke County, Georgia. Two farmers rescued a black man wanted for the rape of a white woman from a mob and turned him over to the sheriff, who brought his prisoner to Savannah for safekeeping. Two weeks after the alleged crime the trial began. It lasted forty minutes. After deliberating for five minutes, the jury found the defendant guilty and imposed a death sentence. The man was electrocuted in the Georgia state prison four weeks later. The *Atlanta Constitution*, the leading daily newspaper in the state, celebrated the case as a victory of the "dignity and integrity [of] the law." Due to this kind of prompt and efficient administration of criminal justice, the paper maintained, "the day is not far distant when the rope of the lyncher will be as strange in modern life as is the stake of the Salem witchburner." It never occurred to the writer that the black rapist might be no less a figment of popular hysteria than the witches of old.

Not surprisingly, such travesties of justice provoked resistance from civil rights activists. From its founding in 1909, the NAACP waged a protracted legal battle to secure due process of law for black defendants. In 1923 it obtained a ruling from the U.S. Supreme Court that trials held under the menace of mob violence violated the constitutional right to due process guaranteed by the Fifth and Fourteenth amendments to the Constitution. In the 1930s the NAACP and the leftist International Labor Defense (ILD) successfully fought the execution of the "Scottsboro Boys," eight black youths who had been sentenced to death in 1931 by the state of Alabama for the alleged rape of two white girls. The case exposed the barefaced racism of the Southern criminal justice system and made both national and international headlines. But spectacular trials, which veteran civil rights lawyers were able to carry to the U.S. Supreme Court, remained rare exceptions and had little impact on the daily routine of Southern criminal justice. It continued to discriminate against black defendants and relentlessly employed capital punishment as an instrument of white supremacy.

Legal executions served as a substitute for lynching only if they were held in public. At public executions the people experienced the venerable rituals of communal punishment, such as prayer, singing, and sermons, and born witness to criminals receiving their proper punishment. Defenders of public executions thus argued that they helped prevent lynchings by "appeasing and quieting the people who are ready to take this matter in their own hands." In other words, public hangings constituted a reward of sorts for refraining from mob justice. The advocates of a "modern" system of criminal justice, on the other hand, demanded that executions be confined behind prison walls and carried out in a detached, scientific manner, preferably by the electric chair which supposedly minimized physical pain. Yet the South stubbornly resisted this trend as long as possible. Even where the law mandated capital punishment to be administered in restricted spaces, crowds often demanded public executions. In 1920 a gathering of five thousand people in Tupelo, Mississippi, broke down a fence that had been built around the gallows to shield an execution from open view. The last official public hanging in the United States took place in Kentucky in August 1936, when an African American convicted of murder and rape died before ten thousand cheering onlookers.

Some legal executions got completely out of hand. In March 1934 Mississippi officials executed three young black men in the jail of Hernando. They had been sentenced to death for armed robbery and an attack on a white girl. The trial had been particularly speedy because angry crowds repeatedly threatened to break through the barbed-wire entanglements set up in the courtroom. After the death sentence, Mississippi legislators introduced a special bill that would allow the father of the raped girl to serve as the hangman. The chairman of the judiciary committee of Mississippi's House of Representatives, however, vetoed the proposal, declaring his oppostion to what he termed "legalized butchery." To avoid trouble during the execution, the responsible officers decided to hold the hangings in the early morning, several hours before the official schedule. Because journalists learned about the change, the plan failed. A throng, including several schoolgirls, besieged the jail to catch a glimpse of the spectacle, laughing and mocking the condemned men as they dropped to their deaths. Spectators jumped on top of the coffins when the bodies were taken to the graveyard; people chanted cruel rhymes like "Bye Bye Blackbird" and "I'll be glad when you're dead."

Even when the death penalty was carried out behind closed doors using the electric chair, authorities were sometimes willing to meet the expectations of popular voyeurism. After the electrocution of a convicted black murderer in Cleveland, Mississippi, in 1934, officials exhibited the body in the lobby of the jail. Before the trial and execution, Mississippi authorities had scrupulously taken precautions to forestall a possible lynching. Exhibiting the corpse thus served as a reward to the good citizens of Cleveland for their patience and orderly conduct.

Reformers who sought to arouse Americans to the evil of lynching entertained an optimistic faith in the power of reason, morality, and education. Social critics condemned mob violence as a blot on American civilization but continued to hope that Americans would eventually reconcile their practices with their ideals. The brave struggle of anti-lynching crusaders deserves admiration; whether their optimism was justified is a different question. The tireless propaganda campaign of the NAACP, the ASWPL, and many other groups and individuals probably contributed to the gradual change in public awareness. Yet lynching did not decline because American society generally, and Southern society in particular, underwent a moral catharsis. Rather, a combination of enhanced law enforcement, both against lynchers and criminal suspects, and the expansion of the death penalty gradually curtailed lynch law. For African Americans, the main victims of mob killings, the effects of this transition proved highly ambivalent. All too often a lynching prevented by the police merely presaged a legal lynching by a kangaroo court. Blacks thus faced a double bind: while weak legal institutions failed to protect them against lynching, strict and "efficient" law enforcement hit them harder than any other racial or ethnic group.

Most white Americans, however, preferred to ignore the racial bias of the criminal justice system and complacently noted that lynching, at least as a public spectacle, had virtually ceased by the mid-twentieth century. On May 9, 1940, the Association of Southern Women for the Prevention of Lynching declared that the first full year without a lynching had passed since records were maintained. A month later the Tuskegee Institute confirmed the ASWPL's accounting, though other anti-lynching organizations disputed the good news. The ILD claimed that there had been at least five lynch victims during the period surveyed by the ASWPL, and it called for the immediate passage of a federal anti-lynching law. All the same, in 1942 the ASWPL dissolved, ostensibly because it had accomplished its mission. The group did not deny that deadly racial violence persisted, but it argued that it had become indistinguishable from ordinary homicides. Of course the boundaries between the two were extremely volatile. Whether lynching had really stopped, and what kinds of killings should be classified as a lynching, remained contested issues for several decades.

8

From Lynching to Hate Crime

IN JANUARY 1940 Senator Robert F. Wagner, Democrat of New York, and Senator Arthur Capper, Republican of Kansas, two leading supporters of anti-lynching legislation in Congress, sponsored the publication of a report entitled "Lynching Goes Underground." The author, who introduced himself as a white Southerner but preferred to remain anonymous, had investigated lynchings for several years. The phenomenon, he insisted, was not disappearing but rather "entering a new and altogether dangerous phase." The declining numbers of recent years were misleading. "Countless Negroes are lynched yearly," the report stated, "but their disappearance is shrouded in mystery, for they are dispatched quietly and without general knowledge. In some lonely swamp a small body of men do the job formerly done by a vast, howling bloodthirsty mob composed of men, women, and children."

The NAACP and other organizations dedicated to anti-lynching distributed the document in support of their long-standing demands for a federal law against mob violence. The problem of lynching persisted, they argued, albeit in a different shape that was more difficult to identify than the undisguised action of mass mobs in the past. The new method of "quiet lynching" was as malicious as the older variety and called for determined action. Critics of the NAACP's focus on federal legislation, including Jesse Daniel Ames, leader of the ASWPL, and other moderate white Southerners strongly objected to the arguments made in the "Lynching Goes Underground" report. Secret killings, they maintained, were not at all new but had occurred for many decades; there was no evidence that their numbers had increased as public lynchings declined. And the fact that the killers saw a need to conceal their deeds indicated that the overwhelming majority of white Southerners no longer condoned lynching.

As throughout the sordid history of racial violence, political interests affected the new dispute over how to define lynching. A narrow
definition—that included only killings perpetrated by a sizable crowd
in full public view and open defiance of the law—kept the numbers
low and thus created the impression of racial progress. A broad definition—that encompassed all racially motivated homicides of blacks by
whites, including those committed by officers of the law—promised to
raise public awareness of racial violence as a larger problem.

In December 1940 representatives of all major anti-lynching organizations convened at Alabama's Tuskegee Institute to resolve their differences. After intense debate the conference participants issued the
following definition of lynching: "There must be legal evidence that a
person has been killed and that he met his death illegaly at the hands of
a group under the pretext of service to justice, race or tradition." This
vague description, however, satisfied no one, and disagreements over
what killings should be classified as lynchings continued. Both the narrow and the broad factions had valid points. By 1940 lynching as mass
spectacle and public ritual had indeed come to an end. Yet white supremacists continued to employ violence as an instrument of terror against an
increasingly assertive black population in the South.

In the decades after World War II American attitudes toward lynching changed in important ways. These shifts came slowly, but they affected individual institutions as well as American society at large. Both
state and federal agencies began to make more determined efforts to
bring perpetrators to justice. Open support for lynching all but ceased
among white Southerners, and community approval of racist violence
crumbled, though all-white local juries remained receptive to appeals
for white solidarity. Most important, the African-American civil rights
movement triggered a profound political and cultural revolution in the
South and in the nation. At first the movement's challenge of Jim Crow
provoked a fierce backlash from white supremacists. But the black
struggle eventually succeeded in transforming both the law and popular attitudes toward racial hatred. In the post–civil rights era, racial
violence has completely lost its former legitimacy. Thus hate crimes—a
term for violent attacks on racial, ethnic, religious, and sexual minorities, which entered the vocabulary of Americans in the 1980s—do not
represent the continuation of lynching in a different guise. Lynchers of

old could count on impunity because the larger community condoned their deeds and shared their attitudes toward the victim. The perpetrators of hate crimes, in contrast, express their anger and frustration over the social acceptance of the particular minority they hate. They may try to reenact the rites of Judge Lynch, but they can no longer claim to be executioners of popular justice.

In addition to the assiduous propaganda work of anti-lynching activists, larger historical forces contributed to the weakening of popular backing for mob violence. New Deal reforms of the 1930s accelerated the industrialization and urbanization of the South, bringing it closer to the American mainstream. Equally important, the New Deal demonstrated the new powers of the federal government as an agent of economic development and, potentially, of law enforcement too. Southern elites became increasingly concerned that continued mob violence would damage the economic prospects of their region and provoke federal intervention. Although Congress repeatedly failed to pass an anti-lynching bill in the late 1930s, racial liberals in the Roosevelt administration attempted to expand federal authority. In 1939 Attorney General Frank Murphy established a Civil Liberties Unit, later renamed the Civil Rights Section, within the Department of Justice. Department lawyers revived the Ku Klux Klan Act of 1871 as a legal weapon against lynching. The law from the Reconstruction era, long considered a dead letter, had made it a federal crime for anyone acting "under color of law" to deprive a person of rights guaranteed by the Constitution. In 1944 the U.S. Supreme Court agreed that the Klan Act provided a basis for federal law enforcement against mob violence. But the Court also ruled that federal prosecutors had to prove the defendants' intent to deny their victims specific civil rights, such as the right to vote, thus establishing an impossible standard of evidence. Nevertheless from the 1940s on the Federal Bureau of Investigation began to take a more active part in investigating alleged lynchings and racially motivated murders.

World War II, serving as a catalyst for racial change, further undermined the social and cultural edifice that had sustained lynching. During the war more than a million African Americans migrated from the South to the North and the West, where they found wartime jobs and began forming a substantial electoral bloc. The wartime boom also brought new economic security to blacks. They thus became more assertive in claiming their rights. Black soldiers, who had helped defeat a self-proclaimed "master race" on European battlefields, returned home with newfound self-confidence. As one veteran put it bluntly, "I'm hanged if I am going to let the Alabama version of the Germans kick me around when I get home." Likewise, the ideological struggle between democracy and fascism had raised the awareness of many white Americans that they had to practice what they preached. Clearly, racism and lynching exposed the United States to embarrassing charges of hypocrisy.

In January 1942, after a mob in Sikeston, Missouri, had burned a black man to death, German and Japanese propaganda broadcasters immediately touted the event to listeners around the world. The ideological challenge continued after the war when the United States became the leader of the "Free World" in the global contest with communism. As President Harry S Truman acknowledged in a speech he delivered to the annual convention of the NAACP in June 1947, America could preach democracy to the world only if it could show "that we have been able to put our own house in order." A few months later Truman's presidential Committee on Civil Rights issued a report that called for sweeping measures to curb racial violence and discrimination, including a federal anti-lynching law. In 1948 Truman proposed key items of the report to Congress but failed to overcome the resistance of Southern lawmakers.

In the postwar years most Americans looked optimistically toward the future. Unprecedented economic growth and spectacular technological progress promised new opportunities for everyone. Most African Americans shared the grand expectations of their white compatriots and were no longer willing to accept the racial caste system of the South. White supremacists, however, stubbornly resisted change, if necessary through violence. Yet in contrast to earlier decades the American people could no longer dismiss the "race question" as a regional problem. The advance of television, which entered 90 percent of American homes by the 1950s, created national news networks and produced vivid images of the crisis that unfolded as nonviolent civil rights activists confronted the massive resistance of white Southerners fighting desegregation. Watching news reports of police dogs attacking black schoolchildren during the 1963 desegregation marches in Birmingham, Alabama, made him "sick," President John F. Kennedy confessed. The news media had reason to report plenty of ugly stories and images documenting that both Judge Lynch and Jim Crow died hard.

Immediately after World War II, a wave of racist violence swept through the South as black veterans proudly donned their uniforms and demanded their rights as Americans citizens. In many communities former soldiers led voter registration drives demonstrating that African Americans were no longer willing to accept "their place" as second-class citizens. Fearing that voting was the first step toward racial integration and "miscegenation," white supremacists struck back. In the 1946 electoral campaigns, violent attacks on black voters became commonplace. In Georgia gubernatorial candidate Eugene Talmadge, a longtime standard-bearer of white supremacy, openly warned blacks to stay away from the polls. Some of his supporters celebrated Talmadge's victory by abusing African Americans who had tried to cast a ballot.

This climate of racial tension provided the background of a multiple slaying in Monroe, Georgia, in the summer of 1946. Roger Malcolm, a black sharecropper, got into a fight with Barney Hester, the son of his employer, possibly because the young white man had harassed Malcolm's pregnant wife Dorothy. Malcolm wounded Hester with his knife, albeit not seriously. While Hester went to the hospital, the black man went to jail, facing threats of retaliation from Barney Hester's friends. In this situation the Malcolms needed help. Dorothy Malcolm asked a white planter named J. Loy Harrison for work. Harrison, who also employed Dorothy's brother George Dorsey and his wife Mae, agreed to bail out Roger Malcolm. After he had posted bond for Malcolm, Harrison left Monroe with the two couples in his car. When the party came to a bridge across the Apalachee River, they were suddenly trapped by several cars and surrounded by a mob of roughly twenty men, according to the account Harrison later gave to the police. At first the attackers grabbed only the two black men, but when the women desperately protested the abduction of their husbands the mob leader ordered them taken out of the car too. The lynchers then pushed their victims forward into the woods and shot all four of them. Harrison later claimed that the mob allowed him to leave the scene after he had sworn that he did not recognize any of the men.

The murderers may have planned a "quiet lynching," but the quadruple slaying raised a national storm of indignation. President Truman

After their acquittal by an all-white jury, the lynchers of Willie Earle celebrate in the court room, Greenville, South Carolina, 1947.

directed the Department of Justice to investigate the case. FBI agents descended on Monroe but ran into a wall of silence and were unable to uncover any usable evidence. A federal grand jury called more than one hundred witnesses yet in the end issued no indictments. State prosecutors considered the case hopeless and declined to spend more time and effort on it. As the Monroe affair demonstrated, spectacle lynchings were no longer fashionable, but the culture of mob violence lingered on in the rural South, including the unwritten rule that white men would not punish other white men for abusing and killing black people.

Elsewhere the efforts to apprehend and punish lynchers proved more vigorous, though they also came no avail. In February 1947 a passenger robbed and stabbed to death a taxi driver in Greenville, South Carolina. Shortly after the murder, police arrested a suspect, a twenty-four-year-old black man named Willie Earle, and locked him in a jail in nearby Pickens. The following night a convoy of taxi drivers from Greenville drove to Pickens to avenge their colleague. Apparently the jailer did not offer even token resistance. The lynchers took Willie Earle across the Greenville county line where they beat, stabbed, and finally killed their victim with several shotgun blasts. When they were finished, they returned to Greenville for breakfast.

Twenty years earlier the coroner most likely would have ruled that Earle had suffered death at the hands of persons unknown, and that would have ended the investigation. But the times had changed. South Carolina's new governor, J. Strom Thurmond, immediately condemned the lynching, promised to bring the perpetrators to justice, and welcomed FBI assistance in the investigation. Thurmond was a segregationist and a states' rights advocate (the following year he ran for president on the ticket of the Dixiecrats, who had bolted the Democratic party because of Truman's liberal civil rights platform), but the governor was also committed to law and order and to a progressive image of his home state. Within a few days state and federal investigators arrested thirty-one suspects and obtained twenty-six signed confessions. Several statements identified the man who had fired the deadly shots.

In May the courthouse in Greenville became the site of what *Time* magazine called "the biggest lynching trial the South had ever known." All major national newspapers and magazines covered the proceedings; reports of the case made the news nationally as well as overseas. Armed with written confessions, the prosecution was confident that it could win at least some convictions. The defense, however, successfully played the race card, pleading with the all-white jury that the defendants had rendered their community a great service by eliminating a dangerous black criminal. One of the defense lawyers compared the killing of Willie Earle to the shooting of a "mad dog." Curiously, state law permitted the families of the defendants to sit next to them in the courtroom, thus creating a powerful visual image of the lynchers as staunch family men and well-respected community members. The strategy worked. The jury acquitted all defendants of all charges. The crowd in the courtroom greeted the verdict with wild cheers while the judge could barely conceal his disgust with this blatant defiance of the law.

In the Willie Earle case the state of South Carolina made a good-faith effort to bring the lynchers to justice, but the prosecution foundered on local resistance and tradition. White men would not convict other white men for visiting revenge upon a black criminal who had allegedly murdered their friend. The same pattern of local and racial solidarity determined the outcome of similar trials held in Southern courtrooms during the 1950s. Unquestionably the most prominent of these cases was the murder of Emmett Till in Money, Mississippi, in late August 1955. The events in remote Leflore County in the Mississippi Delta region appalled Americans throughout the country and made international headlines. Beyond this the story of Emmett Till, a fourteen-year-old black youth from Chicago who courted disaster by talking fresh to a white woman, has become enshrined in American memory as a symbol of racial injustice.

As in previous summers, in 1955 Till's mother, Mamie Till Bradley, sent her son on a vacation to Mississippi where he stayed with his great-uncle and –aunt, Moses and Elizabeth Wright. Spending his days with other black youths, including several of his cousins, the kid from Chicago tried to impress his friends by bragging about flings with white girls back home. Taking Emmett at his word, his companions dared him to walk into the local general store and ask the white cashier for a date. Of course this was a bad joke, but young Till did not wish to lose face and went into the store. There he and Carolyn Bryant, a twenty-one-year-old former beauty queen and the wife of the owner Roy Bryant, were alone for a few minutes. According to the white woman's testimony, Till bought bubble gum and suddenly squeezed her hand when she handed him the change, boldy asking, "How about a date, baby?" When she ran away, he allegedly touched her waist and "wolf-whistled" at her. It will never be known whether Till really acted this brazenly or merely stuttered a few embarrassed words, as his cousins later claimed. Whatever he did, the young boy from Chicago had inadvertently made the most dangerous mistake a black male could commit in the Deep South.

Trying to avoid trouble, Carolyn Bryant, though upset, decided not to tell her husband about the incident. But when Roy Bryant returned home in the evening he heard about the encounter anyway, supposedly from one of Till's cousins. In the heyday of Judge Lynch, the offended husband might have led a mob to punish Emmett Till for his insolence. Those days had passed, however. Nevertheless, knowing that the story had made the rounds in the local black community, Bryant believed he had to vindicate his honor as a Southern white man. Accompanied by his half-brother J. W. Milam, he broke into the Wrights' home in the middle of the night and demanded to see the boy who had allegedly harassed his wife. Despite the apologies of Till's relatives, the two intruders grabbed the young man and took him away. Three days later Emmett Till's body was found in the Tallahatchie River, maimed and bloated almost beyond recognition. Apparently the killers had beaten their victim relentlessly before shooting and then dumping him into the river with a weight tied around his neck.

The discovery of the corpse instantly brought the town of Money into the focus of the national media. Murdering an adolescent for a foolish joke cast a glaring light on the brutality of racism in the Magnolia State. In Chicago Emmett Till's aggrieved mother held an open-casket funeral service attended by ten thousand people and vowed that she would do anything to bring her son's slayers to justice. Outrage at the killing was universal among blacks and whites. No white Mississipian openly justified the murder.

The police quickly arrested Bryant and Milam and, remarkable by Mississippi standards, the grand jury indicted them for murder. In September 1955 the trial began in the town of Sumner, the Leflore County seat. Massive media interest in the case, including throngs of radio and television reporters, made Sumner "the most talked about town in the country," according to *Newsweek*. Would an all-white Mississippi jury convict two local white men for a crime against a black person, or would the traditional impulse to close ranks prevail? Despite threats to his life, Moses Wright testified against Bryant and Milam, who did not deny they had abducted Emmett Till but insisted they had only scared him a little and let him go unharmed. The defense surmised that the disfigured body found in the Tallahatchie River was not even Till's. The NAACP and other "northern radicals," the defendants' lawyers insinuated, had contrived a conspiracy to discredit Mississippi. Their appeal did not fall on deaf ears. After one hour of deliberation, the jury acquitted both men. Later one of the jurors related that the jury could have come out after ten minutes but took its time to make things look good.

If the verdict shocked Americans unfamiliar with the racist criminal justice system of the Deep South, the follow-up was even more dismaying. In January 1956 Bryant and Milam, immune from a second indictment for their crime, granted a paid interview to *Look* magazine in which they freely admitted to having killed Emmett Till. They had not planned to kill him, the men explained, but Till's defiant behavior and the picture of a white girl in his wallet had incited their implacable wrath. Said J. W. Milam in defending his deeds, "When a nigger even gets close to mentioning sex with a white woman, he's tired of living."

The NAACP and the African-American press called the death of Emmett Till a lynching while Mississippi authorities insisted it was an ordinary murder. Clearly the events differed from a "classic" lynching. There was no mob, though Bryant and Milam may have had help from their wives. Rather than publicly displaying the body of their victim, the killers disposed of the corpse secretly. The two men were prosecuted and indicted, and, except for a brief moment at the end of the trial, they were not celebrated as heroes. In fact the Bryant and Milam families left Mississippi shortly after the acquittal because their businesses went bankrupt and other whites ostracized them. Then again, the murderers had acted from the same ideology that had driven lynchers for more than a century. And the jurors acquitted them because they were still committed to the tradition of defending white supremacy at all costs.

The murder of Emmett Till was an act of personal revenge tolerated by the community, but it lacked key characteristics of popular justice. In contrast the lynching of "Mack" Charles Parker in Poplarville, Mississippi, in April 1959 revealed that the spirit of popular justice had not yet expired. Parker, a twenty-three-year-old black truck driver, stood accused of a particularly brutal rape that he had allegedly perpetrated on a white woman named June Walters in the presence of her little daughter. Although Parker maintained his innocence, the rape victim identified him as the assailant the day after the rape. At this point a police officer reportedly offered his gun to Walters's husband, who declined to shoot the suspect on the spot. To preempt a lynching, the sheriff of Pearl River County had the prisoner removed to Jackson until the start of the trial.

All local residents, black and white, expected a swift trial ending with a death sentence. But Parker's mother, worried that the state of Mississippi would railroad her son to the electric chair, hired an experienced black defense attorney, R. Jess Brown, who had argued civil rights cases for the NAACP. Brown immediately filed a motion to dismiss the case because no blacks had sat on the grand jury that indicted his client. Brown's tactics caused considerable alarm among local whites because recently a federal Court of Appeals had voided the death sentence of a black man from Mississippi for the same reason. Moreover Parker's legal counsel announced his intention to cross-examine June Walters. Fearing that an "impudent" black lawyer might publicly embarrass a white woman and aid a black rapist in escaping punishment, a mob of several local white men broke into the Poplarville jail on the night of April 25. They encountered no resistance from the guard, but Mack Parker fought back frantically. The lynchers had planned to hang their victim from a bridge across the Pearl River. Unable to restrain the sturdy black man, they instead killed him with several gunshots and dumped his body into the river. Nine days later the corpse was found.

The traditional coroner's statement that "unknown persons" had caused Parker's death no longer sufficed to end the affair. As soon as news of the abduction transpired, the FBI entered the case based on the 1932 Federal Kidnapping Act, passed after the spectacular kidnapping and murder of Charles Lindbergh, Jr., the little son of the famed aviator. The law allowed federal authorities to pursue kidnappers who had crossed state lines. Because the Pearl River borders Mississippi and Louisiana, the FBI took charge of the investigation. Over several weeks sixty FBI agents collected evidence and testimony on the lynching and produced a report of almost four hundred pages. But because federal agents could not prove that the lynchers had actually carried Parker into Louisiana, the Department of Justice did not seek indictments under federal law and instead handed the report to state authorities. The state district attorney, however, ignored the FBI investigation and withheld the report from the grand jury. Although it was an open secret that former deputy sheriff J. P. Walker had organized the lynching party, the jurors failed to issue any indictments. Even had the grand jury seen the FBI report, it is doubtful that the result would have differed. Whites of Pearl River County, though they did not necessarily support the lynching, had become so incensed by what they considered an FBI "invasion" that local pride seemed to demand obstruction of the prosecution. A later attempt by the Department of Justice to bring charges under federal law also failed.

Many white Southerners regarded the Emmett Till and Mack Parker cases as embarrassments that reinforced old stereotypes of the South as a hopelessly backward region populated by violent "rednecks." As much as they wished to share in American postwar prosperity and progress, however, the vast majority of white Southerners refused to consider substantial

racial change. They reacted with hostility and anxiety to the challenge
the civil rights movement mounted against the Jim Crow system in the
1950s. Opinion polls found that between 80 and 90 percent of white
Southerners opposed desegregation. One contemporary study estimated
that perhaps 25 percent of all white Southerners condoned violent resistance to racial integration. Not surprisingly then, when the U.S. Supreme
Court, in its momentous 1954 decision *Brown v. Board of Education of
Topeka, Kansas*, ordered the desegregation of public schools, a wave of
"massive resistance" ensued, including deadly terrorism and large-scale
riots. In some parts of the South the Ku Klux Klan experienced a revival
and thrived on brazen acts of racial violence.

Attacks on civil rights organizers occurred regularly before the *Brown*
decision. Because white supremacists viewed the NAACP in particular as
a conspiracy of Communists, Jews, and "outside agitators," many of the
association's activists faced constant threats to their lives. In September
1948, for example, Jim and John Johnson, two brothers who enjoyed a
reputation as trigger-happy racists, killed NAACP member Isaac Nixon of
Montgomery County, Georgia, for organizing a voter registration drive.
The Johnson brothers were indicted for murder but acquitted by an
all-white jury. In another incident occurring on Christmas Eve 1951, a
bomb exploded in the home of Harry T. Moore, president of the Florida
NAACP state conference, killing both Moore and his wife. No one was ever
charged with the crime.

After the *Brown* decision, both black activism and white supremacist terrorism burgeoned in the Deep South. In 1955 Mississippi's NAACP
organized a voter registration campaign that succeeded in signing up
black voters in some of the most repressive areas of the state. The backlash followed quickly. In May the Reverend George Lee, who had led
the registration drive in Humphreys County in the Delta region, was
killed in a drive-by shooting. The local white press dismissed the assassination as a traffic accident while the sheriff cynically declared the
shotgun pellets in Lee's face to be "fillings from his teeth" and declined
to launch an investigation. In August an unidentified assailant gunned
down Lamar Smith, a sixty-three-year-old farmer who had been active
in mobilizing black voters in front of the courthouse in Brookhaven
in southern Mississippi. Although the sheriff had reportedly watched
a white man covered with blood absconding from the scene, he did not

pursue the suspect. A subsequent arrest of three men in connection with the murder resulted in no indictments.

These murders were not lynchings in the traditional sense of the word. The assassins ambushed their victims and fled the scene of the crime. Obviously they did not pretend to mete out popular justice. Isaac Nixon, Harry Moore, George Lee, and Lamar Smith had committed no crime other than to defy white supremacy by demanding their civil and political rights. Yet racist terrorists who fought nonviolent civil rights activists with dynamite and bullets instead of the rope and the faggot could rely on tacit backing from local white communities as well as the collusion of local law enforcement.

In addition to the assassination of individual civil rights workers, massive resistance against desegregation produced startling images of rioting mobs. In September 1957 Americans and the world watched with disbelief as jeering crowds attempted to block the integration of Central High School in Little Rock, Arkansas, forcing President Eisenhower to dispatch the U.S. Army's 101st Airborne Division to protect nine black schoolchildren from violent attacks. Five years later the attempt of a black student to enroll at the University of Mississippi pursuant to a court order provoked a riot that one eyewitness described as resembling a "state-sized civil war." Two people died in the confrontation between federal marshals and segregationist rioters, but many more people might have lost their lives if the army had not restored order. Still, this violent resistance to racial change could not halt the black freedom movement; on the contrary, it speeded the demise of Jim Crow. Racist terrorism and riots thoroughly discredited the segregationist cause in the eyes of most Americans, including many white Southerners, forcing the federal government to intervene, and paving the way for the sweeping civil rights legislation of the mid-1960s which outlawed racial segregation and secured black voting rights in the South.

The triple murder of three civil rights activists in Mississippi during the "Freedom Summer" of 1964 was a key event that helped turn the tide of public opinion. For years the civil rights movement had plugged away at increasing the number of black voters in Mississippi, where merely 5 percent of all eligible African Americans were registered. Exasperated with the harassment of white supremacists and the indifference of the federal government, civil rights leaders decided to bring into the state hundreds of white volunteers from the North—mostly college students—to conduct registration drives and education projects among the rural black population during the summer of 1964. This "invasion" by Northern "radicals," among them many young white women who freely socialized with young black men, infuriated white supremacists. Sooner or later a terrible incident was likely. On June 21, 1964, three volunteers disappeared after they had taught "freedom schools" in Philadelphia in Neshoba County. One of them, twenty-one-year-old James Chaney, was a black student from Meridian, Mississippi; the other two were Jewish Americans from New York, twenty-year-old Andrew Goodman and twenty-four-year-old Michael Schwerner.

As the FBI investigation later revealed, the three activists became the targets of a conspiracy by the local Ku Klux Klan and the Neshoba County police. Deputy Sheriff Cecil Price first arrested the civil rights workers on spurious speeding charges, then held them in jail for several hours without allowing them to telephone their friends. After nightfall he suddenly ordered them to pay a fine and depart. Shortly after the volunteers had left Philadelphia, the deputy, accompanied by a group of Klansmen, again pulled over their car and hauled them away to a hidden place off the highway. Yelling racial slurs at their victims, they shot Schwerner, Goodman, and Chaney execution style. The Klansmen had carefully planned ahead. They used a bulldozer to bury the three bodies under a dam, then burned the car and hid it in a swamp. It took six weeks until the FBI discovered the remains of the three men on August 4, following a tip from a paid informant.

As soon as the leaders of the Freedom Summer project realized that the three activists had disappeared in Neshoba County, they contacted the FBI and demanded action. The fact that two of the missing persons were white Northerners may have put special pressure on the federal government. For weeks the case figured prominently in the national news. Yet President Lyndon B. Johnson needed little prodding. Trying to demonstrate his commitment to advancing civil rights and quelling lawlessness, Johnson ordered the FBI to launch an all-out search for Chaney, Goodman, and Schwerner. Largely because of leads the Bureau received from informers inside the Klan, federal agents first recovered the car and then found the bodies. After four months of investigation they arrested nineteen suspects, including Deputy Sheriff Price and his superior, Sheriff Lawrence Rainey.

As expected, the criminal prosecution of the conspirators proved an uphill battle. Because the Department of Justice did not trust Mississippi's resolve to try the defendants for murder, it sought an indictment under federal law, charging them with a conspiracy "under color of law" to deprive the three victims of their civil rights by murdering them. It took an affirmative ruling by the U.S. Supreme Court, delivered in March 1966, to move the trial forward. Still, conviction in federal court was not a foregone conclusion, given that the judge, William H. Cox, was an avowed segregationist and the jury consisted of twelve white Mississippians. Remarkably, on October 20, 1967, the jury returned guilty verdicts against seven of the defendants, including Deputy Sheriff Price. Sentences varied between three and ten years in a federal penitentiary. The *New York Times* editorialized that the convictions signaled "the quiet revolution that is taking place in Southern attitudes." Then again, the outcome of the trial hardly amounted to a triumph of justice. Sheriff Rainey and a local minister named Edgar Ray Killen, who were widely regarded as the masterminds behind the murders, went free. None of the convicted men served their full sentences.

Many historians consider the 1964 triple slaying in Neshoba County as a lynching because the victims undeniably died at the hands of a mob—albeit a small one compared to the standards of the early twentieth century—and because the lynchers acted in collusion with law officers. Moreover in the eyes of the murderers their deed constituted an act of communal self-defense because Goodman and Schwerner, in particular, had come from New York to stir up trouble among the state's black population and to destroy the so-called "Southern way of life." Presumably many white Mississippians, who felt under siege from a hostile federal government and the national news media, agreed that the three slain civil rights workers had brought the tragedy upon themselves and that the civil rights movement was responsible for destroying "harmonious" race relations in the South. But the case also demonstrated that the bonds between the self-proclaimed vindicators of the community and their presumed constituents had weakened. By the mid-sixties most white Southerners had become exasperated with the ongoing violence and wanted a return to law and order. Extremists such as the lynchers of Neshoba County could no longer count on impunity, if only because ordinary white Southerners understood that brash lawlessness threw their communities into turmoil and provoked further federal intervention.

Still, racist terrorism against black civil rights activists continued. In January 1966, Vernon Dahmer, an NAACP leader from Hattiesburg, Mississippi, fought back against a gang of Klansmen who firebombed his home. Dahmer died of his burns one day after the attack. Six months later snipers wounded James Meredith, who had integrated the University of Mississippi in 1962, when he began a "March Against Fear" through his home state. Most dramatically, the assassination of Martin Luther King, Jr., America's most prominent and revered black leader, in Memphis, Tennessee, on April 4, 1968, reminded African Americans that in the struggle for civil rights "murder may come at any time," as NAACP leader Roy Wilkins wrote in his obituary for the martyred civil rights hero. Yet Wilkins, with bitter cyncism, also noted that King's assassination represented "change." "It used to be that a white killer had nothing to fear. In fact, if he announced a projected killing of a Negro, he could recruit a band of assistants," Wilkins observed, recalling the heyday of Judge Lynch. "Things are different today. Assassins make plans . . . they seek cover. . . . They hide because in this time there is no guarantee that law officers will not track them down, or that courts and juries will not convict." Of course there was no guarantee of prosecution and conviction, either.

In the 1970s race relations in America entered a new phase. Many African-American activists made the transition from protest to politics, and most former supporters of segregation, often grudgingly, accepted that the Jim Crow system had to go. Racial hatred and violence did not disappear, but they became increasingly marginalized. Lynching as popular justice had rested on the participation and support, or at least on the acquiescence, of local communities willing to concede that the lynchers represented the "people's" true feelings about certain types of crimes and criminals. Throughout the twentieth century this attitude had gradually lost its hold on American culture and become closely associated with the violent defense of white supremacy. The civil rights revolution served to discredit open racism. Although many white conservatives opposed what they called "forced integration" or "reverse discrimination," they nevertheless took pains to distance themselves from extremists who clung tenaciously to the white supremacist past. In March 1981 the death of Michael Donald, a young black man, at the hands of two Klansmen in Mobile, Alabama, tragically highlighted these changes.

On the night of March 20, Henry F. Hays and James "Tiger" Knowles, members of the Mobile Ku Klux Klan, spotted Donald, a nineteen-year-old African-American student, walking the streets of a black neighborhood. Pretending to ask for directions, they lured Donald toward their car and then forced him into the vehicle at gunpoint. The two Klansmen took their victim to a remote place outside the city, tied a rope around his neck, and beat him unconscious. To make sure Donald was dead, they cut his throat. Hiding the body in the trunk of their car, the killers returned to the home of Hays's family where they hanged their victim from a tree across the street and left it dangling until it was found the next morning. Evidently the Klansmen were not interested in covering up their crime. On the contrary, their actions suggest that they deliberately created a lynching scene. Their motive for killing Donald, whom they chose randomly and had never met before, also fit in the picture. Knowles and Hays made their victim the scapegoat for an affair that underscored the demise of the old racist order.

Shortly before the two Klansmen killed Michael Donald, the second trial against Josephus Anderson had ended with a hung jury. Anderson, a black man, had been charged with the murder of a white police officer. But at two consecutive trials, the second one held in Mobile, racially integrated juries failed to agree on a verdict. In the heyday of Judge Lynch, such a "miscarriage of justice," as the Klansmen saw it, would have been inconceivable. Either Anderson would have been lynched right away or he would have been quickly convicted and executed. After racial integration had been "forced" upon the South, white supremacists concluded that blacks could get away with murdering whites because black jurors allegedly refused to convict one of their own—an intolerable reversal of Jim Crow justice. Yet the days of the lynch mob had passed. Many whites in Alabama may have resented the outcome of the Anderson trial, but it no longer occurred to them that they had a right or even a duty to take the law into their hands.

All the same, the Klan leaders of Mobile were unwilling to face the new reality and called for revenge. Allegedly Bennie J. Hays, Henry's

father, personally ordered the killing of a black man to serve notice on
the black community that the Klan had not lost its mettle. By deciding
to kill the next African-American man they could find, Henry Hays and
James Knowles, perhaps unwittingly, remained true to the spirit of lynch
law. In the old Jim Crow South, racial lynchings had never simply been
punishment of individuals but a warning to others and an affirmation of
white supremacy. In this sense all black lynching victims were scapegoats,
regardless of whether they had committed the crimes of which they were
accused. And yet the murder of Michael Donald was not so much a reen-
actment of the past, when Judge Lynch had reigned supreme, as a defiant
protest against white Alabamians' forgetfulness of their duties in service
to race and tradition. By hanging their victim in front of the Hays home,
the perpetrators seemed to challenge the white community of Mobile
whether they had the determination to prosecute the Klan.

At first the local police denied the racial background of the slaying and
speculated that black drug dealers had dispatched Donald. It took demonstrations by angry African Americans and the involvement of the FBI
to put Mobile law enforcers on the right track. Eventually police arrested
Henry Hays and James Knowles. Because Knowles agreed to testify
against his accomplice, the prosecution had a solid case. At the 1984 trial
the jury sentenced Henry Hays to life in prison, but, pursuant to a new
state law, the judge overruled the jurors and imposed the death penalty.
The Alabama Supreme Court confirmed the decision. On June 6, 1997,
the state of Alabama put Henry Hays to death in the electric chair; he became the first white man executed in Alabama for killing a black person
since 1913. In addition, Michael Donald's mother sued the United Klans
of America, headquartered in Tuscaloosa, Alabama, for complicity in the
wrongful death of her son. In 1987 an all-white jury awarded her seven
million dollars in damages, bankrupting Alabama's Klan.

In order to underline the enormity of the crime, many observers called
the murder of Michael Donald a lynching. In fact Donald's killers and
their instigators wanted to be seen as lynchers, that is to say as enforcers
of popular justice and keepers of tradition. But their claim no longer res-
onated among the larger society. As Americans embraced racial equality
and diversity as part of their national identity, the once-respectable defenders of America as a "white man's country" became the lunatic fringe,
malcontents who committed "hate crimes" to vent their anger and frus-

tration against minorities. Beginning in the late 1970s, activists began lobbying for legislation against the harassment of and violent attacks on people because of their race, skin color, religion, national origin, or sexual orientation. The purpose of these laws has been to enable jurors and judges to impose harsher sentences for such crimes and to oblige state and federal authorities to keep track of them, as, for example, prescribed in the Hate Crime Statistics Act passed by Congress in 1990.

In some respects the debates over hate crime legislation resembled the controversy over anti-lynching legislation in the early twentieth century. Critics denounced them as special privilege for vociferous minorities. In an age when even former segregationists shunned open racism, opposition focused on the inclusion of sexual orientation. Jesse Helms, the conservative senator from North Carolina, succeeded in adding a section to the 1990 act, stating that the law did not "promote or encourage homosexuality." Opponents also argued that hate crime laws were unconstitutional because they violated the First Amendment protection of free speech and punished beliefs.

In contrast to the long and abortive struggle for a federal anti-lynching bill, the campaign for hate crime laws succeeded relatively quickly, both at the state and federal levels, beginning in 1981 when Washington and Oregon adopted such laws. In 1994 Congress ordered the enhancement of sentences for hate crimes punishable under federal law. Whether these laws have been effective remains uncertain. Surely they have not ended hate crimes. Perhaps their most important consequence has been the repudiation of the beliefs and attitudes that nourished lynching and mob violence for so long.

In 1998 Americans were shocked by the news of a particularly gruesome murder of a black man in Jasper, Texas. Many people thought it resembled a lynching. Three white supremacists abducted forty-nine-year-old James Byrd, Jr., beat him ferociously, tied him behind their car, and dragged him for several miles until his head was severed. As in the Michael Donald case, the killers had randomly chosen their victim and, after their arrest, proudly posed as defenders of white honor. Again, there is no question that the three men, social outcasts and ex-convicts aged between twenty-three and thirty-one, tried to make sense of their actions by claiming the mantle of Judge Lynch. But outside their own delusions and fantasies, this world no longer existed. Condemnation was universal, and criminal justice officials dealt quickly with James Byrd's murderers. Following their arrest and trial, one man received life in prison while his two accomplices were sentenced to death. The case also led to tougher hate crime legislation in Texas, despite initial opposition from then-governor George W. Bush. In 2009 Congress strengthened federal hate crime statutes in a new Hate Crimes Prevention Act, named after James Byrd and Matthew Shepard, a homosexual hate crime victim murdered by homophobes in Wyoming in 1998.

By the late twentieth century lynching as the practice of extralegal punishment meted out by the "people" had faded into history. Yet the term "lynching" has continued to enjoy wide currency in American debates on crime, punishment, and race relations. It has also served as a metaphor to denounce all kinds of abuse, even if no physical violence was involved. During his 1991 confirmation hearings before the Senate Judiciary Committee, Supreme Court nominee Clarence Thomas, a black conservative, cast himself as the victim of a "high-tech lynching." Thomas faced accusations of sexual harassment from Anita Hill, a black lawyer and Thomas's former special assistant at the U.S. Department of Education. Referring to voyeuristic media reports on these accusations, Thomas cited the history of black men being lynched for alleged sexual transgressions. Then again, most observers, regardless of whether they supported Thomas's nomination to the Court, insisted that he deserved a fair hearing and must be presumed innocent. Thomas had every opportunity to defend himself, and eventually the Senate confirmed his nomination.

Not surprisingly, interracial violent crime has also repeatedly provoked the use of lynching as a rhetorical weapon. During the sensational O. J. Simpson trial of 1995, in which the former football player and movie actor stood accused of murdering his ex-wife Nicole Brown and her friend Ronald Goldman, defense lawyers portrayed O. J. Simpson as the victim of a racist police force trying to frame a black man in the murder of a white woman, conjuring up the darkest days of lynching and racial prejudice. On the other hand, some feminists have claimed that Nicole Brown must be considered a lynch victim because her alleged killer went free.

Because it brings to mind a host of horrible images, the term "lynching" lends itself to polemical use. Like genocide, lynching epitomizes evil.

If people wish to express their condemnation of a terrible act of violence, they call it a lynching. But the tendency to make lynching into some kind of "gold standard" for suffering may lead to trivializing history. If the public inquisition of Clarence Thomas's conduct toward a female employee was tantamount to a "lynching," what happened to Sam Hose, Jesse Washington, Mary Turner, Emmett Till, and countless others who were hanged, riddled with bullets, and beaten or burned to death? Nor does it diminish the suffering of Michael Donald and James Byrd, Jr., or, for that matter, the culpability and depravity of their killers, to point out the differences between a lynching and a hate crime.

9

Lynching in American Memory and Culture

ON JUNE 13, 2005, the United States Senate, by unanimous voice vote, passed a resolution for the purpose of "Apologizing to the victims of lynching and the descendants of those victims for the failure of the Senate to enact anti-lynching legislation." The resolution acknowledged that African Americans had been the principal group of lynch victims and that lynching had been "the ultimate expression of racism in the United States." The senators also recognized that "protection against lynching was the minimum and most basic of Federal responsibilities" but that their predecessors had failed to live up to that responsibility, though nearly two hundred anti-lynching bills had been introduced in Congress during the first half of the twentieth century. Coming to terms with the history of lynching, the resolution asserted, was essential for the United States in order to champion human rights abroad credibly and to achieve racial reconciliation at home. By rendering an official apology the Senate also wished "to ensure that these tragedies will be neither forgotten nor repeated."

The Senate apology was not an unprecedented act. In 1976 President Gerald Ford had symbolically revoked the 1942 executive order by President Franklin D. Roosevelt calling for the summary internment of Japanese Americans on the West Coast after the Japanese attack on Pearl Harbor. Four years later the U.S. Congress commissioned an inquiry that found that the internment had been a "grave injustice" motivated by "racial prejudice and war hysteria." Pursuant to this report, in 1988 Congress passed the Civil Liberties Act that included an official apology by the U.S. government and a $1.6 billion fund earmarked for individual compensation to surviving victims of the internment and for educational purposes.

Senator Mary Landrieu of Louisiana (who sponsored the 2005 apology by the U.S. Senate) with the survivor of a 1930 lynching.

The United States has not been alone among nations in revisiting past injustices. In the 1990s many nations engaged in debates about righting the wrongs of history, inspired by the end of the cold war, the breakdown of Communist dictatorships, and the fall of the South African apartheid regime. The willingness to face painful historical legacies and to admit guilt became a new standard of international morality. The nineties turned into a decade of apologies for historical injustices. The Vatican officially apologized for the historical anti-Semitism of the Catholic church. British Prime Minister Tony Blair expressed remorse over his country's failure to aid the population of Ireland during the terrible famine of the 1840s, and French President Jacques Chirac apologized for the collaboration of French authorities in the deportation of French Jews to the Nazi death camps during the German occupation from 1940 to 1944.

Critics have complained that apologies remain hollow gestures unless they are followed by material redress. Responding to international pressure, especially from the United States, Germany in 2000 agreed to compensate surviving forced laborers of the Third Reich. At the same time

South Africa grappled with the legacy of its former apartheid regime, especially with the question of how to bring the perpetrators of human rights violations to justice without jeopardizing the goal of racial reconciliation.

International debates over compensating "slave laborers" under the Nazis and the work of the South African Truth and Reconciliation Commission have provided new impulses for African-American activists to demand that American society, at long last, accept responsibility for centuries of slavery as well as for the discrimination and violence blacks suffered in the age of Jim Crow. A large majority of Americans, however, have rejected the idea of paying reparations for slavery. Obviously all slaves and slaveholders are dead and can neither be compensated nor made to pay. The claim that present-day African Americans still suffer from the consequences of slavery strikes most Americans as implausible and has made little headway politically.

Reckoning with the legacy of racial segregation and lynching is a different matter. The civil rights reforms that ended the Jim Crow system occurred only in the 1960s. Many older Americans vividly remember the postwar era when white supremacists and the civil rights movement battled over America's future. By now the movement's heroic struggle for racial justice has become a celebrated part of American history. Yet Americans have found it easier to honor Martin Luther King, Jr., by designating his birthday a national holiday than to confront the history of lynching and racial violence. Historians have only begun to look seriously at lynching from the late 1980s on, and their work has had a limited impact on the historical awareness of ordinary Americans.

In 2000, however, an exhibition of lynching photography unexpectedly aroused the interest of the general public and the media. Over fifteen years James Allen, a white antiques dealer from Atlanta, had collected photographs of lynchings he found in family albums, attics, and flea markets. The images documented lynchings of black and white victims from the late nineteenth to the mid-twentieth centuries throughout the United States, though most pictures illustrated mob killings in the South. To make his collection accessible to the public, Allen persuaded a small gallery in Manhattan to display it. As soon as the exhibition opened in January 2000, it attracted large crowds, forcing the gallery owner to limit the number of visitors to two hundred a day. All major news media reported on the startling photographs. To accommodate the crowds, the New York Historical Society agreed to accept the exhibition under the name "Without Sanctuary: Lynching Photography in America." The title, Allen explained, reflected the fact that most of the photographs had been reproduced for commercial reasons. "Even dead," he writes, "the victims were without sanctuary."

Between 2001 and 2005 the organizers sent the exhibition on a national tour that included Atlanta, Chicago, and Jackson, Mississppi. James Allen also published a book with roughly one hundred images that has gone through nine editions so far, and he created an interactive website. Many viewers have been appalled not only by the macabre images of dangling and mangled bodies but by the sight of ordinary citizens proudly posing in front of lynch victims. "I cannot believe the photos I saw," one visitor of the "Without Sanctuary" website confessed, "and how people could enjoy watching another living, breathing human, be tortured and killed for a crime that they may or may not have committed." After viewing the photographs, Senator Mary Landrieu, a Louisiana Democrat, decided to sponsor the Senate apology of 2005; the resolution explicitly praises the exhibition for fostering "greater awareness and proper recognition of the victims of lynching."

The "Without Sanctuary" exhibition and the Senate resolution were attempts to incorporate the history of lynching into American memory. There have also been efforts to seek compensation for the victims of lynching and racial violence. The most publicized case of financial recompense occurred in Florida in the early 1990s, when the state legislature awarded $2.1 million to the survivors of the 1923 Rosewood massacre. Sparked by rumors that a black man had raped a white woman, a mob lynched a resident of the all-black hamlet of Rosewood in north central Florida. When the black community fought back, hundreds of white men from the vicinity descended on Rosewood, staging a riot that lasted for several days and claimed the lives of at least six blacks and two whites. The assailants burned down the entire village and drove out its population. No one ever returned to Rosewood, and the incident was later surrounded by silence.

In 1993, however, survivors who as children were displaced from their homes sought compensation for property loss and emotional trauma. The Florida legislature commissioned a report by historians who confirmed that officers of the law had colluded with the mob in destroying Rosewood. In response to the report, the legislature in 1994 acknowledged a "moral obligation" and passed a bill to compensate survivors and those descendants of the Rosewood victims who could demonstrate property loss as a result of their family's expulsion. The statute also established a scholarship fund for the offspring of former Rosewood residents. In a similar vein the Oklahoma legislature in 2001 appropriated an educational fund for the descendants of black residents of Greenwood, a black district of Tulsa and the scene of a murderous race riot in 1921. Unlike Florida, Oklahoma refused to make direct payments to survivors and their progeny.

Opponents of the Rosewood bill warned that compensation for an injustice that had occurred seventy years earlier might set a precedent for reparations for slavery for all blacks. As in the case of the Japanese-American internment, political support for the Rosewood claimants hinged on the fact of identifiable surviving victims of the riot. Limiting compensation to survivors of historical injustices precludes financial redress for lynch victims because few of them survived their encounter with the mob. Still, there were exceptions. In 1930 James Cameron, a black man, was nearly lynched along with two other blacks in Marion, Indiana, for the murder of a white man, when suddenly an unidentified person shouted that Cameron was innocent. Miraculously the mob let him go. Cameron never sued for damages, but he spent much of his life telling his story. He wrote a self-published book and opened a small local museum in Milwaukee, Wisconsin, dedicated to the history of lynching. Fortunately Cameron lived long enough to witness the 2005 Senate apology as a visitor in the U.S. Capitol. One year later he died at age ninety-two.

The passage of time has also been a major impediment in bringing lynchers to justice in the post–Jim Crow era. As the 2005 Senate resolution correctly pointed out, "99 percent of all perpetrators of lynching escaped from punishment." Nothing can be done to change this historical fact. Like their victims, most lynchers are long dead. Nevertheless civil rights activists, investigative journalists, and prosecutors have successfully pressed for a reopening of some of the most notorious cases of racist terrorism committed during the civil rights era.

In 1994 an interracial jury in Mississippi convicted Byron De La Beckwith of first-degree murder in the assassination of Medgar Evers, a Mississippi NAACP leader, in June 1963. In 1964 two trials against De La Beckwith had ended with hung juries, though the Klansman had openly boasted of the murder. In 1998 Mississippi retried Samuel Bowers, a former Imperial Wizard of the Ku Klux Klan, for the 1966 mob killing of NAACP leader Vernon Dahmer in Hattiesburg. While four trials in the late 1960s had resulted in mistrials, the 1998 jury sentenced Bowers to life in prison for instigating a group of Klansmen to firebomb Dahmer's home and kill him. Between 1970 and 1976 Bowers had already served time in federal prison for his part in the 1964 murder of James Chaney, Andrew Goodman, and Michael Schwerner in Neshoba County. In 2005 that case made headlines again when a majority-white jury convicted Edgar Ray Killen, a Baptist preacher, of manslaughter for masterminding the mob killing. The judge sentenced the eighty-year-old man to sixty years in prison. Killen's 1967 trial had produced a deadlocked jury.

In 2004 the Department of Justice reopened the murder case of Emmett Till, the Chicago teenager killed in Money, Mississippi, in 1955 for making inappropriate remarks to a white woman. In the following decades about 150 history books, novels, poems, plays, songs, and movie scripts enshrined Emmett Till's fate in American cultural memory. Reinvestigating his death was a symbolic act and attracted much attention. Although Roy Bryant and J. W. Milam, Till's confessed killers who were acquitted by an all-white jury, had died years before, investigators attempted to find out if other people had been involved in the killing. Authorities ordered the exhumation and autopsy of Till's body, but the investigation produced no new evidence, let alone criminal charges.

The reopening of cases dating back several decades entails enormous problems, including the death of witnesses and the loss of evidence. Moreover legal barriers, such as the statute of limitations, restrict criminal prosecutors in bringing charges. Critics have therefore questioned the wisdom of what they see as resurrecting old ghosts. Nevertheless in 2008 Congress passed the "Emmett Till Unsolved Civil Rights Crime Act," creating two new offices in the Department of Justice charged with reinvestigating pre-1970 cases. The law's mandate will expire in 2017.

The legal consequences of such actions are less important than their symbolic message that the victims of racist violence have not been forgotten. Public recognition of victimhood and suffering has been a major goal in the quest for historical justice in the United States and internationally. Honoring the victims' memory, the argument holds, will restore their dignity and promote reconciliation. Many advocates of this approach welcome apologies from national leaders but insist that facing the truth and, as the next step, healing old wounds must be local concerns. One way of acknowledging the victims of lynchings and hate crimes at the local level has been to dedicate public spaces in their memory. Hattiesburg, Mississippi, for example, named a street and a park, including a memorial, in honor of Vernon Dahmer; in 2006 Mobile, Alabama, renamed a street after Michael Donald, randomly killed by two Klansmen in 1981. But support for recovering the memory of lynchings and racial violence is far from unanimous. Many white Americans would prefer to let bygones be bygones.

Studies of how local communities remember lynchings have identified a conspicuous gap between the collective memories of blacks and whites. Among African Americans, stories of lynchings are part of oral traditions passed on in families. Yet blacks are reluctant to share their stories with whites, perhaps mirroring the times when speaking out on lynching could be very dangerous. In contrast, whites often claim ignorance or amnesia. As one elderly woman from South Carolina informed an interviewer: "There were lynchings in the county in my lifetime, but I did not see them. I heard about them. I do not remember the names or anything about the lynchings. I just heard that they happened." There is no reason to question the personal sincerity of such statements because collective denial always was an important part of lynching. Once law and order had returned, the blame fell on "parties unknown" and "out-of-town troublemakers." Even today some whites refuse to see African Americans killed by lynch mobs as victims who deserve to be honored. They see them rather as criminals who succumbed to rough popular justice. When a 2007 article in the *Charleston City Paper* reminded the readers of the 1947 lynching of Willie Earle, the black man killed by a mob of taxi drivers for allegedly murdering one of their colleagues in Greenville, South Carolina, one letter writer protested: "It was my great-grandfather, Thomas Watson Brown, who was the cab driver that was murdered by the poor Wille Earl Ray [sic]. Why is there such focus on the death of Willie Earl Ray. . . and NOT [on] the man HE MURDERED?"

Because of this racially fragmented historical memory, attempts to commemorate lynchings may easily result in divisions rather than reconciliation. In September 2003 an interracial group of ministers in Marion, Indiana, proposed to hold a ceremonial atonement for the 1930 lynching of two black men, the same lynching from which James Cameron escaped. Yet the reaction among most whites and blacks was less than enthusiastic. Many Marion residents preferred to "leave it alone." African Americans, in particular, objected to putting up a plaque that, while acknowledging that "hatred, violence, and bigotry" had scarred the town, avoided any reference to the 1930 incident as well as the word "lynching." White opponents of the commemoration contended that present-day whites were not responsible for the lynching and owned no one an apology. Eventually the ministers held an atonement service. No historical marker commemorates the 1930 lynching in Marion.

The dispute in Marion illustrates that historical memory has more to do with negotiating the present than with remembering the past. Far from automatically producing healing and closure, efforts to come to terms with a painful history inevitably spark controversy about whose memories should be privileged. Many white Americans condemn lynching as a terrible deviation from American ideals, but they also insist that the nation has changed and should not dwell on its past sins forever. In contrast, many African Americans consider lynching the epitome of a century-long history of racial oppression that has left an indelible legacy on race relations in American society. James Cameron called his lynching museum in Milwaukee the Black Holocaust Museum because he wanted to send the message that African Americans should be entitled to the same recognition as victims of crimes against humanity as the Jewish victims of Nazi death camps. Other black reparation activists have appropriated the language of the Holocaust for their own causes. But the Holocaust analogy has not proven conducive to a fruitful conversation about how to incorporate the history of lynching into American memory. Most white Americans—and most historians—reject analogies between American racism and slavery on the one hand and Nazi Germany's genocidal murder of six million European Jews in less than five years on the other. In addition to equating crimes of different magnitude and character, the polemical use of Holocaust terminology provides those Americans who would like to forget about racist violence in American history with an excuse for ignoring the cultural legacies of lynching altogether.

Today Americans repudiate lynching as a national disgrace that belongs to the dustbin of an unfortunate past. But while racism is officially discredited in the multicultural society of the twenty-first century, some legacies of popular justice linger on and continue to enjoy considerable support among many Americans. In particular, the tradition of popular justice manifests itself in two salient features of American culture, at least in comparison to all other Western democracies.

First, the United States maintains the most draconian criminal justice system in the Western world, epitomized by the death penalty and the highest incarceration rate worldwide. The American penchant for harsh retributive justice reflects the popular-justice ideal that in punishing criminals the state must execute the will of the people. Second, no other Western nation entertains such a wide-ranging tolerance for private violence, including a broad concept of legitimate self-defense and virtually unrestricted access to firearms for ordinary citizens. The underlying belief that citizens cannot trust the state with a monopoly of force but must be prepared to defend themselves against both criminals and a tyrannical government is deeply rooted in the vigilante tradition and the myth of the frontier.

As a ritual of retribution, the death penalty has had a close historical relationship with lynching. In the first half of the twentieth century, extralegal mob justice declined in part because legal executions became a substitute. Many Americans remained convinced that the forestalling of mob violence demanded the death penalty. When in 1972 the Supreme Court temporarily suspended capital punishment because of the arbitrary ways in which it was being administered, Justice Potter Stewart explained why he did not object to the death penalty on principle: "The instict for retribution is part of the nature of man," Stewart reasoned. "When people begin to believe the organized society is unwilling or unable to impose upon criminal offenders the punishment they 'deserve,' then there are sown the seeds of anarchy—of self-help, vigilante justice, and lynch law." Four years later the Supreme Court reinstated capital punishment after several states had revised their death penalty statutes. Since then state and federal authorities have executed roughly twelve hundred persons, including about four hundred African Americans. Indisputably the death penalty enjoys broad popular support. Responding to a crime wave during the 1970s and 1980s, up to 80 percent of Americans told pollsters that they favored capital punishment for convicted murderers. In recent years support has declined to an average of 65 percent, still a solid majority. Meanwhile more and more countries have abolished the death penalty either in law or in practice. In 2009 only eighteen countries worldwide carried out official executions, with China, Iran, Iraq, and Saudi Arabia leading the way, followed by the United States.

American proponents of the death penalty remain undisturbed by the international company they keep, and they deny any historical continuity with lynch law. Capital punishment in America, defenders argue, represents a legitimate and essential instrument of criminal justice. The Supreme Court has never declared the death penalty per se a violation of the Eighth Amendment, which prohibits cruel and unusual punishment; executions are carried out pursuant to laws passed by democratically elected legislatures; defendants in capital cases enjoy all protections of due process and have the right to appeal their sentences before state and federal courts. In short, death penalty supporters consider legal executions the opposite of mob violence. They admit that, historically, capital punishment was used in a patently racist fashion, but they insist that in the post–civil rights era the death penalty has become "color-blind." Although studies have shown that black defendants convicted for murdering white persons are significantly more likely to receive a death sentence than whites who murder blacks, a Supreme Court majority has consistently refused to strike down capital punishment as racially discriminatory. Statistical proof of discrimination, the Court has maintained, is irrelevant; petitioners must demonstrate that they have personally experienced intentional racial discrimination during their trial.

In contrast, the historian Michael Pfeifer argues "that the history of lynching and the history of the death penalty in the United States are deeply and hopelessly entangled." Critics contend that capital punishment today, even when inflicted by the pseudo-sanitary procedure of lethal injection, serves the same archaic concept of popular vengeance and disproportionately targets social outcasts and racial minorities—as did Judge Lynch in his heyday. The fact that more than 40 percent of all death-row inmates are black and that the Southern states account for nearly 90 percent of all executions since 1976 demonstrates a striking historical continuity between lynching and the death penalty that cannot be dismissed as coincidence. The death penalty, the Reverend Jesse Jackson asserts, is a direct successor to lynch law and the "legal lynchings" of the Jim Crow era. Critics of capital punishment also see the death penalty as a dangerous instrument in the hands of a potentially oppressive government. Given the common distrust of government among Americans, including many of those who favor the death penalty, it is amazing that most citizens are willing to grant government power over life and death.

At the same time many supporters of a strong government that is "tough on crime" are also firm believers in the vigilante tradition, according to which citizens have a right and duty to take the law into their own hands if the need arises. Since the 1980s extremist militia groups have repeatedly staged violent standoffs with state and federal law enforcement agencies, claiming to defend the liberty of the people against what they see as as the tyranny of government in the United States. In recent years vigilante groups have begun to patrol the U.S. border with Mexico in an effort to track down illegal immigrants. Their action, they argue, is a democratically inspired grassroots project to enforce the law that the government is either unwilling or unable to enforce. In the view of these self-appointed border patrols, protecting themselves against an invasion of immigrants amounts to legitimate self-defense of the people.

The American vigilante tradition requires a good citizen to be armed. The Second Amendment to the Constitution, protecting the right to bear arms, enshrines American liberty and democracy, according to its advocates. As a consequence of nearly unlimited access to guns, Americans have become the best-armed civilians in the Western world; the United States also has the highest homicide rate among Western nations. Fear of violent crime, in turn, fuels demands for tougher punishment of criminals and induces citizens to buy more guns to defend themselves.

Of course it would be a gross exaggeration to depict all gun owners as potential lynchers. But sometimes the line becomes uncannily blurred, as, for example, in a 2007 case from Texas that made national headlines and attracted international attention. In November that year a senior citizen from Pasadena, Texas, reported to police that two men had broken into the house of his neighbors. He told the operator that he had a shotgun and intended to stop the burglars. Although the officer implored the caller to refrain from taking action on his own, the man announced, "I'm not going to let them get away with it. I'm going to shoot. I'm going to kill them."

As a police officer was arriving on the scene, the caller confronted the fleeing burglars who were running across his front yard in bright daylight. Shouting, "Move, you're dead," he fired several times into their backs, killing the two men who were later identified as illegal immigrants from Colombia. It turned out that they had carried no guns. When testifying before a grand jury, the man claimed he had no choice because the criminals came running onto his property. The grand jury

1983), and *National Association for the Advancement of Colored People* (Washington, D.C., Library of Congress Manuscript Division). The magazine *The Crisis: A Record of the Darker Races*, New York, 1910 [...], also contains numerous accounts and background information on [...]ings and on the anti-lynching struggle.

[...]m the 1880s to the 1940s the practice of lynching elicited numerous [...]s by scholars and anti-lynching activists. Hubert Howe Bancroft, *Pop-[...]Tribunals*, 2 vols. (San Francisco, 1887), a history of the vigilante move-[...]s in the Far West, defends the need for and the legitimacy of popular [...]e. In contrast the African-American journalist and anti-lynching cru-[...] Ida B. Wells exposed both the brutality and the hypocrisy of white [...]emacist lynchers. Her most important writings are available in several [...]ints: *On Lynchings: Southern Horrors*; *A Red Record*; and *Mob Rule in [...] Orleans* (New York, 1969). See also Jacqueline Jones Royster, ed., *South-[...] Horrors and Other Writings: The Anti-Lynching Campaign of Ida B. Wells, [...]2–1900* (Boston, 1997). In 1905 James E. Cutler published his seminal [...]k *Lynch-Law: An Investigation into the History of Lynching in the United [...]es* (reprint New York, 1969), which remains of great value because of its [...] documentary evidence and its treatment of many key issues. Other im-[...]rtant contemporary writings and documentaries by anti-lynching authors [...]d groups include National Association for the Advancement of Colored [...]ople, ed., *Thirty Years of Lynching in the United States, 1889–1919* (New [...]rk, 1969; orig. ed. 1919); Walter White, *Rope and Faggot: A Biography of [...]dge Lynch* (New York, 1969; orig. ed. 1929); James H. Chadbourn, *Lynch-[...]g and the Law* (Chapel Hill, 1933); Southern Commission on the Study of [...]nching, *Lynchings and What They Mean* (Atlanta, 1931); Arthur Raper, [...]he Tragedy of Lynching* (New York, 1969; orig. ed. 1933); and Jesse Daniel [...]mes, *The Changing Character of Lynching: Review of Lynching: 1931–1941* [...]New York, 1973; orig. ed. 1942).

From the 1980s on, historians began to take a keen interest in lynching, which has generated an abundance of monographs and articles. Yet con-[...]iderable gaps remain. Most publications focus on the lynching of African Americans in the Jim Crow South. Only recently have historians paid more attention to other parts of the United States and to other victim groups while lynching in the colonial, Revolutionary, and antebellum eras has been ne-glected. No broad synthesis is so far available. Christopher Waldrep, *The Many Faces of Judge Lynch: Extralegal Violence and Punishment in America* (New York, 2002) is the closest approximation. Philip Dray, *At the Hands of Persons Unknown: The Lynching of Black America* (New York, 2002) treats only the plight of African Americans.

refused to indict him, supposedly on the basis of a Texas law that excuses deadly force to protect someone else's property if the actor reasonably be-lieves that such force is immediately necessary.

The incident stirred much controversy over racial bias and the limits of legitimate self-defense. Observers wondered if the Pasadena resident might also have shot at two white burglars, or if the grand jury might have treated a nonwhite defendant with equal leniency. The case highlights the extremely broad concept of self-defense in American law. As a rule, citi-zens have a right not only to defend themselves against imminent threats of violence but also to defend their property. And Americans have no legal duty to retreat from a confrontation when they feel attacked or threatened. Whereas gun rights advocates celebrate such "Stand Your Ground" laws as true to the spirit of American liberty and manliness, skeptics fear they may encourage citizens to take the law into their own hands and kill crimi-nal suspects whenever they see fit. The Pasadena incident fails to qualify as a lynching case because it did not involve the action of a mob, but the grand jury's dismissal of the case casts into sharp relief the extraordinary degree of private violence American society is willing to accept. This willingness also suggests that many Americans consider the state's monopoly on the use of force a threat to their democratic rights.

Noting these contemporary cultural legacies of the lynching era does not mean that nothing has changed. Americans abandoned Judge Lynch long ago. Yet other forms of personal and collective violence persist and remain problems for American society and for every other society in the world. Surely a society without violence will remain a utopian vision. Many people reject this goal because they see violence as a wellspring of progress. Others contend that humans by nature are inherently and unalterably violent, and not much can be done about it. The history of lynching in America suggests a different conclusion, however. As the Preamble to the Constitution phrases it aptly, governments must uphold the rule of law to "establish justice, insure domestic tranquillity . . . and secure the blessings of liberty." Over the course of American history, state and federal governments all too often have failed to redeem this promise. The Senate's apology in 2005 was thus a belated yet appropriate act.

A Note on Sources

Lynching in America is part of a larger history of r
vigilantism. For two richly documented introductions,
stadter and Michael Wallace, eds., *American Violence:*
History (New York, 1970), and Christopher Waldrep a
lesiles, eds., *Documenting American Violence: A Sourceb*
2006). Ronald Gottesman, ed., *Violence in America: An En*
York, 1999) and Michael Newton and Judy Ann Newton
ligious Violence in America: A Chronology (New York and
are useful reference works. Richard Maxwell Brown, *Stra*
Historical Studies of American Violence and Vigilantism (Ne
and Richard Maxwell Brown, *No Duty to Retreat: Violence*
American History and Society (New York, 1991) are classic
culture of vigilantism and private violence in American his
William C. Culberson, *Vigilantism: Political History of Priv*
America (New York, 1990); Paul A. Gilje, *Rioting in America*
ton, Ind., 1996); and Michael A. Bellesiles, ed., *Lethal Imag*
lence and Brutality in American History (New York, 1999).

For specific periods, see David Grimsted, *American Mobbing,*
Toward Civil War (New York, 1998); Michael Feldberg, *The Tu*
Riot and Disorder in Jacksonian America (New York, 1980); John N
Reaping the Bloody Harvest: Race Riots in the United States Duri
of Jackson, 1824–1849 (New York, 1986); George C. Rable, *But*
No Peace: The Role of Violence in the Politics of Reconstruction (At
1984); and Herbert Shapiro, *White Violence and Black Response:*
construction to Montgomery (Amherst, Mass., 1988). For a compara
spective, see Pieter Spierenburg, ed., *Men and Violence: Gender, Ho*
Rituals in Modern Europe and America (Columbus, Ohio, 1998).

For collections of documents on lynching, see Ralph Ginzburg,
Years of Lynching (Baltimore, 1988; orig. ed. 1962), and Christophe
drep, ed., *Lynching in America: A History in Documents* (New York,
The materials gathered by anti-lynching groups are invaluable s
My own work has benefited from two collections in particular: *Asso*
of Southern Women for the Prevention of Lynching Papers, 1930–1942

The lynching scholarship of the past thirty years has pursued different approaches. Robert L. Zangrando, *The NAACP Crusade against Lynching, 1909–1950* (Philadelphia, 1980) and Jacquelyn Dowd Hall, *Revolt Against Chivalry: Jessie Daniel Ames and the Women's Campaign Against Lynching* (New York, 1993) focus on two major anti-lynching organizations. Recently Christopher Walrep published a documentary history of black resistance against lynching: *African Americans Confront Lynching: Strategies of Resistance from the Civil War to the Civil Rights Era* (Lanham, Md., 2009). On the anti-lynching struggle of the radical Left, see Rebecca N. Hill, *Men, Mobs, and Law: Anti-lynching and Labor Defense in U.S. Radical History* (Durham, N.C., 2008).

Other historians have been primarily interested in mining quantitative data and establishing causal explanations for lynchings. The most important econometric work is Stewart E. Tolnay and E. M. Beck, *A Festival of Violence: An Analysis of Southern Lynchings, 1882–1930* (Urbana, Ill., 1995). W. Fitzhugh Brundage, *Lynching in the New South: Georgia and Virginia, 1880–1930* (Urbana, Ill., 1993) compares the two Southern states with the highest and the lowest numbers of lynchings, respectively. Michael J. Pfeifer, *Rough Justice: Lynching and American Society, 1874–1947* (Urbana, Ill., 2004), argues that the struggle over lynching was part of a larger cultural war over the nature of criminal justice. My own interpretation echoes that argument. For a collection of essays representing recent research and approaches, see William D. Carrigan, ed., *Lynching Reconsidered: New Perspectives in the Study of Mob Violence* (London, 2007).

Several studies situate lynching in the cultural and historical context of particular regions or states. Not surprisingly, the South looms large in this approach. See W. Fitzhugh Brundage, ed., *Under Sentence of Death: Lynching in the South* (Chapel Hill, 1998); Julius E. Thompson, *Lynchings in Mississippi: A History, 1865–1965* (Jefferson, N.C., 2007); Bruce E. Baker, *This Mob Will Surely Take My Life: Lynchings in the Carolinas, 1871–1947* (New York, 2008); John H. Moore, *Carnival of Blood: Dueling, Lynching, and Murder in South Carolina* (Columbia, S.C., 2006); Walter T. Howard, *Lynchings: Extralegal Violence in Florida During the 1930s* (London, 1995); and George C. Wright, *Racial Violence in Kentucky, 1865–1940: Lynchings, Mob Rule, and "Legal Lynchings"* (Baton Rouge, 1990). In addition, the West is now receiving more attention. See William D. Carrigan, *The Making of a Lynching Culture: Violence and Vigilantism in Central Texas, 1836–1916* (Urbana, Ill., 2004); Stephen Leonard, *Lynching in Colorado, 1859–1919* (Boulder, Colo., 2002); and Ken Gonzales-Day, *Lynching in the West, 1850–1935* (Durham, N.C., 2006).

A NOTE ON SOURCES

Even more authors have written individual case studies and taken what anthropologists might call a "thick description" approach in looking at particular community settings. Again, the Jim Crow South has received much attention. See, for example, Dominic J. Capeci, *The Lynching of Cleo Wright* (Lexington, Ky., 1998); Monte Akers, *Flames After Midnight: Murder, Vengeance, and the Desolation of a Texas Community* (Austin, Tex., 1999); Patricia Bernstein, *The First Waco Horror: The Lynching of Jesse Washington and the Rise of the NAACP* (College Station, 2005); William Ivy Hair, *Carnival of Fury: Robert Charles and the New Orleans Race Riot of 1900* (Baton Rouge, 1976); James R. McGovern, *Anatomy of a Lynching: The Killing of Claude Neal* (Baton Rouge, 1982); Cynthia Skove Nevels, *Lynching to Belong: Claiming Whiteness Through Racial Violence* (College Station, 2007); and Howard Smead, *Blood Justice: The Lynching of Mack Charles Parker* (New York, 1986). The 1915 lynching of Leo Frank has been the subject of several monographs, including Leonard Dinnerstein, *The Leo Frank Case* (Athens, Ga., 1987); Robert Seitz Frey and Nancy Thompson-Frey, *The Silent and the Damned: The Murder of Mary Phagan and the Lynching of Leo Frank* (Lanham, Md., 1988); Jeffrey Paul Melnick, *Black-Jewish Relations on Trial: Leo Frank and Jim Conley in the New South* (Jackson, Miss., 2000); and Steve Oney, *And the Dead Shall Rise: The Murder of Mary Phagan and the Lynching of Leo Frank* (New York, 2003). For the post-1945 South, there are several case studies on hate crimes that many insist should be classified as lynchings, especially the 1955 murder of Emmett Till in Mississippi. See Laura Wexler, *Fire in a Canebrake: The Last Mass Lynching in America* (New York, 2003); Stephen J. Whitfield, *A Death in the Delta: The Story of Emmett Till* (Baltimore, 1988); Christopher Metress, *The Lynching of Emmett Till: A Documentary Narrative* (Charlottesville, 2002); and Joyce King, *Hate Crime: The Story of a Dragging in Jasper, Texas* (New York, 2002).

Case studies of mob violence and lynching in the North and the West include two books on the 1930 lynching in Marion, Indiana: James H. Madison, *A Lynching in the Heartland: Race and Memory in America* (New York, 2001) and Cynthia Carr, *Our Town: A Heartland Lynching, a Haunted Town, and the Hidden History of White America* (New York, 2006). See also Dennis B. Downey and Raymond M. Hyser, *No Crooked Death: Coatesville, Pennsylvania, and the Lynching of Zachariah Walker* (Urbana, Ill., 1991); Michael W. Fedo, *The Lynchings in Duluth* (St. Paul, 2000); and Harry Farrell, *Swift Justice: Murder and Vengeance in a California Town* (New York, 1992).

In recent years the study of lynching has been strongly influenced by the new cultural history that concentrates on ideologies and discourses (especially those related to gender and race), on visual and literary representations, on the performative and ritualistic spectacle of lynching, and on lynching in cultural memory. Important contributions to this field are Trudier Harries, *Exorcising Blackness: Historical and Literary Lynching and Burning Rituals* (Bloomington, Ind., 1984); Orlando Patterson, *Rituals of Blood: Consequences of Slavery in Two American Centuries* (Washington, D.C., 1998); Gail Bederman, *Manliness and Civilization: A Cultural History of Gender and Race in the United States, 1880–1917* (Chicago, 1995); Grace Elizabeth Hale, *Making Whiteness: The Culture of Segregation in the South, 1890–1940* (New York, 1998); Crystal N. Feimster, *Southern Horrors: Women and the Politics of Rape and Lynching* (Chapel Hill, 2009); Dora Apel, *Imagery of Lynching: Black Men, White Women, and the Mob* (New Brunswick, N.J., 2004); James Allen, et al., eds., *Without Sanctuary: Lynching Photography in America* (Santa Fe, 2000); Sandra Gunning, *Race, Rape, and Lynching: The Red Record of American Literature* (New York, 1996); Anne P. Rice, ed., *Witnessing Lynching: American Writers Respond* (New Brunswick, N.J., 2003); Harriet Pollack and Christopher Metress, *Emmett Till in Literary Memory and Imagination* (Baton Rouge, 2008); Jacqueline Goldsby, *A Spectacular Secret: Lynching in American Life and Literature* (Chicago, 2006); Amy Louise Wood, *Lynching and Spectacle: Witnessing Racial Violence in America, 1890–1940* (Chapel Hill, 2009); Sherrilyn A. Ifill, *On the Courthouse Lawn: Confronting the Legacy of Lynching in the Twenty-first Century* (Boston, 2007); and Jonathan Markovitz, *Legacies of Lynching: Racial Violence and Memory* (Minneapolis, 2004).

This book emphasizes the character of lynching as "popular justice" and therefore its close relationship to the death penalty and the criminal justice system at large. In particular, my views have been informed by the following books: Paul Finkelman, ed., *Lynching, Racial Violence, and the Law* (New York, 1992); Margaret Vandiver, *Lethal Punishment: Lynchings and Legal Executions in the South* (New Brunswick, N.J., 2006); Lawrence M. Friedman, *Crime and Punishment in American History* (New York, 1993); Charles J. Ogletree and Austin Sarat, *From Lynch Mobs to the Killing State: Race and the Death Penalty in America* (New York, 2006); Stuart Banner, *The Death Penalty: An American History* (Cambridge, Mass., 2002); Randall Kennedy, *Race, Crime, and the Law* (New York, 1997); and Christopher Waldrep, *Local Matters: Race, Crime, and Justice in the Nineteenth-Century South* (Athens, Ga., 2001).

Credit is also due other key sources on which the individual chapters of this book draw. For Chapter 1, on crime and criminal justice in the colonial era, see Eric H. Monkkonen, *The Colonies and Early Republic: Crime and Justice in American History* (Westport, Conn., 1991); Douglas Greenberg, *Crime and Law Enforcement in the Colony of New York, 1691–1776*

(Ithaca, 1976); and Donna J. Spindel, *Crime and Society in North Carolina, 1663–1776* (Baton Rouge, 1989). On the punishment of slaves I found Kirsten Fischer, *Suspect Relations: Sex, Race, and Resistance in Colonial North Carolina* (Ithaca, 2002) especially insightful. On tarring and feathering, see Benjamin H. Irvin, "Tar, Feathers, and the Enemies of American Liberties, 1768–1776," *New England Quarterly* 76 (2003): 197–238. Pauline Maier, "Popular Uprisings and Civil Authority in Eighteenth-Century America," *William and Mary Quarterly* 27 (1970): 3–35, remains a highly influential analysis of mob violence in colonial and Revolutionary North America. My comparative references to the French and Russian revolutions draw on Jeffrey L. Short, "The Lantern and the Scaffold: The Debate on Violence in Revolutionary France, April–October, 1789" (Ph.D. dissertation, SUNY Binghamton, 1991); and Orlando Figes, *A People's Tragedy: The Russian Revolution, 1891–1924* (New York, 1997).

Chapter 2 draws heavily on Grimsted, *American Mobbing* as well as on the classic study by Bertram Wyatt-Brown, *Southern Honor: Ethics and Behavior in the Old South* (New York, 1982). See also Edward L. Ayers, *Vengeance and Justice: Crime and Punishment in the 19th-Century South* (New York, 1984) and Diane M. Sommerville, *Rape and Race in the Nineteenth Century South* (Chapel Hill, 2004). On the Christiana Riot, see Thomas P. Slaughter, *Bloody Dawn: The Christiana Riot and Racial Violence in the Antebellum North* (New York, 1991).

Chapter 3: On Turner's frontier thesis, see Frederick Jackson Turner, *The Frontier in American History* (New York, 1920). On crime and punishment in nineteenth-century California and on the San Francisco vigilante movements, see Clare V. McKanna, *Race and Homicide in Nineteenth-Century California* (Reno and Las Vegas, 2002) and Kevin J. Mullen, *Let Justice Be Done: Crime and Politics in Early San Francisco* (Reno and Las Vegas, 1989). On violence in the West generally, see Marilynn S. Johnson, *Violence in the West: The Johnson County Range War and the Ludlow Massacre* (New York, 2008) and Richard Maxwell Brown, "Violence," in *The Oxford History of the American West*, ed. Clyde A. Milner, Carol A. O'Connor, and Martha A. Sandweiss, 393–425 (New York, 1994).

Chapter 4: On the New York City draft riots, see Iver Bernstein, *The New York City Draft Riots: Their Significance for American Society and Politics in the Age of the Civil War* (New York, 1990). My account of the events at Gainesville, Texas, follows James Smallwood, "Disaffection in Confederate Texas: The Great Hanging at Gainesville," *Civil War History* 22 (1975): 349–360. On violence and slavery during the Civil War and after emancipation, I refer extensively to Leon Litwack's classic *Been in the Storm So Long: The Af-*

termath of Slavery (New York, 1979); see also Armstead L. Robinson, *Bitter Fruits of Bondage: The Demise of Slavery and the Collapse of the Confederacy, 1861–1865* (Charlottesville, 2005). On the lynching of Saxe Joiner, see Joan E. Cashin, "A Lynching in Wartime Carolina: The Death of Saxe Joiner," in Brundage, *Under Sentence of Death*, 109–31. The standard account of the Ku Klux Klan during Reconstruction is Allen W. Trelease, *White Terror: The Ku Klux Klan Conspiracy and Southern Reconstruction* (Baton Rouge, 1971).

Chapter 5: The classic interpretation of race relations in the postbellum South is C. Vann Woodward, *The Strange Career of Jim Crow* (New York, 1974, 3rd ed.). My interpretations also draw partly on Joel Williamson, *The Crucible of Race: Black-White Relations in the American South Since Emancipation* (New York, 1984) and Leon Litwack, *Trouble in Mind: Black Southerners in the Age of Jim Crow* (New York, 1998).

Chapter 6: My account of the lynching of Mexicans is based on William D. Carrigan and Clive Webb, "The Lynching of Persons of Mexican Origin or Descent in the United States, 1848 to 1928," *Journal of Social History* 37 (2003): 411–438. On the lynching of Sicilians, see Clive Webb, "The Lynching of Sicilian Immigrants in the American South, 1886–1910," *American Nineteenth Century History* 3 (2002): 45–76. On the Robert Prager lynching, see Franziska Ott, "The Lynching of Robert Prager," in *German-Americans in the World Wars: The Anti-German Hysteria of World War One*, ed. by Don Tolzmann, 239–365 (Munich, 1995).

Chapter 7: All my lynching statistics are based on the figures in *Historical Statistics of Black America*, ed. Carney Smith and Carrell Peterson Horton, 2 vols., I, 488-495 (New York, 1995). The Death Penalty Information Center has recently compiled a list of all known legal executions in America; see http://www.deathpenaltyinfo.org/documents/ESPYyear.pdf. The numbers on and narrative accounts of prevented lynchings are drawn from the ASWPL Papers.

Chapter 8: On racial and social change in the New Deal, World War II, and cold war eras, see Harvard Sitkoff, *A New Deal for Blacks: The Emergence of Civil Rights as a National Issue* (New York, 1978); Mary Dudziak, *Cold War Civil Rights: Race and the Image of American Democracy* (Princeton, 2000); and James T. Patterson, *Grand Expectations: The United States, 1945–1974* (New York, 1996). On the violence against NAACP activists in the 1950s, see Manfred Berg, *"The Ticket to Freedom": The NAACP and the Struggle for Black Political Integration* (Gainesville, Fla., 2005).

Chapter 9: On the general context of apologies and reparations for historical injustices, see John Torpey, *Making Whole What Has Been Smashed: On Reparations Politics* (Cambridge, Mass., 2006); Manfred Berg and Bernd

Schaefer, eds., *Historical Justice in International Perspective: How Societies Are Trying to Right the Wrongs of the Past* (New York, 2008); Michael T. Martin and Marilyn Yaquinto, eds., *Redress for Historical Injustices in the United States: On Reparations for Slavery, Jim Crow, and Their Legacies* (Durham, N.C., 2007); and Renee C. Romano and Leigh Raiford, eds., *The Civil Rights Movement in American Memory* (Athens, Ga., 2006). My account of the Pasadena, Texas, incident is based on the reporting of the *New York Times*; see http://www.nytimes.com/2007/12/23/us/23texas.html?sq= and http://www.nytimes.com/2008/07/01/us/01texas.html?sq=.

Index

A NOTE ON THE AUTHOR

Manfred Berg was born in Wesel, Germany, and studied at Heidelberg University, where he received a Ph.D. in history. He has also written *The Ticket to Freedom: The NAACP and the Struggle for Black Political Integration* as well as three monographs and several edited volumes. Mr. Berg has received the David Thelen Award from the Organization of American Historians. He is now the Curt-Engelhorn Professor of American History at Heidelberg University and lives in Heidelberg.